New River Vanity

The Love and Adventures of Calamity Vanity

Tami Noftz

New River Vanity, The Love and Adventures of Calamity Vanity by Tami Noftz

Library of Congress Control Number: 2023916211

ISBN: 979-8-9890364-2-4 (hardcover)

ISBN: 979-8-9890364-1-7 (paperback)

ISBN: 979-8-9890364-0-0 (ebook)

TamiNoftz.com

Contents

Prologue

Under the warm, golden light of a North Carolina sun, a lush, green expanse of land stretched as far as the eye could see. Vanessa "Vanity" Jane VanBuren stood in the heart of her verdant farm, smiling as she watched her horses graze lazily under the summer sky. There was a certain magic in the air, an invisible thread that connected her to the land and the creatures she called family. Her bright green eyes sparkled with wisdom and a quiet strength she had cultivated over the years.

Having lived on this land for thirty years, Vanity had become an integral part of her small, rural community, but unknown to her neighbors, Vanity's heart had once belonged to a man who lived across borders, in a world far beyond the sandhills of North Carolina. The summer they had spent together, sharing laughter, conversation, and daring adventures, had bloomed into an immortal love story. She had planted the fertile memories of their short time together in soil so rich, nothing could stop it from flourishing and nourishing all living beings around her.

News of her former love had finally reached Vanity, in the most coincidental of ways, and exposed some unexpected truths that threatened to dismantle the delicate fortress she had built around her memories of the past.

As the sun dipped lower, bathing the farm in a warm, orange glow, Vanity stood at the edge of her porch, reminiscing about the indelible summer of 1989 spent with her lover.

She had a decision to make that could alter the course of her life once again. Bound by both fear and hope, she contemplated the consequences of her choice, knowing whatever path she took, the revelations of her story would forever be entwined with it.

Vanessa "Vanity" VanBuren was left standing at a crossroads, her heart whispering of a love long past while the lessons of her life hummed steadily in her thoughts. As Vanity contemplated rekindling her past, she took a seat on her colorful, egg-shaped rattan lounge, reached for her laptop, and poised her fingers above the keyboard. And so her journey through the years began, a memoir to be forged from a flame that once burned bright, each word becoming a bridge to her past.

Part I – The Memoir

THE LOVE AND ADVENTURES OF CALAMITY VANITY

A Memoir by Vanessa "Vanity" Jane VanBuren

To the forever love of my life, I have not forgotten either.

Epigraph

Nothing can compare to the moment life throws a simple surprise your way. That's what happened to me.

Chapter One

White Water Getaway

Annie and I completed our check-in at the reception counter inside the rafting lodge. It was a functional place with unstained bare wood walls, walnut-stained hardwood floors, and a couple of benches to the right and left of the only entrance door. The counter had a dark walnut finish with a thick layer of polyurethane. Rafting photographs were permanently preserved underneath the coating. I wanted to linger and look at each photo, but there were other people waiting. Instead, I took a seat with Annie on one of the benches.

Just as I started to ponder my choice of vacation, the door to the lodge creaked open, the joyful sound of laughter and camaraderie tumbling in like a fresh breeze. In that instant, the room seemed to shift, the air suddenly electrified with an ephemeral energy. Craig Bjorn Eriksen entered, his warm and genuine smile radiating a mystical aura of grace and kindness that instantly drew the eyes of every person in the room. I tried to pretend like I hadn't noticed him, but the sound of his rhythmic Scandinavian accent was hypnotizing. It reverberated deep into my soul like a voice I had been longing to hear my entire life.

He could easily have been a lead in a Hollywood blockbuster or a famous model. That would certainly explain why everyone was staring at him, but I really didn't know if there was a celebrity in our midst.

As someone who often got stuck at their desk, crunching numbers for a public accounting firm, I had missed, especially over the last twelve months, activities other people enjoyed. I hadn't been able to go to the movies or read the latest gossip magazines, but, moved by an inexplicable curiosity when my friend Anastasia "Annie" Preston had first proposed this trip, I decided it was time to leave my spreadsheet-laden desk job for a weekend and embark on a daring adventure. Against my cautious nature, I signed up for a rafting expedition, entrusting my safety to the capable hands of those running Rapid River Adventures in New Hill, West Virginia.

Regardless, this was not a movie set, and this man wasn't here as an actor; he was a real person, and he was standing just ten feet in front of me. I was a solid, accountable person, not overly prone to affairs of the heart, but the emotions stirring inside me at just the sight of him were tantalizing. Although our eyes had not yet made contact, the analytical portion of my personality had already started to evade me, and what felt like a new and improved me began to emerge.

His demeanor was as strong and confident as the whitewater rapids we were all eager to conquer. He was tall with an athletic build, slender but not thin. He had nice, stylish short- to medium-length hair that looked like it took little effort, maybe a toss of his head and a comb through with his hand. He had a square face with an angular, masculine jawline but with boyish good looks and one dimple. His teeth were perfectly straight and white, which just added to his overall allure.

My heart pounded and I wished I had lost ten pounds before this trip.

"I knew I should have worn makeup today," I said to myself loud enough for my best friend, Annie, to hear me.

I felt self-conscious as it occurred to me that I would be wearing a bathing suit on this trip and this mysterious man was going to see me in it. As I watched a group of young women flirt effortlessly with him, I reassured myself he would end up on someone else's raft. His charm and easy smile were captivating, but I knew I couldn't compete with this swarm of gorgeous ladies in their colorful bikinis surrounding him. Their giggles and whispers filled the air, and I felt a pang of envy at their youth and vitality.

I took a deep breath, shrugged off my worries, and decided to make the most of this special day. I would do my best to enjoy myself, regardless of who accompanied me on this journey. After all, I was there for an adventure, not to compete over a man, so I turned my attention to the task at hand. If the mysterious man ended up on my raft, then so be it.

Chapter Two

The Bus Ride to My Future

An employee of the rafting company blew a whistle just outside the door to get our attention. Annie and I transitioned to the outdoors and joined a group that had gathered around to listen. The employee went over basic rules and information before directing us to load onto one of the three buses headed for a twenty-mile drive to a drop-off point along the New River.

Once we reached our destination, we would launch twelve rafts and begin our adventure. Each raft accommodated six rafters plus a guide. Single file, we loaded onto the buses. I climbed the bus steps, turned to my left, and followed Annie down the narrow aisle to our worn and torn, but still padded, green seats. I hadn't ridden a bus since grade school, so it felt oddly nostalgic.

Annie took a seat by the window seven rows back, on the right. I took the aisle seat next to her. A dozen people walked past us, mostly filling the seats towards the back of the bus first and working their way forward. I glanced around to look for the young man with the Scandinavian accent, and just as I assumed he had gotten on another bus, I saw him walking up the aisle towards me. He was looking directly at me.

My heart began pounding. I reminded myself he was just looking for a seat. As he approached, he looked right into my eyes and smiled without looking away. His gaze was so intense I averted my eyes as he stood right next to me. I wondered where he would sit. With the seats across the aisle occupied, I knew he wouldn't be sitting next to me.

As he took the seat directly behind me, I couldn't shake the feeling that something important had just happened. I told myself there was no way fate would put us on the same raft together, but deep down I hoped for it anyway.

You could never get this guy, I said to myself. *He is out of your league.* I was reiterating those things we sometimes tell ourselves to avoid the pain of rejection.

"He's right behind you," Annie said as she interrupted my thoughts.

I gave her my best "be quiet" look, but that did not work. Funny how your close friends know what you are thinking before you are ready to admit it. Annie had noticed my physical reactions to Craig, and she sensed the mental gymnastics taking place within me from the moment I first saw him.

I tried to play it off like I didn't know what she meant, but my sly grin revealed my true feelings.

"Who?" I asked.

Annie leaned over to whisper to me, "I saw you walk out the door of the rafting lodge. You weren't even aware we had transitioned to the outdoors. And I just saw your face when he entered the bus."

Annie was not going to let me squirm out of this one.

"He's right behind you," she said again. "Say something to him!"

I listened to the rhythm of his accent as he spoke to the girl sitting next to him. He spoke English, but his accent was clearly Norwegian. I recognized it as such because I had briefly known a person from Norway. The only Norwegian words I remembered were "Jeg Elsker Deg," pronounced by me as "Yi El Ski Die," which meant "I love you."

I could tell from the conversation he was having with the girl sitting next to him, he did not know her well. He told her he was visiting from Oslo, Norway, and he had a friend who owned the rafting company. *The owner of the rafting company must be his girlfriend,* I thought.

"If you don't say something to him, I will," Annie said.

With her good-natured threat, I turned around in my seat and faced him. Then in a life-altering decision I said, "Jeg Elsker Deg."

It was too late to take it back. I said it. To me, the words were meaningless, but to him they meant "I love you." I instantly berated myself for letting those words come out of my mouth. I had mispronounced the words, so he attempted to help me pronounce them correctly. I practiced the words with him. First, he would say them, then I would repeat them. During this brief exchange, I had somehow gotten the most beautiful man I had ever seen to say "I love you" over and over. This was a feat I had not been able to accomplish throughout a recently terminated relationship of nearly four years. I was Superwoman now. I was soaring.

Quickly, however, the little voice returned. He was just being polite, but that would be okay. It would be great to spend even a day with a nice guy. It was something I had not had the opportunity to do in a long time, and I know I had never done it without makeup.

"Hi, I'm Annie and this is Vanity," Annie said. I was relieved she spoke for both of us and filled in the lull in our conversation.

"Nice to meet you. I'm Craig."

Craig. I even liked the sound of his name, and the way he said it made me like it even more.

The driver pumped the brakes, and the bus slowed as it pulled onto an unpaved, bumpy road. I somehow felt the bus's hydraulic brake fluid pumping through my veins as if I had become one with the bus. I wanted to stay in my seat. I wanted my captive audience to stay in his seat. I wanted the lighthearted conversation we were having to continue. Inevitably, though, the bus came to a stop and with it my fantasy of spending the day with this man.

***

"It's time," one of the rafting instructors said, "to exit the bus and gather with your group."

Annie and I stood by ourselves twenty feet from the bus.

"Are you alone?" the instructor asked Craig.

"I'm with them," he said as he looked our way, smiled, and walked towards us.

I smiled a close-lipped smile, nodded at him, and mumbled a barely audible "hi" but otherwise remained speechless. My heart pounded so hard I was afraid he might notice my chest thumping or even hear it. I could feel the blood rushing up through my neck and into my face and ears.

His eyes locked with my eyes, and they stayed locked on me. He moved to stand next to me. I was looking forward, but he was still looking at me. *What is happening here and why,* I wondered.

For the next twenty minutes, we got the rafts off the trailer, put on our life vests, and prepared to launch the rafts into the water. I often caught him looking at me, and he did not look away. It was not an uncomfortable stare. It was as if he had become mesmerized by me.

I was still not sure why it was happening or what exactly *was* happening, but I was certain it was better than any car I had ever driven, any house I had ever lived in, or any food I had ever eaten.

CHAPTER THREE

The Launch

Although I looked up and down the river, I could see no sign of whitewater or hear the rush of river rapids as we waited along the bank to meet our assigned rafting guide. Within minutes he approached and introduced himself. He announced he would accompany us on our raft for the entire day, remaining seated in the back of the raft no matter what. He wanted three of us to sit on the left side and three on the right. I was too distracted to catch his name.

He mentioned a get-together or after-party back at the rafting lodge, then dining at a local restaurant and sports bar as a suitable end to our adventurous day. The sports bar caught my attention. I already wanted this day, which had barely begun, to last forever.

"We'll have to do that," Annie said.

"Yes, that sounds like fun."

Our guide explained the areas of the river we should pay particular attention to or avoid, and he reiterated basic safety instructions. I caught the key facts of what our guide was saying and nodded my head occasionally in agreement, but I wasn't listening closely.

I got more nervous the closer we got to the water, and visibly shaken the closer Craig got to me. I tried to channel my inner athlete and focus on enjoying the day.

Individual teams launched their rafts, one at a time, creating a bottleneck situation that slowed the line down to a crawl. Three young ladies from the lodge used this as an opportunity to gather around Craig once again and chat. He reintroduced himself, because at least one of the three had not been privy to the conversation the girl named Christie had with him on the bus. He was more familiar with Jodi than Megan or Christie. I wondered how well he knew the three of them, if at all.

I could now see Christie in her full form. She was about twenty-two, older than I thought she was back at the lodge. She had a perfect figure, smooth complexion, and long dark hair. I wanted her to return to her place in line.

Christie's two friends were equally attractive. I wanted them to all go back to their places in line and leave Craig alone.

"If I don't eat lunch, maybe I'll lose some water weight and those jeans I brought to wear tonight might actually fit," I said to Annie, who was standing next to me. "I almost didn't pack jeans and almost brought those black sweats with that bleach stain on the leg that I wear around my apartment."

"Aren't you glad you packed your just in case pants," Annie said. She was looking at me smiling.

"Just in case what?" I asked Annie.

"Oh, you know, just in case he goes to the sports bar tonight?"

"Do you think he will?" I asked her.

Annie shrugged her shoulders and shook her head like "you never know."

I stood still, facing forward, and tightened my life vest so it was covering as much of my now exposed body as possible, wrapping my towel around my waist as well. I could tell the three young ladies and some fellow rafters had already noticed Craig's near constant staring at me and were curious about his apparent and sudden infatuation with me. I thought they were probably noticing we were a mismatched pair.

"Are you two together?" Christie had walked around and behind Craig to ask me while her friends Jodi and Megan engaged Craig in conversation.

"Yes," I replied. "I'm Vanity. This is my friend Annie."

"No, I meant are you here with him?" She pointed to Craig, whose back was turned slightly towards us.

"No, I just met him on the bus."

"Oh, okay," she said flippantly as she walked back around him to re-enter her circle of friends.

I overheard Craig telling Megan he was a student from Norway, studying in England, and interning in the U.S. as part of a college exchange program. He had made travel plans while visiting and said he was going to visit San Francisco and walk across the Golden Gate Bridge just before he returned to college in Bath, England, at the end of the summer.

As we continued to wait on people in front of us to awkwardly board their rafts and float downstream clearing the way for the next group to launch, I finally mustered up the courage to speak an entire sentence to him in front of Christie and Company.

"Do you know how far San Francisco is?"

"I do," he said. He smiled that gorgeous smile as he looked directly into my eyes. I averted my glance. I noticed he had used this opportunity to turn his back on the girls, which abruptly ended their conversation.

"Do you know what else I know?" he asked.

"What else do you know?"

"You are going with me," he said.

I laughed a disbelieving "you must be crazy" kind of laugh, which caused him to add, "And we're going to hold hands the entire way across the bridge."

With that, the spurned Christie and Company disbursed back to their original positions in the queue in seemingly utter disbelief at what they had just heard.

I briefly wondered if Annie might have hired him as an escort to cheer me up.

For the next few minutes, I just let the thought of walking across the Golden Gate Bridge, holding Craig's hand, take hold of me.

Chapter Four

Slippery When Wet

I believed as soon as we launched the rafts, we would get pulled by the current into whitewater, but that was not the case. We had to start out slowly, get our balance, and learn how and when to use the oars. We needed to do all this on fairly smooth water, and we would need our experienced guide to orchestrate and choreograph this dance so when we approached the rapids, we would be able to safely, as a team, maneuver our way through them.

My plan to stay dry and keep my poofy eighties-style hair from getting wet was thwarted within minutes as the New River had opposite intentions for me and my hair. I was drenched right from the start, along with everyone else on the raft.

Now I was grateful I hadn't worn makeup. I didn't need black stripes running down my face with one eyebrow painted on and another missing. My thoughts went back to a time when I had front row seats and meet-and-greet tickets to see the Rolling Stones with Annie. I won them by being the tenth caller and answering an obscure question about the band on a radio program. Once we arrived at the venue, just after sunset, I parked the car using a special valet pass that was included in our prize. We quickly refreshed our makeup in the car before we tucked our purses out of sight under the back seat and made our way to the stadium.

We walked past thousands of fans, most of whom had camped for days. I thought how lucky I was to have landed such good seats. Annie and I arrived at the last minute and strutted past everyone to the front row and took our seats just before the concert started. We felt like VIPs wearing our backstage all-access badges around our necks. We had that "we're with the band" kind of vibe.

We were practically walking on air. Under the brightly lit stadium lights, just before a stagehand dimmed the lights completely and announced the warmup act, Annie looked at me and started laughing so hard she had trouble explaining why she was laughing. She had crammed a compact with a built-in mirror into her pocket. She pulled it out, opened it, and showed me my face.

While refreshing my makeup in the car, I had used red lip liner on my eyebrow, only one eyebrow, instead of my light-brown eyebrow pencil. My other eyebrow was fine as I had drawn it on correctly in the car before I fumbled and dropped my eyebrow pencil into my deep, cluttered makeup bag. Reaching into the bag, without enough light to see, I had inadvertently felt around and pulled out my lipstick liner.

There was no time to fix it and no way to get back to the car, where my eyebrow pencil was. I went to the venue's restroom and used toilet paper and hand soap to remove the red lipstick from my eyebrow and had to remove the brown liner from my other eyebrow as well along with a good portion of my forehead foundation and eye shadow. The area around my eyebrow remained red where the lipstick stained my skin and from my vigorous scrubbing. Remnants of the thinnest toilet paper ever manufactured remained stuck on my face. Annie removed all the pieces of toilet paper she could find.

Annie brushed my face multiple times with her hands during the intermission as she spotted more tiny pieces of dried paper on my face. Right before we met the band, we were ushered through a brightly lit hallway. Annie started laughing again as she spotted one more piece had dried on my dangling topaz earring. I took the earring out of my ear to scrape off the piece of toilet paper.

The door opened and we were ushered inside. There stood Keith Richards, my favorite band member. I crammed the earring in my pocket and became engaged in an interesting conversation with this musical icon. He enjoyed my eyebrow story and laughed aloud when I told it.

Keith was wearing only one dangling earring. Just before we left, he took it out of his ear and handed it to me. I reached into my pocket and handed him mine as we walked out the door.

The door closed behind us. Annie started laughing in a way that made me want to laugh with her, but I wasn't sure why.

"Your earring," Annie said as she paused long enough to control her case of the sillies, "still had toilet paper on it."

We staggered back down the long hallway to exit the building, not because we were intoxicated but because we were laughing so hard. No words could express how embarrassed I felt, but the genuine laughter and memories we shared were something I would always treasure.

I glanced at Annie across from me on the raft. Thinking back to the day of the concert, I could not contain my outburst of laughter. Everyone on the raft probably assumed I was just having that much fun on the water, but at that moment, all I could think about was Annie and Keith and my lipstick-red eyebrow.

Except for the few occasions where I let my mind wander to places other than the slippery rubber raft, I was wholeheartedly committed to the rafting adventure as there was no turning back, rafting upstream, or disembarking along the bank. A sense of tranquility and peace permeated my normally overactive nerve endings as I gazed up at the blue sky, watched the clear water in the shallows trickle over flat rocks, and listened to birds chirping in the rustling green landscape. I used these moments of calm not only to reflect and gather my thoughts, but also to adjust my bathing suit, and re-tuck body parts that were trying to escape the confines of my bikini.

Coming back into focus and being present in the moment, I listened a little more carefully to our guide as the day progressed. He asked us to paddle in unison backwards or forwards as we approached the rapids. No surprise at this point, Craig had taken a place right next to me on the raft. I had no way to escape him, nor did I truly long for freedom *from* him. Our bodies touched as we paddled rhythmically, and it felt as natural as if I had known him my entire life.

Not long after we got comfortable and lazy, our emotions mimicking the ebb and flow of the river, we heard the water rushing through the rocks. Then the water got rough and bumpy, tossing rafters onto various other rafters. We all laughed uncontrollably at times as we forcibly drifted downstream, tossed side to side by currents and white foaming water rushing over jagged rocks, sometimes traveling backwards in the raft around the twists and turns of the New River.

"Remember what I told you, everyone needs to work together, paddling in sync with each other!" our instructor bellowed above the roar of the rapids, his gaze scanning as much of the group as possible.

"Are you ready?" he asked the group, the question ringing with thrilling promise. Without thinking, I found myself nodding, eager for the waves to crash against me, taunting me to embrace a new world beyond the comfort of my home and office, hurdling myself into the dangerous pull of both love and adventure.

"Ball up," our guide said. "If you get tossed from the raft and find yourself stuck against a rock underwater by the force of the current, ball up and chances are, you will roll up the rock and back to the top. Do not panic and don't try to push yourself away from the rock."

He recounted a story of a recent drowning where a rafter had fallen overboard and gotten trapped against a rock underwater and held by the pressure of the oncoming rapids. Our guide was still visibly reeling with anxiety and grief over that experience as he guided us through that infamous part of the river that had taken the rafter's life. I did not ask if the deceased had been on our guide's raft, but his lingering look as we passed the site where the accident occurred made me believe it was likely.

Shortly afterwards, I flipped backwards overboard, and not on purpose. The rafting company had set up cameras at locations where the rapids swell, and the water is swift where rafters commonly fall overboard. Annie later bought the photo of our near-death experience. I like to think of it as a near-life experience because I have never been more alive than I was that day.

Soon after, the water calmed for about ten minutes, and I dared to glance to my right. Craig was staring and smiling at me again, just like he did on the bus. It was the kindest smile, warm, comfortable, and sexy, yet it was a smile that did not overtly indicate he was thinking of sex. He was smiling like a soulmate. I prefer not to describe it in those words, but that is exactly what it was. I kept thinking throughout the day, *What if this is real? Is this how it happens? Could he be the one?* They say you always find true love when you stop looking for it.

Chapter Five

My Collision with Coincidence

Morning hours had slipped by like minutes as the sun transitioned to high noon. Our guide instructed us to bank our raft on a tiny sandy beach that lay ahead. The rafting company had a picnic lunch set up for us.

What if I eat lunch and then I have to go to the bathroom? Will I rush into the woods? My anxiety always accompanied me on my adventures; it was like a loyal friend. I was never alone.

What had also crossed my mind as we were approaching that sandy beach and concerned me far more than bathroom urges, was what would happen when my captive audience got to mingle with all the now soaking wet bikini girls who had gathered around him before we left. Would he still be mine?

I wished we could remain on the raft and go downstream a little further to eat our picnic lunch in private. My fantasy of a secluded island rendezvous with him was not going to happen as it was already too late; we were unloading.

When I saw a small buffet of sandwiches, chips, and drinks, I realized just how hungry and exhausted I really was. Any notion I had of skipping lunch dissipated as I eagerly made my way over to the table. In that moment, I decided to put some distance between the charming man I'd just met and myself so I could overanalyze the morning's events in peace and test our four-hour relationship.

Yet, with each passing moment, I couldn't help but feel an overwhelming sense of happiness and excitement bubbling up inside of me. Whatever was happening between us was no longer explainable using one's normal senses of touch, sight, hearing, smell, and taste. There was something bigger going on here and beyond the scope of what we can reason or understand.

Craig kept glancing at where I was sitting with Annie and smiling at me. As if we were in a magnetic field where opposites attract, we found ourselves side by side once again.

"Are you trying to get away from me by sitting with Annie?" he asked.

"Yes," I admitted. "I was."

"Do you think it worked?"

"It did not," I answered.

We both laughed. I changed the subject.

"Why are you in West Virginia?"

He explained what I had overheard him saying on the bus earlier while I was eavesdropping. He said he had a friend who owned the rafting company.

It was an unusually sweltering day in May. After being waterlogged by sprays from the rapids and unexpected back flips into the water for most of the morning, we were all drying quickly in the heat of the sun. The entire rafting party, including Annie, who was making conversation with two other people from our raft, began seeking shelter further back into the cove, leaving Craig and me alone at the edge of the woods.

We were sitting just a few feet under a mixture of white oak and silver maple trees, which seemed to grow right up and into the edge of the water except for that small patch of white sandy beach perfect for launching the rafts. I assumed that because the sand looked out of place in the natural green setting, the rafting company had brought in the sand and manufactured the beach to provide a perfect place for rafters to dock for lunch.

The sun was shining brightly through the leaves on the trees surrounding us and making patterns on the sparse sand and on our legs and feet. I slowly stood up with the intention of refilling my drink as Craig used the lull in our conversation as an opportunity to take a bite of his sandwich.

As I stood over him, I noticed the light of the sun as it danced across his face and tan shoulders. He had nice smooth skin. How I wanted to reach down and touch him and trace the sunlight pattern dancing on his face. This was the first time I really looked at him. I got quickly and deeply lost in thought as I examined his facial features.

Craig looked up at me and realized I had been standing over him and staring. He didn't seem to mind. I broke the awkward silence first.

"If you don't live in West Virginia, then where do you live?" I blurted out the question too quickly, as if I had planned to ask him that question anyway, to cover up why I was still hovering. What he told me next sealed our fate, although I now believe our fate was sealed long before we ever met.

"I'll be working as a corporate intern at NCR Corporation in Dayton, Ohio for the entire summer."

The moment Craig's words hit me, it was as if the earth had opened and swallowed me whole. I was rooted in place, unable to move even as my heart raced in my chest. How was it possible he would be working in my hometown all summer, 250 miles from where we were in West Virginia? My mind struggled to wrap itself around the coincidence, and I couldn't help but wonder if fate was at work here. But as I stood there, feeling the weight of his words, all I could think was how I desperately wanted to spend the summer getting to know this man who had somehow grounded me with a single sentence.

"That is where I live," I said.

As the news had shaken me just moments before, he was now processing this information. We stared at each other in disbelief, both trying to wrap our heads around the magnitude of such a discovery. I was barely able to take it all in as my brain processed every scenario and implication that could come from this, from good to bad, from days to years.

***

"How old are you?" I asked.

"Twenty-five."

"I am thirty, about to turn thirty-one. This is not going to work. I am too old for you. Look at all these young women around you, every one of them is dreaming about being with you tonight at that party and you know that."

That was my failed attempt to run and hide.

He agreed about the other women openly flirting with him, but he didn't say it in an arrogant manner. People fawning all over him everywhere he went must have been something he had gotten used to by his age. He simply could not look like he did without having people notice him. He seemed slightly reserved, not loud or boastful, like the kind of person who avoided the ever-present spotlight.

"Why me," I asked, "instead of her?" as I nodded towards Jodi, a female version of him who had been practically stalking him since we docked.

"I know Jodi's attracted to me, but you have an adventurous spirit. I like that." He added, "I care about what is on the inside of a person. I am attracted to you. I'm not attracted to Jodi." He spoke with confidence as if he knew Jodi already and he remembered her name, but I was still too nervous to ask him how he could be so sure.

I couldn't see anything clearly about myself at the time, and any need I had for daring adventures had been crushed by an all too recent tragedy. The purpose of this trip, planned by Annie, was to break my recent routine of going to work and going home and nothing more.

No matter what my thoughts were about what was happening and why, and whether it would end in heartbreak or a lifelong love, I knew there were only two forks in this road. There was no middle ground.

Chapter Six

A Leap of Faith

We lined up in groups and relaunched our rafts into the river. Now all I could think about was the possibility of spending the summer with Craig. I could hear the rushing water slamming against the rocks and frequent shrieks from my fellow rafters, but my ears were humming to the beat of Craig's heart.

I was absorbing the latest information. It was slowly sinking in, but it was still going to take time. We kept looking at each other and smiling, both obviously, thinking about how bizarre this news we had just learned really was.

"Do you want to jump off that cliff?" Craig asked. He pointed towards a rock ledge about two stories in the air where fifteen or so people had lined up to jump. "Do you want to jump off that cliff?" he asked again, this time nudging my shoulder with his shoulder because he knew I was ignoring him on purpose.

"Yes."

I didn't let him know I was contemplating the danger, but he must have sensed it.

"You'll be fine," he said.

The guide pulled the raft to the bank, and four of us climbed our way up the side of the cliff. Annie opted to remain on the raft.

Every inch of my body charged with excitement as we climbed higher, feeling the rough texture of the rock against my hands and feet. The danger that lurked below only added to my adrenaline rush.

"It looks higher from here," I said.

I noticed for the first time Craig was much taller than me, about six foot. I felt safe standing next to him and terrified at the same time.

"Do you want to jump together?" he asked.

"Yes," I nodded. He reached for my hand. By the time I had a chance to process the thrill of holding his hand, off the cliff we ran.

I took a deep breath and plunged into the water, feeling the rush of the cool liquid enveloping my body as I entered the depths. It took longer for me to reach the surface than I anticipated. I was relieved once I did, but the delay caused a small amount of fear to envelop me as I was swimming towards the light. Once I broke through the surface water, I gasped for a breath of air.

I had taken a leap of faith that resulted in Craig holding my hand for all of a few seconds, and that was the first thing my mind processed. Warm oxygen reached my lungs, and I realized I was fine, but I also realized my bathing suit bottom was missing. I caught Craig's face, his head bobbing just above the water ten feet from me.

"I lost my bathing suit," I shrieked and then I laughed an awkward and worried laugh, and momentarily suffered self-consciousness and embarrassment on a grand scale.

I was grateful the deeper, slower-moving water under the cliff was murky brown and cloudy as Craig repeatedly dove down to find my missing bathing suit bottom. Fellow rafters from our raft and another raft jumped overboard and assisted Craig in the search and rescue operation. I could not dive to help because my rear end might have popped straight up out of the water, mooning everyone.

"There they are," two people, one of each from the two remaining rafts near the cliff, spotted my bikini bottoms at the same time and pointed and shouted.

Fortunately, my bottoms had floated downstream with the current and caught on a series of broad, flat rocks in the shallow water near the shoreline.

Craig swam downstream and walked over the rocks near the bank of the river to retrieve them. He did not hold them up or make a scene, nor did he swing them around on his finger, as would have been the case with some young men I had met prior to Craig. Instead, he gallantly walked into the deeper water, holding them just below the surface, then swam over to me. When his feet could no longer touch the bottom, he treaded water with me as I slipped the bottoms back on, over one foot and then the other.

He waited for me to signal to him that I was ready, then we swam together side by side back to the raft, which had floated slightly downstream. The rafting instructor had everyone paddle backwards as they slowed the raft enough to wait for us to catch up, and then we attempted to climb back into the raft. Everyone worked together as a team to pull the search party back into the raft, followed by me and then Craig.

Once we settled back into our places and got our oars going in the same direction, we all had a giggle about the incident.

"Can you imagine if we hadn't found them, and you had to complete the rest of the trip naked?" Annie asked me loud enough that the entire rafting party heard her. I smiled at her as I tried to imagine just that.

"There has never been a permanently lost bathing suit on my watch, but there is always hope for tomorrow," the rafting instructor said. With that, everyone on the raft laughed.

"You're bad," I scolded the instructor, trying to be stern and keep from smiling, but I couldn't.

As we floated further down the river, we passed under the New River Gorge Bridge, 876 feet above us. There were people on the bridge getting ready to jump. We realized they were bungee jumping, so we all started cheering. After the first jumper had made the leap, Craig looked at me, then looked up at the jumper and shook his head up and down in an affirmative yes while he pointed to himself, and then to me, and smiled. I immediately knew he was trying to say we should try that leap too, so I shook my head side to side and mouthed "no way."

Soon our raft was well past the dark russet–colored bridge, and we were watching this unfold from downstream. We continued watching until the jumpers were no longer visible and changed our focus forward as we heard the roar of rapids fast approaching.

Chapter Seven

The Sports Bar

At five o'clock in the afternoon, the rafting trip ended. As we were heading back to the headquarters of the rafting company where we had parked our cars, the guides started handing out beer from a cooler sitting next to the bus driver. The people in the front passed them to the people in the back before keeping one for themselves. Annie and I both accepted a beer. We were just trying to fit in with a group of mostly hippie offspring tree huggers, relaxing at the end of a long day on the river.

During the bus ride, the driver reminded us about the place our guide had told us about earlier where everyone was going for dinner and dancing. My hunger and exhaustion had magnified three-fold, but I was running on attraction adrenaline. There was no stopping me now.

Annie and I had rented a suite at a hotel twenty minutes from the rafting facility. Other rafters were camping in tents adjacent to the parking lot near the rafting lodge, but most of the other rafters were ten years younger than us. The lodge itself did not have any rooms for the public; it was only large enough to house a maximum of four seasonal staff members who remained on the campsite throughout the summer. Annie and I didn't know camping was an option when we registered for the trip, but after the day I had, I was grateful to have rented a real bed in a comfortable room with a shower before going out with Craig and our new group of friends. I loved the outdoors if the comforts of home were not far out of reach.

We made plans to regroup at the sports bar. I told Craig, who had planned on camping at the lodge, that Annie and I had rented a suite at a local hotel where we were going to shower and change clothes before meeting the rest of the rafters for dinner. Craig asked if he could come along and shower as well. I was feeling grungy from the river water, sand, and sun. I knew he must be feeling the same, so Annie and I agreed he should come with us.

My heart was doing somersaults in my chest. Annie fit in the back seat of my car easier than Craig, so she hopped in and told Craig to sit in the passenger seat, next to me.

Annie showered first, me next, and Craig last. I decided to dress in the bathroom and put on all my makeup, and dry and curl my hair, before I opened the door. In my imagination, this would be like a 1950s prom where your date is waiting at the bottom of the stairs to see you dressed like a lady with full makeup for the first time since you met.

The clothes I brought with me to wear that evening fit perfectly, not too tight and not too loose. My jeans were no prom dress, but I pulled them up and zipped them without having to lie on the bed. This was a notable improvement from my usual routine, which involved struggling and kicking my feet, lying down, then bending and stretching and squatting to the floor to make them loose enough so I could walk or sit in a car.

I turned around to look at the back of my jeans in the bathroom mirror. *Not bad,* I thought.

I was born in Cincinnati, Ohio in 1959. My father named me Vanessa Jane VanBuren, against my mother's wishes and better judgment. She wanted to name me Janice, but my father insisted on Vanessa. She often recounted the story about how she imagined the nickname Van Van becoming an unwelcome part of my future, and she did not like it, so she nicknamed me Vanity first.

My close friends and relatives often added my middle name Jane to my nickname Vanity because Vanity Jane rhymed with Calamity Jane. It was a loving, humorous jab and constant reminder of my frequent clumsiness. I wore my nickname with honor after I learned Calamity Jane had been an American frontierswoman, sharpshooter, and storyteller who loved to wear men's pants and ride horses. I imagine I would have become good friends with her, given the chance.

I preferred Vanity to Vanessa as it was diametrically different than my insecure personality. I wore it like a mask.

Annie called me Vanity 100 percent of the time.

I was an average-looking person, nothing physically remarkable about me to attract the attention I was receiving from Craig.

Sometimes, with the right clothes and makeup, I could hold someone's attention, but never long enough for a lasting relationship to develop—the exception being the relationship I had with the guy of four years. He had never once told me he loved me. He pushed and pulled on my emotions so many times I felt like a yo-yo by the time I declared enough is enough and called it quits. I had a lot to offer personality-wise, so I comforted myself after previous rejections, with the knowledge they didn't know what they were missing.

I had pale skin and red hair, light eyelashes, and no noticeable eyebrows. Fortunately, on this trip, even though I had gotten hours of sun exposure, I was not sunburned, at least not to the point of pain. I had learned from an earlier mistake. One sunburn was severe enough to earn me a brief stay in a Florida hospital emergency room covered with blisters, while my mom and Annie took a ride on an air boat in the Everglades, without me.

This time, I came prepared. I had taken the time to condition my skin for the upcoming trip by visiting a tanning bed. I started out slowly with only five minutes under the lamps on the first tanning trip, and I maxed out at fifteen minutes. Despite the comments from other rafters who didn't seem to recognize my newly acquired tan, I knew I had done everything in my power to protect myself from the sun's harmful effects.

I'm not sure if the attractive pink hue now on my face was all from the sun or from the glow coming from deep inside of me. I was blissfully happy. I had a wonderful day.

Before exiting the bathroom, I blended a little makeup on my beaming face, and I was ready to meet my man with more confidence than I had earlier in the day. Yes, I was ready to lay claim to him. No more playing coy. And to think, it only took two swigs of bus beer to give me enough confidence to walk out that bathroom door.

I stepped into the hotel room, and I saw Craig was as pleasantly surprised as I was with my transformation. I turned and walked around the room to avoid falling directly into his arms. It was a struggle, but I succeeded. "Here's to You, Mrs. Robinson" by Simon and Garfunkel was playing in my head.

***

"Is Vanity your real name?" Craig asked.

"My name is Vanessa, but friends call me Vanity because it rhymes with Calamity." I briefly explained why "Calamity" suited me, using the loss of my bathing suit bottoms as a prime example.

"I'd like to call you Vanessa," Craig said.

Once again, his accent pierced my heart like Cupid's arrow. Just hearing him say my name in that rhythmic tone was almost too overwhelming for my heart to manage and my head to process.

If all the men in Norway sound like him, I should move there, I thought.

"If I sit next to you at the party tonight and spill something on you, you'll likely start calling me Calamity Vanity." We all laughed, with Annie laughing the loudest, as the voice of experience.

"You won't spill anything on me tonight," he said, almost speaking quietly to himself. *Does that mean he doesn't plan to sit next to me or does this guy know the future?* I quietly pondered his unusual remark.

"I have my money on her spilling something," Annie said.

"What kind of music do you like?" I asked Craig. I brought up the subject because I was wondering what type of music they would be playing at the sports bar. I assumed it would be disco, country, or rock.

"I don't listen to music. I don't really like it," he said.

"I don't think I've ever met anyone who doesn't like music."

"Now you have," he said.

"Okay, get out," I said playfully as I gently put on the brake and pretended to pull over to the curb.

Finally, I found a flaw. Who doesn't listen to music? Who doesn't occasionally find meaning in the lyrics of a popular song or fantasize about being in a band while singing and playing an air guitar? My only escape from my number crunching day-in, day-out reality had been the twenty-minute commute by car to and from my accounting office, listening to the radio and singing along to my favorite tunes.

Well, there you have it, Craig could not be my soulmate. If this relationship didn't go any further, I could always quip, "Well, he didn't like music, so what kind of relationship would that have been?"

The archaic phrase "by and by" had been going through my mind for weeks in an endless loop. I had just finished a Mark Twain novel and couldn't get that phrase out of my head. Suddenly, I knew these were the perfect words to use after finding out Craig didn't like music.

"What am I going to do with you? By and by." Craig didn't grasp the connection to the novel, but he knew by my tone I was teasing him and that's all that mattered. He reached over and rested his hand so the side of his hand touched the side of mine. The sensation of his touch, ever so slight, was music to my ears.

***

We arrived at the venue a few minutes later. It was a typical sports bar with multiple television sets playing the latest games and a menu consisting of burgers and beer. The atmosphere at the venue was not as private as I had hoped. Sixty of the eighty rafters, plus four or five guides and rafting company employees, were already inside. I had expected fifteen or twenty people max.

The chairs were at a premium and hard to find, so our server gave a menu to each of us and pointed to the last table in the far back corner of the room. There was only room for a single file line between the tables and chairs of the other rafters, so Annie led the way, then me, and then Craig.

When we got to our table it was a chair short, so Craig scanned the room. Of course, Christie had her arm raised signaling to Craig that she wanted him to sit in the empty chair they had strategically placed between herself and Jodi. Craig made sure he thanked Christie and Jodi for saving him a seat as he picked it up in the air and walked with it above his head down the narrow aisle back to our table. He placed it down on the floor and squeezed it in next to mine.

As the evening progressed and the number of dining patrons dwindled, the restaurant staff stacked all the vacant tables and chairs into a back corner as the last remaining light struggled to shine through the tinted windows and presented a magnificent sunset with reflective prism arms reaching out to us from over the Blue Ridge mountaintop. I glanced at the illuminated Budweiser Clydesdale clock, which caught my attention due to the horses and its vintage feel. It was almost 9 p.m.

The evening turned into late night and the sports bar transformed into a dance club. Dance-pop songs from the eighties, one of my favorite times in music history, were playing. Annie spent most of the evening on the dance floor. She was an accomplished dancer with natural rhythm and didn't lack for dance partners. We watched Annie dance, but neither Craig nor I took the initiative to join her on the dance floor.

Immersed in a sea of sound, we were engulfed by the competing forces of music and conversation. We found ourselves leaning into each other, drawn closer by an invisible force. Even though words were no longer effective, we were communicating in a way that went beyond language. I didn't want the night to end, but all too soon sleepiness set in to punctuate a perfect day.

Chapter Eight

The First Goodbye

The next morning, Craig, Annie, and I headed to the rafting lodge. It was another beautiful spring morning. Sore from bouncing around in the raft using muscles and body parts I had not used in quite some time, I welcomed the mild and soothing temperature.

The rafters who had camped—I estimated their numbers were about fifty—were moving about, drinking coffee, and eating the complimentary donuts. I wanted coffee. I did not want a donut, I wanted two. I was determined to lose weight, starting that day, but I was nursing mild dehydration and low blood sugar. I had one but resisted having another.

To the locals, it was uncool to stay in a hotel vs. camp near the lodge, but when my head hit that pillow the previous night with Craig's next to mine, I knew I was in the right place, at the right time.

The next morning, we returned to the lodge to drop off Craig. After briefly looking at the decorations, trophies, and photos displayed in the lodge, we decided to walk outside with our coffee. I anticipated the inevitable goodbye that was about to take place.

I resisted that second donut as the door automatically sprung closed behind us. Instead, I followed Annie and Craig down the cobblestone sidewalk leading from the front door. I decided Annie and I should stop and have breakfast on the way home.

Craig and I weren't touching, hugging, holding hands, or anything physical, but our connection remained intact. If he had treated me differently this new day, I would have been ridiculously hard on myself for getting caught up in this fantasy and for not being able to control my own libido.

We were experiencing an energy force around each other as if we had been destined to meet or as if we had known each other for lifetimes beyond what we know or understand. This was happening and I believed Craig could feel it, too.

Craig was the only one who did not seem to be questioning or noticing our differences, but we were, most definitely, the odd couple.

As the three of us approached my car, of course I was wondering if I would ever see him again.

"Can I call you?" Craig asked.

Those were the words my heart had been wanting to hear.

"You don't have my number."

"Yes, I do." Then he said my number aloud.

So, it had been a setup. Annie had arranged for me to meet this guy. As I glanced around the side of my car to see where Annie was standing so I could give her the "I knew you were behind this" look, my heart was secretly breaking.

She walked from behind the car and looked at me.

"I didn't give it to him. I am innocent of this," Annie said.

Craig must have seen the disappointed look on my face and sensed my bewilderment in the conversation with Annie.

Before Annie had a chance to say another word, I turned to face Craig. "How do you know my number?"

"Your car is for sale. I got it off the sign in your window last night when we drove to the sports bar."

A wave of relief washed over me as I glanced over my shoulder at my Red Porsche 944 in the gravel parking lot. The Porsche was at the top end of my budget and now some parts needed to be replaced. They were costly, hard to find, and slow to arrive, which is the reason I had decided to sell it. I had placed the store-bought white, black, and red for-sale sign in the back window about a month prior and forgotten about it.

Annie helped me lift out the sunroof and place it in the back hatch compartment. I smiled at Craig, who was lingering under a shade tree twenty feet away waiting for my answer. I stared at him over the now open top of the car.

"I'm not sure that would be a good idea."

I could tell he knew exactly what I meant. He knew I would fall head over heels in love with him and he had only short-term plans to remain in the United States.

There weren't any "happily ever after" endings possible, or none that I could visualize.

"Would you feel worse if I did call, or if I didn't?"

After pausing a moment, I visualized a summer spent with him, versus never seeing him again. With equal fear of both situations, I made a decision. It really wasn't a decision because I knew, and I believe Craig also knew, we no longer had a choice. What was happening to us had already started and wasn't going to end until fate ran its course.

"It would be worse if you didn't call," I admitted.

I opened my door before I crouched down to get into the driver's seat. Our eyes met again and this time, we smiled at each other directly from our hearts.

I don't believe either of us had stopped smiling for more than a few minutes at a time the entire weekend, and my face muscles were sore, but it was a good pain. Craig watched as Annie and I drove away, our hair tousled in the wind coming in from the sunroof and rolled down windows. I looked in my mirror until I could no longer see him.

At that moment, I was grateful I had sold my 1985 Ford Maverick and bought the red Porsche 944. For the first few minutes of my ride home, I actually considered keeping that car because it had just helped me make the sexiest exit I had ever made in my life. If I didn't hear from him again, maybe that one weekend with him would still be enough.

Once away from Craig, and alone with Annie, I couldn't stop talking about the trip and meeting Craig. On the ride home, Annie and I rehashed and overanalyzed every single moment of the entire weekend. What if he forgets my number? I hope he wrote it down. Wouldn't it be just my luck if he wanted to call, but he forgot my number?

Why didn't we stay until he left? Annie and I discussed all of this on our five-hour drive home. Why didn't we offer him a ride home? Annie suggested he probably had a rental car provided by his company.

I admitted to Annie I had made out with him for hours after she fell asleep, but we didn't have sex and she responded, "I know, I wasn't asleep."

Could this get any more embarrassing? We laughed like high school girls the rest of the way home. Did I go too far with him? Did I not go far enough? Alas, we had no answers.

I finally decided to make peace with the possibility he might not call, to view it like a weekend to remember, and convinced myself to expect no more to come of it. I wasn't sorry I had met him. He was just what I needed when I needed someone the most.

Chapter Nine

Stop and Get Some Gas

Less than a year earlier, my dearest friends, John Danbury and Kyle Heath, and two friends of theirs, Gene Remnick and Luke Chapman, and I had taken a trip to Myrtle Beach, South Carolina over Memorial Day weekend. I took a commercial flight home while my friends flew home in their black and white single-engine 1969 Piper Cherokee.

While we, as a group, were standing outside by the hotel pool saying good night on the evening prior to our departures, I reminded them again to stop and get some gas. They repeated that phrase to me in a mocking way.

"Stop and get some gas; stop and get some gas. You're like a broken record," John said. John held my foot and ankle at a ninety-degree angle to the ground while leaving my other foot planted firmly in the sand, so I had to hop in a circle around him to keep from losing my balance.

"There are not a lot of airplane gas stations on the way home," he added.

My closest friends were quick to pick up on this ingrained trait of mine, accepting it as another quirk in my convoluted personality. They must have seen it as my desperate attempt to control every situation, but little did they know it was rooted in something far deeper. The fear of losing control, especially in relationships, was just one more thing to hold me back from truly connecting with others.

John, Kyle, Cathy Banks, six other friends, and I had made four trips to Myrtle Beach over the years, sans Gene and Luke. This trip, however, was a little different. John had fallen in love with a girl back home and Kyle had fallen in love with me, but my relationship with Kyle had always been platonic, much to Kyle's dismay.

John wasn't acting like himself on this trip, and we all knew, amongst our intimate group of friends, the lazy days of summer this year weren't going to be the same. Our lifestyle of boating, tubing, and water skiing at Brookville Lake in Ohio on one of their two boats and flying around with them in their Piper was facing some major changes.

We knew John was planning to propose to his girlfriend. They would be getting married, after which John would be spending his weekends with his family, instead of our group. John had found love.

Love is really what we all wanted to find, so although we were sad our group outings would become a distant memory, we were happy for John. He had made it to the finish line in a race we were all running, but none of us knew the rules or could remember where the starting line was. We just knew John had made it to the finish line first.

John was missing his new love during the trip to Myrtle Beach. We could tell he was sorry he hadn't invited his soon-to-be fiancé, Beth, to come with us, but I suspect John knew this was his last single outing before he settled into married life. It was a somber trip relative to our previous cross-country escapades.

Somehow, I knew as John was holding onto my ankle and foot to prevent me from leaving, it was John's way of saying I love you, my friend. Please understand my life is changing and I won't be hanging out with you any longer. I knew what he was saying, without him having to say it. He knew I loved him, too, and I understood it was a goodbye of sorts, a goodbye to single life.

I never believed John would be the first of our group to settle down. If I'd had to bet, I would have thought John would be the last.

***

The morning of our departure Gene drove me to the airport so I could catch my flight home. I had given up my seat on the Piper Cherokee for Gene. On the way to the airport, he admitted John wasn't the only person who had done some soul searching on this trip. Gene said he was going to propose to the person he had been seeing for over two years when he got home.

He admitted he had made excuses to leave our dinner party early the prior evening and had made his way alone into a strip club in Myrtle Beach. Gene told me it was at the strip club that his fear of marriage vanished and he knew he was ready for commitment. Continuing as a bachelor was no longer an attractive option for him. I was happy for him. I didn't know Gene as well as I knew John and Kyle, but I liked him. I didn't think we would run into each other again after the drive to the airport because he lived a little further away, in Columbus, and wasn't part of our close core group, but we had a nice time getting to know each other during the trip and I enjoyed his company.

Just as we arrived at Myrtle Beach Municipal Airport, Gene asked me if I would switch planes with him. He wanted to know if he could have my commercial ticket and if I would stay and ride home that evening in the four-seater Piper with John, Kyle, and Luke. He said he was afraid to fly home with John and Kyle. I assured Gene everything would be fine.

Gene asked me twice as I was stepping out of his rental car, once lightheartedly and once nearly pleading. I explained if he had asked the night before, I might have agreed to it, but I had gotten up early, packed, checked out of my room, and since we were already at the airport, I was ready to go home.

"No," I said to Gene as he asked me the third and final time. Then I clicked my heels together twice like Dorothy in The Wizard of Oz and told Gene, "There's no place like home."

I closed the passenger door, leaned down through the open passenger window, smiled, and waved to him. Gene returned my smile, but I could tell he was disappointed I had not agreed to the swap. Luggage in hand, I walked to the ticket counter and checked my bag.

Fourteen hours later, the Piper Cherokee that John was piloting ran out of gas one half mile before John, Kyle, Gene, and Luke made it to their local runway. They snagged a line of trees along the way, which caused the plane to nosedive into the dirt. Gene was decapitated by the plane's propeller blade, which twisted back into the side of the plane on impact and cut through the back right seat, the seat that had always been mine on our trips. The airplane came to land on its top with its nose embedded several feet into the dirt.

John had joined his family's four-generation produce business after graduating college. Since I had not heard from John, I called his work. Bruce, John's father, answered and said John was not at work and he was getting concerned. Immediately, Bruce and I both sensed something had happened.

Bruce said he knew someone at the airport. He placed me on hold while he called to see if his contact had any news about John and Kyle's flight being rerouted or delayed. Bruce took me off hold and told me news I never expected to hear. There had been a small plane crash near their local airport. There was one survivor, but Bruce did not know if it was his son, John. The survivor had been transported to Miami Valley Hospital in Dayton, Ohio.

Bruce was over an hour's drive from the hospital, and he did not have any business driving. I asked him to have someone from his company drive him and I would meet him at the hospital. The hospital was ten minutes from my office. I would arrive first, but I would have no way to contact Bruce to let him know if his son was the sole survivor.

I screamed aloud. My office door was closed, but my boss and coworkers, whose offices were located next to mine, heard my wails, and came rushing to my office to see what was wrong.

When I arrived at the hospital, the emergency room staff didn't know the name of the person who had just arrived by helicopter. Pertinent information had gotten lost in translation between the wreckage, the ambulance ride to a small regional hospital near the accident sight, and the subsequent helicopter flight to the trauma center at Miami Valley. They didn't know he had survived a plane crash; they assumed it was a car accident.

Quickly, hearing the story of the crash, the nurse allowed me to pass through the double doors next to her counter, and someone ushered me to the person they had just admitted.

I saw Luke.

I immediately thought of Bruce, John's dad. I nearly buckled from the weight of knowing John, Kyle, and Gene were all dead.

Since Luke arrived with no identification, the hospital's sole purpose of allowing me, a non–family member, to see him was to identify him. I was able to give the attending physicians all the information I had learned about Luke during the holiday including that Luke was a physician himself. With the information I gave them, they were then able to contact Luke's parents through Luke's hospital personnel records.

His doctor also estimated how long Luke had been in the airplane, based on the time I knew they left South Carolina and the time they were expected to arrive home. Ten hours. Ten hours Luke had been trapped in that plane, with our three dead friends. I hoped he had remained unconscious and not in pain or aware of what had happened, or that his friends had all died.

I held Luke's hand for a moment, just before they wheeled him down the hall. I let go and watched until they disappeared into a room at the end of the long hallway. Luke was comatose. The nurse who had escorted me back to see Luke started talking, but all I heard was wah wah wah, then woosh woosh woosh. Her words faded into nothingness. I heard my own heartbeat as it pounded against my eardrums. I could not comprehend that I was never going to see John and Kyle again.

I awoke in a bed in the emergency room. The nurse explained that I had fainted and hit the floor with a thud. They were administering smelling salts to wake me as I regained consciousness. The nurse prevented me from sitting up on the side of the bed as she administered intravenous fluids through a needle she had placed in my hand.

"Lie down. You are dehydrated and in shock," she explained.

The nurse sat beside me asking questions until an accident investigator arrived and he took over from there. I assured him there were no drugs or alcohol involved in their accident, and answered all his questions, but all I wanted to do was grieve.

Luke's family started to arrive at the hospital, including Luke's longtime girlfriend, whom he had failed to mention anything about during our trip. The physicians were busy working on Luke in the operating room. His confused, distraught family, knowing nothing of my existence prior to this day and suffering complete hopelessness over the condition of their son, didn't need anything further from me.

***

Bruce never arrived at the hospital. I didn't see him in person for two more days. He was a visibly broken man. He met me at the funeral home and let me see John, but he was unable to see his son himself. I offered to hold Bruce's arm and go in with him, but he just couldn't, he explained, he would simply die, right there on the spot. Instead, he sent me and John's only brother into the brightly lit room to view John's remains.

I was grateful Bruce and his family allowed me to say goodbye in person to John, grateful beyond words. I never saw or spoke to John's father, Bruce, again because after attending Kyle's funeral, I was unable to get myself out of bed and dressed on the day of John's funeral.

I later learned the local sheriff, who knew Bruce and John personally, had driven directly to Bruce's work and arrived just as Bruce was leaving his company's parking lot to meet me at the hospital. He then drove Bruce to the coroner's office, where they had just transported John's remains, but John's dad was unable to get out of the sheriff's car.

The sheriff then drove Bruce home, where he also notified John's mom. Bruce was unable to speak those unspeakable words to tell her their son was dead.

Kyle's dad had died eight years earlier. Kyle's mom, Jules, had a heart attack as soon as she learned of Kyle's passing. She spent the next week in a hospital and lived another nine years, but from all accounts from people who knew her well, she never really recovered.

One day, I received a package in the mail from Jules. It was a windsock I had purchased in Myrtle Beach as a gift to my friends. They planned to mount it near their runway so they would always know which way the wind was blowing as they approached for landing. It had survived the plane crash unscathed, still in its original wrapper and gift bag.

It was heartbreaking to think of the despair my friends' parents and family members felt. It crumpled me. It crumpled me into a ball of nothingness. There was nothing further I could do to comfort myself, let alone the survivors, so I disappeared completely, physically and emotionally, until the day I met Craig.

Isolation is not a remedy for despair, and my friend Annie knew she had to help me. She had to get me out of my slump. She planned the rafting trip, and I reluctantly went along with her plan, thinking it would make her happy to see I was going to survive. At least, I wanted to make her believe that and I knew it would make my mom happy, too.

I learned that just before their crash, my friends had detoured and purposely flew over a Fed-Ex airport hub before heading back to their destination. Because it was late and a holiday weekend, the runway lights were not lit, and I can only assume my friends thought the Fed-Ex airport was closed. A pilot employee at the facility, and old friend of John's, took me to dinner one evening and told me if my friends had used their radio to contact the tower to let the Fed-Ex air traffic controllers know they were low on fuel, the controllers would have turned on the runway lights and permitted them to make an emergency landing. For reasons unknown, they did not use their radio, and opted instead to land at their own isolated airstrip, ten miles further.

Their detour cost them just enough gas to miss the runway by one half mile. Did they detour to get gas because of me repeatedly telling them, "Stop and get some gas." Would they have detoured to get gas if I hadn't spent the weekend embedding that thought in their heads? I will never know one way or the other. As a result, I blamed myself. I thought I would never experience a zest for life again.

Chapter Ten

The First Call

I returned home from the rafting trip and immediately called my parents to tell them all about my trip and how I'd met a wonderful guy. My mom answered on the first ring. Mom instructed my dad to pick up the phone in their bedroom, but I heard him tell her to just relay the conversation to him. I knew he would be sitting right next to her and could hear what I was saying.

I told them how I had met Craig and then I summarized the details of the rafting trip itself and the time I had spent with Craig, leaving out the part about him spending the night. Then I told them Craig was going to live and work in Dayton for the entire summer. My parents reacted with concern and trepidation, and I realized the tone in which I'd told them the whole story gave away my feelings. I had already fallen hard and fast for a stranger from a foreign land; my parents were obviously worried.

"What do you think is going to happen?" Mom asked.

"I don't know, but regardless of whether I ever hear from him again, we really had fun and I needed to get out and meet new people."

"Yes," she said. My mom had to agree with that. "Did you sleep with him, Vanessa?"

"Mom!"

"Vanessa!" she said.

"Would you be more worried if I couldn't muster the strength to go out and start living again or if I did finally muster the courage to meet someone and just like that, I found the one?"

I had dodged her actual question and was quite proud of myself for creating such a diversion.

"You didn't answer my question," she said.

Call waiting interrupted us.

"Mom, I'm going to take this call."

My heart started racing, hoping it was Craig. I was thankful I had any way out before the next series of Mom interrogations began.

"Okay, but you better call me right back," she said.

I quickly clicked over to see who was calling, clinging to hope with every breath of my being it would be him, but deep down preparing myself for disappointment. I wasn't preparing myself for a spam call or a phone solicitor, the obnoxious interrupters as I called them, because in 1989, while they did exist, they didn't call as frequently as they do today.

"Hello," I answered.

"Hello," he said.

It was Craig. Thrill, surprise, and relief overcame me.

"What are you doing?" he asked.

"I was just telling my parents about the trip."

"Are you with them now—do I need to call back another time?"

"No, I was talking to my mom on the phone, and she was relaying everything to my dad."

"Did you tell them about me?"

"Of course, it would be hard to describe the trip without including you."

"Did you think I was going to call?" he asked.

"I was hoping, but I wasn't sure."

"I was sure," he said. Then there was a pause.

I was so happy hearing those words, I was momentarily speechless.

"May I take you to dinner, if you haven't already eaten?" he asked.

"I haven't and I'm starving. Annie and I didn't stop to eat breakfast because we missed the exit for the only breakfast place we saw on the way home, and I only had one donut at the rafting lodge for breakfast."

Why was I still trying to justify eating that one donut and why did I always have to account for every bite of junk food that entered my mouth? I internally chastised myself for saying that or even thinking it but as I did, Craig kept the conversation flowing without missing a beat.

"Do you mind driving to my apartment and picking me up?" he asked.

"No, I don't mind, what's your address?"

He gave me his address and I knew exactly where it was. I got ready as quickly as possible and headed out the door just after I made a quick call to let my worried Mom know where I was going. I told her repeatedly I would be fine. My words of reassurance didn't relieve her concerns, but I had to go.

Ultimately, both my parents understood and relented. One, because I gave them no choice. I was going to do what I was going to do regardless, so their best bet to track what I was doing was to keep the communication lines open. Two, they often reminded me they had also been young once. They knew what love was. They could tell by the tone of my voice I was already in it, deep.

"Be careful and call us," Mom said. I agreed.

I briefly wondered on my drive over to Craig's apartment, if he just wanted to finish what we had started back at the hotel, but that fleeting thought didn't have much time to linger. It had no platform on which to rest.

I was nervous when I first entered Craig's apartment. The fear of being in unfamiliar places would sometimes prevent me from accepting invitations. I still had unfounded fears, not fears of Craig himself but of being in someone else's space, especially a place with which I wasn't familiar, and these thoughts often looped around in the back of my mind. But this time, on this day, nothing could have stopped me from seeing Craig again.

I had barely made my way into the small living room when he embraced me, so kindly and gently. I knew I was safe, and I felt I would always be safe in his arms. He invited me to sit on the couch. He went into the kitchen and got himself a glass of water and brought me one, too.

"We both need to rehydrate after being in the sun all weekend," he said.

Worry dissipated in that moment, and I relaxed. I believed he would fully accept me as I was and resigned myself to just keep turning the pages of this fairy tale, in the order written.

The apartment was humble and minimally decorated, better described as drab. It was a dated unit, in an older building, but looked like it had been professionally cleaned before he moved in. It had a refrigerator, stove, couch, lamp, end table, coffee table, and a double bed with headboard and dresser and a large black telephone with a long stretched-out cord. The furniture was a basic, lower-priced, professional style. It revealed no personality of its occupants, past or present.

When someone invites you to their home, you learn more about them, like what they collect, what colors they prefer, and if they are clean, dirty, messy, or neat. Craig's apartment was a blank slate that provided no answers to my many questions. Craig had just gotten keys to this apartment hours before he left for the rafting trip. His employer had put him up in a hotel when he first arrived, before securing this furnished apartment for him. Craig commented he knew his new apartment was a bit dreary, but he obviously had no plans to make any decorative changes to it, nor did he plan to spend much time there, other than to sleep.

As Craig sat in the living room next to me, his apartment suddenly seemed perfectly homey. It was much better than my current place now that I considered the company. I thought about my own apartment, my roommate, her sister, and her sister's new boyfriend. My apartment was crowded. When I first signed a lease, my roommate's sister didn't live there, but somehow during my stay and without my approval or knowledge, we took on an extra roommate, then two. I'm understanding, but I couldn't wait until my lease ended so I could buy a house of my own.

Perhaps the two of us would not be spending much time here either. I fantasized about us taking that romantic cross-country trip to the Golden Gate Bridge.

"Let's go eat. I think we both need a good meal after that adventure," Craig said.

I smiled and nodded in agreement.

"You know the best places around here to eat, so you choose. This will work out just great," Craig said in that lovely accent with a slow emphasis on each of the ending words, "just" and "great."

His accent was mesmerizing. I momentarily got lost in my thoughts just listening to him.

"Are you okay?" he asked.

"I've never been better."

That seemed to make him even happier.

"So, you said on the phone you didn't know if I was going to call?" he said. He was smiling at me and joking and looking at me like I should have known he was.

"I was hoping but I wasn't sure. I didn't expect you to call tonight, but I'm glad you did. I forgot to ask you how long you were planning on staying in West Virginia before I left. I am surprised you are home already. I could have given you a ride."

"Jodi gave me a ride home."

"Jodi?" My heart sank for a moment hearing those words, but I appreciated his honesty.

"Yes, we work together. She let me know the first day of training she was single. And I let her know the first day I don't date people from work."

"Oh," I said, "do you also work with Christie and Megan?"

"No, they are Jodi's friends. She had arranged to meet them. Jodi and I camped there the night before you arrived. Her friends arrived the morning of the trip. The entire situation made me quite uncomfortable. It was supposed to be six of us from work going but when Jodi picked me up, it was just the two of us."

I was relieved that after five hours in the car with Jodi, he called me as soon as he arrived home. Some of the nuances of the trip were starting to make sense.

“I really wanted to ride home with you,” he said. With that simple sentence, I knew there was going to be a real connection between us. As we headed to my car, I couldn’t help but wonder where this might lead.

I reminded him to lock the front door to his apartment, something he admitted he was not used to doing at home.

“Do you think it’s really necessary?” he asked.

“I do. There are no safe places. Everywhere is a high-crime neighborhood.”

Craig looked surprised, but he complied and locked his door.

He put his hand softly on the middle of my back and walked me to the car and opened my door for me. He walked around and got in the passenger side. Once seated, he reached for my hand and held it. Holding his hand felt like we had been separated for years and had finally found our way back to one another. I wanted to keep driving just so I could continue to hold his hand, although eventually I had to let go to shift gears. I knew I should have bought a car with an automatic transmission.

I took him to a local hangout, a restaurant called Mackabee’s in the University District. I could have found a closer restaurant, but I temporarily forgot where I was driving. It worked out well regardless.

At Mackabee’s, the atmosphere was even better than the food. We laughed in between bites, talked about our weekend, and learned more about each other. It oddly felt like we were a well-established couple just having a casual dinner on a Sunday evening before a hectic work week, not two people on their first real date.

Chapter Eleven

Floating on Air

"Happy two-week anniversary!" Craig said, his voice bursting with excitement. I squinted at his beaming face and frowned, still groggy from sleep and failing to understand his enthusiasm. I was a creature of habit, and Saturday mornings were reserved for sleeping, especially before dawn.

Craig revealed his surprise.

"We are going to watch hot air balloons launch at sunrise."

My initial thrilled reaction turned to caution.

"Are we going to just watch?" I asked.

I had begun to realize nothing about being with Craig was ever going to be routine or normal.

"Well, it was going to be a surprise, but we're going to actually take a balloon ride," Craig admitted.

"What? Craig!!"

"It will be fun. You will love it. Trust me," he said.

I experienced vertigo at that very moment, and I hadn't even sat up in bed yet.

Craig had arranged for us to take part in the launch at a festival in Vandalia, Ohio. It was home to the bustling and newly renovated James M. Cox Dayton International Airport, which had brought $50 million in contracts and contributed substantially to the area's growth and employment opportunities.

The town's people were flourishing, and their hobbies were getting bigger and more expensive, along with their cars and houses. Bigger, braver, and bolder was all the rage in the late eighties, so hobbies like hot air ballooning rose in popularity alongside disposable income.

The sun was barely awake, casting its golden glow on sleepy, tree-lined streets as we approached the launch site.

I had always been entranced by the mesmerizing colors of the balloons and the romance of soaring through the skies, but today, I would finally experience it all for myself. Each balloon was a unique masterpiece, more beautiful than the last. The blues and yellows mixed in harmony with reds, oranges, and muted tones; stars twinkling against stripes and polka dots like a heavenly sky. Even an intricate Renoir painting found its way onto one of the vibrant balloons.

Slowly, as the balloons started to fill, their magnificent size became even more apparent. Whoosh, whoosh, whoosh, the noise was all around us. I quickly learned how much noise a balloon makes while it's being filled.

Craig's hand in mine, he reassured me as we stood just outside the basket and prepared for takeoff. The memories of my friends' accident still fresh in my mind, I wasn't full of bravado as I would have been just a year earlier. But secretly, it was something I had always wanted to do.

Craig gave me a playful smile before dropping to one knee so I could use it as a stepladder, and then fake opened an invisible box like he was proposing. I took my foot and gave him a light push to make him unbalanced enough to toss him into the grass. Smiling, he hopped back up on his knee again, this time without the invisible ring theatrics, and invited me to step onto his leg and into the basket. Hopping into the woven haven, I lost my footing as my quivering legs gave way. Craig leaped over the side of the basket and extended his hand to help me to my feet.

There was only one other couple with us on this trip. We had extra room in the basket to maneuver so we'd be able to see a different view from each side. The pilot explained that they often turn the basket onto its side and let passengers crawl into it and then tip it back upright, but we all looked fit enough to climb over the side.

Once we were safely inside the basket, my ordeal with gravity began as I watched the world gradually become smaller. Houses resembled Monopoly tokens, and people appeared no bigger than ants. I gripped the basket's edge, my knuckles threatening to burst through my skin, while Craig wrapped his arms around my waist and placed his hands on top of mine, fully embracing our ascension.

The serenity of hovering above the world was breathtaking. My heart danced with joy as the landscape below resembled a panoramic masterpiece, bathing me in a sense of wonder and freedom I had never known.

In the tranquil skies, an even stronger connection between us was forged, a bond that tethered our souls as strongly as the ropes that held their basket beneath the balloon. The awe we shared as we watched the world from above was a language spoken only by our hearts.

Our adventure was underway. It was much quieter once we were airborne, except for the times the aeronaut fanned the flame on the gas burner. He opened up an insulated chest and served us sesame bagels with cream cheese and butter, fresh fruit, sliced cheese on a tray, and mimosas. I had never tasted anything so good.

"The tradition of serving champagne on hot air balloons started in the late 1700s as did the sport," our aeronaut explained. "Local farmers were afraid of the flying contraptions and didn't like that their crops were being damaged when the balloons would land. So, balloonists would offer a bottle of champagne to the farmers as a gesture of goodwill anytime prevailing winds took them to an improvised landing site and the tradition remains to this day."

You see the horizon from every vantage point on a balloon. It is not like seeing the view from an airplane or a tall building. For the first thirty minutes, we could see other balloons around us, but then we started seeing fewer balloons, and those we could see were moving in a different direction.

I started to worry. I didn't fret to the point where it was noticeable to anyone around me, but it was concerning. I switched from being worried that something could go wrong, to allowing myself to relax and enjoy the view in Craig's loving arms, back to being convinced something was going to happen.

Except for when we were eating or walking around to enjoy the different views, Craig was like a seat belt around me securing me to the side of the basket and keeping me comfortably in place, where I felt safe.

Craig and I each had one glass of champagne. I glanced at the champagne bottle, contemplating pouring another, but our balloon pilot had apparently indulged in the remainder.

I noticed we could no longer see *any* other balloons and then I noticed a concerned look on the aeronaut's face.

"The wind has taken us off course. It will carry us over a group of houses, likely in the Westmore subdivision," he said. "That's where we are going to have to land."

A subdivision? I thought as my heart started racing so strongly the vein in my neck was pulsing. Craig, too, seemed a bit shaken but was quietly reassuring me everything would be okay.

"Do you know something I don't?" I asked. He squeezed me tighter. I trusted him. I felt safe, yet I still scanned the horizon for power lines. I saw several.

We were losing altitude, slowly heading for the rooftop of a house near Stanford Ridge Court. I knew that street, a cul-de-sac because Cathy Banks, my friend who traveled with me and my friends to Myrtle Beach, owned a house there.

The whooshing sound had caught the attention of Saturday morning gardeners, bicyclists, and joggers. People came out of their houses and gazed skyward. I remember seeing pictures on the news, years earlier, of a balloon that had touched power lines with tragic results. The thought of becoming tangled in those metal-wire tentacles I could now see we were headed right towards was enough to send shivers down my spine.

How I wanted to be on the ground with the people now looking up, and not the one in the basket looking down. I scanned the small crowd for Cathy's familiar face, but she was not among them. I needed her at that moment. I wished I had her familiar face to focus on during our descent.

Craig's arms were still cradling me but were now keeping me away from the side of the basket. His reassurances that everything was going to be alright had to be enough. We were going down.

We bounced down hard in a large corner lot, directly across the street from my friend's house. Our pilot placed us in the safest place possible, forty feet to the side of a power line. Relieved we were safely on the ground, we quickly flipped out of the basket as the aeronaut was barking orders for us to evacuate and move away from the balloon as quickly as possible.

We cleared the balloon and made it a safe distance away while the aeronaut started deflating it and tipped it to one side away from the lines.

"You are bleeding," Craig said as he dashed over to me. I had busted my chin on the side of the basket when we landed.

"You need stitches," he said.

"I just need a Band-Aid; I like scars. Something to help me remember you."

I smiled, causing the cut to open wider and start bleeding even more.

"I'm sorry you got hurt. I didn't see that coming," Craig said.

"Neither did I, but it's okay. I'm fine. We lived to tell the tale." Thinking of the friends I'd lost, I knew falling out of the sky could have been much, much worse. I hadn't yet shared the story of losing my friends in the plane crash with Craig. I made a mental note that it was something I needed to do. We were getting closer and if he was going to learn about me and understand some of my fears and anxieties, it might help if he knew about the root causes of some of them.

Still, Craig seemed concerned and responsible for taking me on a trip that resulted in my injury—more concerned than I was.

I told Craig about the missing champagne to ease his mind of any thoughts he was having about our off-course adventure, and the subsequent hard landing being his fault.

The person who owned the property where we landed offered to make a call for the aeronaut. I noticed there was no bottle of champagne offered to the inconvenienced homeowner.

The aeronaut was using a short-wave radio to communicate with his chase crew on the ground, so he declined the use of the homeowner's telephone.

A second spectator retrieved a first-aid kit from his house and offered me some larger chin-sized gauze and some individually wrapped antiseptic wipes while another neighbor handed me some Band-Aids they had retrieved from their house. I doctored myself in the side mirror on a nearby truck. Looking at my chin for the first time, I realized I could have used a couple of stitches. Instead, I just cleaned the wound and taped it closed using the products I had been handed.

A crew arrived to help fold and transport the balloon back for the pilot. A man who looked like he was in charge was taking a report. I heard another balloon passenger tell him the story about the pilot drinking the champagne shortly before the balloon changed course. I listened as I watched from the opposite side of the truck. Leaning down and looking into the mirror as I doctored my chin, I temporarily appeared invisible to the men holding the conversation.

I stood up so they could see me, as I was sure they would want to interview me, but their conversation ceased. Before we departed, the man taking the report did ask for our names and addresses, but did not ask what I thought happened, or if I saw the pilot drinking alcohol. I did voluntarily mention it to him, but instantly regretted saying anything, because I picked up a weird vibe as soon as I said it.

We made our way back by caravan to get our vehicle. Almost half the people who had gathered earlier that morning were still there to welcome us. Most of those remaining were either owners, aeronauts, family, friends, or avid fans of hot air balloons. We were now balloon celebrities.

Everyone wanted to hear about our scary adventure and congratulate us for surviving our hard but successful landing and still being in good enough spirits to talk about it.

Our pilot drinking champagne story was no surprise to the older die-hard veteran balloonists.

"He's always the last launch number, for a reason," one of the men in his early seventies said. The men exchanged looks that expressed thoughts only long-time comrades with history fully understood.

"I reported the drinking to the investigator," I said.

"Investigator?" he asked.

"The man who arrived at the scene asking questions and taking names," I said.

"Oh, Larry," he said smugly, "he's not an investigator, he's your aeronaut's father. Taught him everything he knows about ballooning and, rumor has it, drinking."

"I'll drink to that," one of the old guys in the group said as he held up his glass.

I just shook my head as several of the other old men chuckled.

"You be safe going home," I said. "Nice to meet all of you."

Craig and I headed home.

"Craig, I want to tell you why I'm afraid to fly."

As Craig drove, I proceeded to share the story with him about my friends and their plane crash and the reasons I thought it might be my fault.

Craig was compassionate and reassured me I was not to blame for their accident. I wanted to somehow believe him. I also wanted him to forgive himself for what happened in the balloon that day.

My hands and legs began trembling once we got home. Craig held me as I started to relive the day my friends crashed and realized how close we came to disaster in the balloon that day. I fell asleep in Craig's arms.

***

Craig didn't realize I rarely went outdoors for almost a year before we met. I had ridden horses since the time I could walk and was a talented rider in my teens, but after getting an office job during my senior year of college, I drifted away from my outdoor lifestyle and had spent the last eight years tied to a desk during the weekdays.

The exception was those last few years boating and flying to weekend vacation destinations with my friends. Weekend warriors, we called ourselves, because we all worked Monday through Friday nine to five, like Dolly Parton, John used to say, paying homage to her often talked about hit movie at the time.

Craig got to spend time with the new and improved me, which was a version of the old me Craig was helping me rediscover.

I was grateful Cathy had been at work during our landing because I knew it would have frightened her and brought up the same memories I was now reliving. It was a story best relayed to Cathy over dinner a few weeks later, where she would get to meet Craig for the first time. Cathy had heard about the balloon almost landing in her yard from her neighbors but had no idea I was one of the five people in the balloon. Cathy commented about it being yet another crazy coincidence in a long string of coincidences Cathy and I had experienced since we met. Through Cathy's stories, Craig got to see a small part of me, a part I really liked sharing with him.

CHAPTER TWELVE

Freefalling

Four weeks rolled past me like tumbleweeds. I was still learning new things about Craig and hadn't discovered a single thing about him I didn't like. We both worked during the day and met up at his apartment as soon as our workday was finished. After our first dinner date, I never spent another night at my apartment.

"We need to get a good night's sleep," Craig said. "I have a surprise for you in the morning."

"What do you have planned this time?"

I shot him a suspicious but curious look and was met with a smile and slightly bowed head.

"After that balloon ride, I'm on to you," I said.

I knew he was up to something.

"We are going to do something that will probably scare the crap out of me, aren't we?" I asked, trying to guess.

"I don't want to frighten you," Craig said. "It's to enlighten you, to open you up to more than you ever dreamed possible."

"Thanks for the Zen energy but what you mean is, it's going to scare the crap out of me, right," I repeated.

Craig chuckled.

"Yes, I suppose you are correct, it will."

I then play-poked him in the ribs and tickled him as we wrestled about the living room in his apartment, laughing. His admission took my curiosity to an entirely new level. I couldn't let it go.

"You'll sleep better tonight if you don't know," Craig said.

"If you think I'm going to sleep now, you're wrong. Tell me now, please."

"Skydiving."

"Oh, no we're not."

A shiver spread across my body, starting somewhere in my gut and permeating out of my skin. I immediately began to sweat. I could feel a still unnoticeable tremble trying to wiggle its way to each of my four limbs. I got quiet and I thought long and hard about it.

"I can't do it. I just know myself well enough to know I can't step out the door of an airplane. It could just never happen. I'm not sure I can even step into the door of a small plane. Maybe I'll go and just ride with you to conquer my fear of small planes."

It was a small concession, but one I would attempt to make, not just for Craig, but for my own healing.

Around 11:30 p.m., well past our usual 9 p.m. bedtime, I tossed and turned under the covers in a complete state of panic and dread. Craig, realizing my predicament, turned on the light and took my hands in his hands, and convinced me all I had to do was go with him and watch.

"No one is going to make you jump if you don't want to do it."

I agreed to go, but only to watch Craig jump. Neither of us believed that would be the ultimate outcome. I tried over and over to convince myself I would just go and watch, nothing more, but my thoughts were spinning scenarios of me falling through the sky. I didn't fall asleep until after 3 a.m.

Seven in the morning rolled around entirely too soon. Immediately upon awakening, I realized why the alarm had sounded and where we were going. The first thing that entered my mind when I opened my eyes was the conversation Craig and I had the previous evening about skydiving. I remembered wishing the previous night for sleep to put an end to my apprehension, but I succumbed to restless anticipation for most of the night.

I struggled to gather my purse, sweater, and sunglasses before walking to the car. My thoughts were still spinning, my hands shaking, and my brain wasn't processing information efficiently. I was terrified and sleepy. Craig convinced me once more that I could just watch, but he wanted me to come with him.

Of course, being head over heels in love with him, and relishing every minute I got to spend with him, even just driving in a car sitting next to him, I couldn't say no. I wanted to be with him but didn't want to leap to my death for him. I hesitantly got into the passenger seat for the thirty-five-minute drive to the Drop Zone in Bellbrook, Ohio.

Craig reached for my hand as we were driving, but this time, he held a slightly sweaty one.

"Nervous?" he asked. "You are just going to watch. Relax."

I convinced myself there was a definite possibility I would not end up jumping, and that was what kept me planted in the passenger seat beside Craig. I had to believe I could still back out of the jump. Otherwise, I might have shaken right out of the seat or opened the car door and leaped from the moving vehicle.

We arrived at the facility and entered a white building made of concrete block construction. A store inside sold skydiving equipment including parachutes, one-piece zip-up jumpsuits that reminded me of coveralls painters wore over their clothes, goggles, safety head gear, and smaller collectible items like key chains and souvenirs.

We were greeted by a young man named Brad, who I later discovered was a twenty-year-old with over 10,000 skydiving hours. His mom, a lifelong avid skydiver, owned the facility. *Kudos to Brad's mom,* I thought.

"Two for skydiving?" Brad asked.

"One," I said. "I'm just here to watch."

"A watcher, I see," Brad said with a wink. He and Craig both smiled. I knew they had spoken on the telephone previously, but I had missed most of their conversation.

"I saw that wink."

Craig and Brad exchanged glances and shrugged their shoulders like they had no idea what I meant.

Brad was super cute with dimples. He won me over immediately with his witty, charming personality. I could tell he appeared a bit confused by our mismatched coupling, as he first thought we were siblings, although I knew Craig had told him he was bringing his girlfriend. That part of their telephone conversation, I had overheard. Brad couldn't quite put the pieces of our love puzzle together as evidenced by his face when he met me and then glanced back and forth between me and Craig several times before apparently surrendering to the great unknown.

"Cool, let's go," Brad said.

Craig explained to me that they were going to give me the full skydiving experience without forcing me or expecting me to jump. I looked at them both with a suspicious glare before falling for their story lock, stock, and barrel.

"Do you need jumpsuits, or did you bring your own?" Brad asked Craig.

"I have one, but it's in Norway right now, so yes, I'll need one."

"What size?" Brad asked. Craig answered him, and they both waited for me to respond. My heart sank. I was going to have to tell them my size. I wanted to run through the door crying. My legs were vibrating so hard, my knees would have made a drumbeat sound if it hadn't been for the cotton material of blue jeans muffling the sound coming from between them. I was mortified.

I was in the presence of two men who were so kind and understanding as they both responded to my hesitation and obvious fear by taking immediate action. I was hoping they would believe my strange reaction to the size of my jumpsuit was because putting one on would indicate I would actually agree to jump from a plane.

I was facing the three biggest fears of my life. My first fear was going up in a small plane. My second fear was admitting what size I wore. My third fear was losing Craig due to him finding out what size I wore. Anxiety was clinging to me like sweat that day.

Before I answered, Brad had brought me a white jumpsuit that fit perfectly. I'm not sure what size it was, XL probably, but it fit. I wasn't happy it was white or that I had to wear it over my already bulky clothes.

Relieved that the jumpsuit fit and I didn't have to return it for a larger size, and in a hurry to have the "what size do you wear" conversation far behind me, I realized I had quickly stepped into and zipped up the jumpsuit. I was nervous all over again, but this time it was about the jump.

"Why do I have to wear a suit if I'm not going to jump?"

"It's for safety. We're not allowed to take you up in the plane unless you are properly suited up with safety gear since the door will be open," Brad said.

It made sense. I accepted his answer. Brad pushed a VHS tape into a television. We watched the safety video and signed a release saying we had watched it and took full responsibility if we happened to end up in a hospital or morgue.

Before any of us were allowed to approach the plane, we walked across a field where they had an empty shell of a plane where we could practice jumping.

"We're going to practice landing while jumping from this platform," Brad said.

"I'll just watch Craig practice since I'm not going to jump," I said.

Brad explained that because Craig had over 4,000 jumps, he wasn't required to practice landing. Since I was going to be in the aircraft with them, and I had never gone up before, I had to know the safety drill in case something happened to the aircraft while we were gaining altitude and I had to jump. It made sense. I was suspicious, but I complied.

"Vanessa, it will be fun to practice anyway and there is no harm in it, right? It's not like you are jumping from a real airplane. Be a good sport and do it for me," Craig said.

"Did you just say be a good sport? Because I know you didn't just say that."

He was batting his eyes at me and smiling in an exaggerated manner.

"If I jump, it will be for me, understand?"

He nodded in agreement, but we both knew everything was for him. The only thing standing in the way of me, my slippers, a cup of coffee, and a couch throw keeping me warm right now, was him.

Thankfully, I needed only a little practice jumping and falling, and instead paid closer attention to the training tips, which consisted of keeping my arms crossed on my chest and my mouth closed so my saliva wouldn't enter the face of my tandem partner, who would be strapped to my back.

We also jumped to the ground to go over the five points of contact rule. If you hit the ground, you need to disburse the energy of the fall through your body by dropping and rolling in a way not to break your neck. I was familiar with this technique because I learned it early in my life as an equestrian, how to take the safest fall off a horse if that dreaded day presented itself.

First, land on the balls of the feet, drop down to the side of your calf, then the side of thigh, followed by your hip and buttocks, and then the side of your back. I didn't have to practice long, and I complied in good spirit. I was a bit proud of myself for performing the test falls correctly. I could tell my hidden athleticism and knowledge of the five points of contact surprised both Craig and Brad.

We finished practicing. My nerves were once again off the chart, immeasurable, because I knew what was coming next.

We headed towards the plane that would be hauling us to 13,000 feet. Craig smiled at me and nodded his head towards the large, custom-made, square entrance. He reached for my hand and helped me climb in after him. How could I resist?

"Would you jump off a cliff if he asked you?" I could hear my mom saying to me, all the while thinking to myself, "Yes, Mother, I already did jump off a cliff for him."

Ten jumpers were on board. The pilot spoke loudly over the roar of the engines and told us we had to sit in double rows of five facing the tail of the plane. We had to sit up against each other, back to stomach, and crunch up toward the front of the small, seatless single-propeller plane as tightly as we could.

Brad handed me a harness and yelled into my ear, "Put this on."

I shook my head no.

"It's for safety so you don't fly out the door with all the other jumpers when they open it. You don't want to go up with them without being hooked to someone with a parachute, do you?" Brad asked.

I shook my head to indicate no; I definitely did not want to go out the door without a parachute.

I didn't want to go anywhere near the door, with a parachute or without a parachute, but I quickly put the harness on like a jacket and buckled it.

"I don't want to jump," I reminded him. I had to turn my head sideways and speak loudly so he could hear me, although his face was only inches from my face. We wore leather helmets that covered our ears, and the noise of the plane drowned out normal conversation.

"When they open the door, you can decide, but I can't have you sitting back here without being strapped to a parachute, and right now, that parachute is on me, so you have to be strapped to me, understand?"

Still looking at Brad with my head turned back towards him I nodded yes, I understood.

"You don't have to jump if you don't want to. Just relax and breathe. It will take about fifteen minutes to get to altitude. You'll have plenty of time to decide."

My thoughts were racing. I wanted to believe that I still had a choice and I tried to relax by telling myself I had at least fifteen minutes more to live, which seemed like a blessing. Even fifteen minutes, if that was all I had, seemed sacred to me as I looked at Craig and thought of all we had done and how alive I felt. I felt the plane's wheels as they parted from the runway. We were airborne.

Time seemed to pass faster in the air than it did on earth, because sooner than I anticipated, the pilot made an announcement that the plane had reached altitude and was in position over the landing zone. My body trembled to the beat of the pilot's every spoken syllable. It would be time to jump in sixty seconds, then the pilot announced thirty seconds. The videographer stood up and slung open the door. Then the pilot announced fifteen seconds, then go, go, go.

It was a large door for such a small plane. It was an amazing view. I realized I had never been in a plane with an open door and although I was fascinated by the exhilarating new experience, I was equally grateful to be hooked securely and safely to Brad's harness.

"I'm not going to jump," I said as I reached back to unsnap my harness from his.

"You have to stay connected to me for safety. Do not touch that buckle. We'll let everyone jump and then we'll walk over so you can look out the door and then you can decide." I nodded, as if I still somehow believed that would be the case, although my faith in Brad's truthfulness was more than wavering.

One by one, everyone jumped. Craig smiled at me as he exited the door and disappeared.

"Stand up," Brad said. I somehow managed to use my legs. The videographer was still with us, taping me, so I was thinking we weren't jumping. I thought they were just going to videotape me being a complete chicken until we landed on the ground.

"Look out the door," Brad said loudly so I could hear above the rushing wind noise. "It's fantastic. You'll never see anything like it." I shook all over from head to toe. I did not want to go near the door or see out the door.

I reluctantly made my way over to it but braced both my feet and hands against all four corners of the frame like a cat refusing to go into a cat carrier. My bracing was only a feeble attempt not to fall or be pushed out into the endless beauty of the clear blue sky, which I was now seeing in all its infinite glory, in a unique way, for the first time.

"Jump," Brad said. "We have to jump now."

"No, no."

I shook my head and braced harder.

"We must jump now, or we'll land somewhere off-course and that will be dangerous. Jump now and we'll be fine." Again, I braced. "On the count of three," he said, then, "one."

On the count of one I was floating like a feather through the air. It was the most incredible feeling I've ever experienced. Brad tapped me on my shoulder and pointed for me to look up because the videographer had jumped and was floating directly across from us. I smiled at the camera and waved, but what I really wanted to do was look down and enjoy every minute of this noisy feeling of floating on air. I can't call it a fall because it did not feel like falling. I was weightless and I liked that feeling. Barely had I started to enjoy this, just thirty seconds into the freefall, that Brad pulled the rip cord on the parachute, and it felt like we shot straight up into the sky.

In actuality, we were still falling, but our speed had slowed due to the opening of the parachute. Immediately, there wasn't a sound to be heard.

It went from feeling light as air with loud wind rushing past my ears, to silence. That wonderful feeling of weightlessness had now abandoned me. I was now dangling about ten inches below Brad, with him still strapped to my back. After thirty seconds of total silence and taking in the scenery, it got a little boring compared to the rush of adrenaline I had just experienced.

I asked, "Can we cut the parachute loose, fall again, and then open the reserve before we hit the ground?" I was serious. I was apparently an adrenaline junkie locked in a scared girl's body.

"No, we are not cutting the parachute loose," Brad said. It was a firm no, and I think it surprised him I had even asked. I was hooked on the feeling of floating.

After two or three awkward silent minutes, with me dangling down in front of Brad, facing the ground in complete stillness, I had taken in all the views around us and could see the landing site. We still had three or four more minutes before we reached the ground.

"How old are you?" I asked.

"Twenty," Brad said.

"How old are you?"

"Thirty, I'll be thirty-one next month."

"How old is Craig."

"Twenty-five."

"Cradle robber," he said, teasing me about the age difference between me and Craig.

"I could turn around and we could kiss until we land, to pass time, you know," I said as a joke in response to Brad's cradle-robbing jab. Brad, who had just admitted to being ten years younger than me, took it accordingly.

"Or I could just unsnap these," he said using both of his hands to point to my harness buckles, "and cut you loose."

Point taken. We both giggled. He couldn't wait to tell Craig I asked him for a kiss during the quiet, more boring part of the under-canopy ride. Everyone in the group laughed and teased me, including Craig. I blamed it on a freefall high and lack of oxygen to my brain due to high-altitude poisoning.

"You can't blame me for asking for a final kiss on my presumed deathbed, right?" I asked, defending myself. Craig knew I only had eyes for him, and he knew I was only toying with Brad.

Our joking around with each other, coupled with the adrenaline high we were experiencing, caused any and all age differences to quickly fade, and I felt a genuine camaraderie with Brad and my new skydiving buddies. We talked for hours after our jump. Craig and I stayed at the landing zone and watched Brad make a few more solo jumps and what the guys called his signature hot dog landings. Adrenaline and exhaustion finally got the best of us, so we said our goodbyes.

Brad gifted me with a VHS tape recording so I'd never forget my leap of faith. The skydiving part was amazing and life changing. Except for the jump itself where I was facing the camera, my backside—highlighted by the oversized white jumpsuit—was center stage during most of the filming. Any retained memories I may still have about being a hot skydiving babe are quickly put into perspective when I rewatch that tape.

I wore a smile on my face for days after my skydiving experience, a remnant of which remains to this day.

***

One evening after work, six weeks after we went skydiving, Craig and I were relaxing on the couch and catching up on the news on a three-channel television with a rabbit ear antenna. The news anchor announced a group of nine skydivers had died in a plane crash in Arizona while practicing for a national competition. He said a local man was among those who perished in the accident and then he said Brad's name. Brad was dead.

"Oh no, no, not our Brad," I cried out as I turned around and buried my head into Craig's chest.

Craig had caught Brad's name at the same time. Although neither of us wanted to believe what we had just heard, we both remembered Brad had mentioned he was practicing for a national competition.

We both held each other and remained silent after our initial exclamations of disbelief. I called my mom and she had heard the news the same time we did.

"I was just getting ready to call you and ask you isn't that the name of the boy who jumped out of an airplane with you?" my mom said.

"Yes, Mom. Craig and I were just sitting here hoping it wasn't the Brad we knew."

"Honey, I think it was him because I heard the name of the skydiving facility where you jumped on the other channel earlier today. I'm so sorry." My mom started to cry knowing how losing yet another person in a plane crash was going to affect me.

"I love you, Mom. I'll come and visit you and Dad this weekend."

"I love you, too. Call me anytime you want to talk."

The local newspaper wrote up Brad's life story, and although it was a short life, it was a life full of family love, commitment, adventure, and accomplishments. There is no one I would have wanted to share my first skydiving experience with, or to push me out of a perfectly good airplane, than Brad.

Our hearts and thoughts were with Brad's family and the people we had recently met at the skydiving facility. We mourned his loss, along with an entire skydiving community, and felt a deep connection to him, as if we had known him much longer than the one morning and afternoon we spent floating through the air with him and his friends.

Chapter Thirteen

Spelunking into Darkness

On July 1, 1989, Craig and I set out on an adventure to Mammoth Cave National Park in Kentucky. The journey was thrilling, but the real excitement lay in the simple act of holding hands with the person I loved. It felt like an unspoken vow, a promise to stay close no matter where life took us. The thought of letting go felt like admitting defeat, like conceding to the inevitable end of our love story.

As we drove down I-75 South, the scenery morphed into miles of majestic mountains looming directly over us and other mountains as far as I could see off in the distance with towering peaks that reached towards the sky. The thick tree-covered landscape was painted in various shades of green. It was hard not to feel small and insignificant in the presence of such grandeur.

As we drove, my mind wandered and I contemplated our impending separation. In just a few short months, Craig would be whisked away to Greece as part of a university exchange program, and then off to England to finish his degree before he returned home to Norway. It was becoming difficult to visualize a future without him. But I felt safe and content knowing that in that moment, we were together.

The drive to Kentucky took three hours but felt much shorter, as did most of our time while traveling together. The weather was cooler than normal for a warm summer day. Fortunately, we remembered to bring our jackets because the caves stay close to fifty-four degrees Fahrenheit, which, to me, is freezing. I prefer around eighty degrees Fahrenheit; another reason I knew deep inside my heart Norway was not a suitable place for me.

We entered the cave and followed along behind a line of people. At first, we walked through a wide opening and proceeded down a wide natural stone hallway with light pouring in through the cave entrance. It quickly became darker than I expected. I hadn't anticipated the complete and total darkness, but I should have because it was, after all, a cave.

We were inside the belly of the world's longest cave with nearly one thousand miles either already explored or still undiscovered. The lights mounted along the initial path and the helmet lights and lanterns were yellow and dim and didn't illuminate the interior well.

On our first day, we chose to take the two-mile guided tour that began shortly after we arrived. It ended in the tuberculosis ward and had 160 stairs, which felt to me like 560, but I wasn't counting. The tuberculosis ward is where doctors housed sick patients, incorrectly believing the chilly air would be good for them. The disease was incurable when the ward was used in 1858, because penicillin wouldn't be discovered for another seventy years. Many people died in the caves, either from tuberculosis or from getting disoriented or stuck in small spaces while spelunking.

During the tour, the guides turned off all the lights to give tourists the experience of being in a dark cave without any hint of light. During the short blackout, the guides told us ghost stories that had become local folklore. Visitors regularly reported experiencing strange sensations and discovering orbs in their photographs. Just thinking of being in a dark cave where many people had perished created an aura of eeriness.

I was relieved when they turned on the lights. Their stories spooked me, but that was their intended purpose. Pioneers discovered the caves in 1790, but the caves had been used by humans for thousands of years prior to the arrival of the pioneers. I visualized early man and wild animals competing for shelter in the very spot where I was standing.

In 1925, a thirty-seven-year-old avid cave explorer got his leg wedged in between two rocks. Although other spelunkers and family members were able to reach him and brought water and food to him for fifteen days, they were not able to free him or save his life.

When he died, they dislodged his body and then displayed the dead body outside the cave's main entrance with a glass lid so tourists could watch him decay, and he decayed unusually slowly. It wasn't until 1989, the same year we were in the cave, that he was finally laid to rest at Mammoth Cave Baptist Church Cemetery. They had a sign outside the visitors' parking saying "Here used to lie the body of Floyd Collins, America's Greatest Cave Explorer."

Nothing Craig and I ever did was dull, so the following day we decided to go spelunking on the more adventurous crawling tour, called the Wild Cave Tour. This involved actual crawling, complete with knee pads. We were trying to stick close to the second half of our group, which consisted of me, Craig, and three other people we met outside the cave. They were slightly more experienced at spelunking than Craig was, and far more experienced than I was. Craig had explored a dozen caves in his travels, but this was my first. Our new companions knew Mammoth Cave well, so regardless of the number of cave crawls Craig had, the locals earned the lead.

I was covered in dirt. The rocks were damp and cold. Bats occasionally buzzed past us when one of us would inadvertently disturb their sleep. Three months prior to this, I would never have believed I would crawl miles through a dark cave all in the name of love.

"Bats have a magnificent sense of echolocation which prevents them from landing on you. The superstition is if a bat takes off with a piece of your hair, you will die," our guide said.

Good to know.

He added, "Normally the bats do not roost where the tourists crawl, but today, we must take a path which isn't frequently used. The normal route is blocked with water from exceptionally heavy rainfall last week, so I apologize in advance if we see more bats or even minor flooded areas during our crawl. We may run into some water, but it shouldn't be too hazardous. One of the guides already crawled it this morning to be sure it was clear."

"We saw an ambulance yesterday. Did someone get hurt?" I asked.

"Well, yeah, sorta, yesterday, spelunkers on the normal route ran into some water and got stranded for an extended time. One of them experienced mild hypothermia and was hospitalized, so we've opted to not make the same mistake today. The guy is going to be fine, but as a result, y'all get to explore a rarely visited, but drier section of the cave."

Lucky us.

Did this make me happy? Not a bit.

Conversation was limited during the latter half of our crawl because even the most experienced crawlers of the group were getting a bit winded. We were just trying to concentrate on placing our hands and feet in the right spot using only the small lantern on our headgear to make our way through. The lead spelunker spoke occasionally to reassure us we were fine. He gave us coordinates as to how far we had come and how far we had left to go. I was not entirely convinced our guide had as much confidence as he claimed.

I was nearing perceived hypothermia, wet, tired, and cold, and was ready to see daylight at the end of the tunnel. I fantasized about a heavy parka wrapped around me. I wanted to bask in the sun. I envisioned a nice dinner and a long night's sleep fueled by exhaustion, lying in Craig's arms. Love kept me going. I felt fit and strong and fueled by that mysterious source of energy only being in love provides. As a result, I persevered.

As my mind continued to wander, we came to an opening in the cave where we could all stand and walk for half a mile. It was a welcome relief. Crawling on rocks is not for the faint of heart. It was still very black, and this section of the trip did not have low-level lighting mounted all along the cave walls like the walking tour had.

We formed a circle and shone our headlamps into the center of the circle. It made it easier to see one another and do a head count. I could see how dusty and dirty our faces, hands, and clothes were. I was still in good spirits as we rested for a moment.

"You alright?" Craig asked.

"Yes, how about you?"

"I'm fine. I'm really enjoying this," Craig replied.

Our guide pulled out a backpack with bottled water and Snickers bars. It was a welcome surprise. I swallowed the Snickers bar in three bites, maybe two. I figured I had worked off more calories than I had consumed on this trek, so no worries. I washed the candy bar down with a bottle of water.

"You want some of mine?" Craig asked.

"No, I'm fine. You drink yours."

I realized I must have seemed a bit parched for him to notice how my candy bar and water disappeared so quickly while the others were still chewing and drinking. Then I realized he was offering me half of his Snickers bar. I declined, but I wanted it.

"I've never had one of these," Craig said holding up his Snickers candy bar. "It's good."

We handed the empty water bottles and candy bar wrappers to our guide. He put them in his backpack as he gave us an overview of where we were in the cave, where we were heading, and how long we had to go before we began another crawl. Suddenly, the lights on all our headsets flickered, dimmed, lit up again, and repeated. The lights stayed on for a minute at the most, and the guide said he had never had that happen before because they were all using portable independent batteries. My brain tried to get a sense of what was happening to our headlamps.

All I could think of was the tour guide telling us the caves were rumored to be haunted. That was enough to scare me. I was ready to get out of that cave.

When the lights flickered again, I reached again for Craig's hand and held it. Just after I'd grasped his hand our headlamps went out and this time, they did not come back on for what I estimate was ten minutes.

The guide told us to place a hand on the back of the person in front of us and he would guide us along the left cave wall for the next half mile. He said again he could not explain why our headlamps were not working, that it wasn't a planned part of the tour, but everything would be fine. He knew the way out of the cave in the dark and he had been through this path at least one hundred times. He told us not to worry.

All I could think was, *he has been through here a hundred times but never have the headlamps simultaneously failed.* My hand was sweating in Craig's hand, yet I was freezing.

Craig placed his left hand on the back of the person in front of him while still holding my left hand in his right hand. The person behind me placed their hand on my back and we started to move slowly forward. I carefully placed my feet down, one by one, to avoid tripping or stepping on Craig's feet, which were in front of mine. I quickly fell into a rhythm as we picked up the pace.

I wondered what would happen if our headlamps stayed out for the rest of the trip and if we had to crawl without headlamps. I tried not to let future-oriented worries get too embedded in my thoughts.

I wanted to whisper to Craig to tell him how cold I was, but I didn't want to add any additional burden to the trip or be a complainer. The cave seemed to get suddenly colder but I assumed it was psychological because it was pitch black and the inherent fear of being in a cold, dark place was causing poor circulation in my limbs. I started to shiver.

I wondered if Craig could feel me shaking through his hand. I expected I would start to warm since we were keeping a good pace at the time, but I did not. Just when I thought I couldn't tolerate it any longer, our headlamps all started to work at the same time. Craig turned, put his hands on my waist inside my jacket, and hugged me. I could feel the warmth of his hands against my skin, and it was comparable to having a hot stone massage. My tense muscles relaxed from the warmth of his touch.

"You are freezing," he said.

I turned with a nervous, but relieved, smile to make small talk with the person behind me. I knew they were as cold as I was because I felt their cold hand in the middle of my back. When I turned, there was no one there. We did a head count. All the spelunkers were in front of me.

I never told Craig. I stayed close holding on to him or to a piece of his clothing the rest of the trip and despite being afraid, I warmed up quickly and my shivering subsided. We eventually made it out safely. I didn't turn to look behind me again until we were outside, in broad daylight.

I wondered if Craig sensed something because of the way I was clinging to him for the second half of the trip. He somehow seemed to know. We ate at a local restaurant where we talked about the lights and how weird it was that they all went out at the same time and then without explanation returned to normal. Craig looked at me in a peculiar way during the rehashing of events, as if he were waiting for me to tell him something more, but I did not.

We decided to make the three-hour drive home instead of staying in Kentucky that night. It was as if we couldn't put enough time and distance between us and that cave. When we got into the car, I took off my jacket and sat it on my lap. I looked down at my jacket and saw an imprint of a large bony-looking handprint, in the middle of the cave dust still covering the back of my jacket.

I quickly tossed the jacket into the backseat. I think Craig looked down long enough to see the imprint, or maybe he saw it on my back in the restaurant and was curious if I had an explanation or an experience in the cave that would account for that handprint. I was afraid to talk to Craig about anything supernatural, although I sensed he would have believed me.

We sat quietly in the car next to each other and I remained deep in thought for the entire ride home. It was as if the cave was a metaphor for my life; full of twists and turns, with glimpses of incredible beauty scattered with unexplained events throughout. And just like I had survived before I met him, I knew deep down I would survive again. Because even in the midst of darkness, there is always a glimmer of light called hope.

Chapter Fourteen

Fear of Flying

Months later, we drove to Indianapolis to board a flight to San Diego with a stop in Denver. Our trip to walk across the Golden Gate Bridge was underway, but the Golden Gate was just one stop on our cross-country adventure. The car ride to Indianapolis International Airport was uneventful. When we arrived, we parked in long-term parking. I did have preflight jitters, but nothing, especially my anxiety, was going to stop me from experiencing this adventure with Craig.

We boarded the Boeing 747 and sat in the first seats on the left as you are walking down the aisle to board, right behind first class. We talked as we waited for other passengers to board. The plane looked and smelled new and there was extra leg room in those first two seats.

"We got great seats," Craig said as he squeezed my hand and smiled. He seemed to sense just when I needed a smile and squeeze of encouragement. Craig and I never ran out of things to talk about, and we never got tired of being together. It was a magical time.

We landed in Denver and changed planes. We still had time to get to our destination and check into our hotel, but it seemed like we sat on the tarmac for hours. Our patience was wearing a bit thin as we were excited with anticipation and ready to get on with our trip.

Denver was in the middle of a freakishly early snowstorm. It would have been considered a blizzard in Ohio. I decided right then I would never be able to live in Denver.

The thick white snow reminded Craig of Norway. Craig and I had our first real conversation about my preference for hot, sunny weather and his preference for freezing, snowy weather. It was our first crack, but not one strong enough to cause a rift. It weighed heavily on my mind, as I knew I would never be able to live in a frigid environment.

An hour passed and we could hardly see the wings out the window. We could see airport employees dressed in neon yellow and orange safety jackets moving around the exterior of the plane, checking and double checking. They de-iced the wings twice before the pilot announced the control tower had cleared us for takeoff. I had never flown in inclement weather, so watching them de-ice the wings was new for me. I had already had enough tragic experiences with airplanes, without throwing severe weather into the mix. I was good through the first de-icing, but by the second de-icing, I was ready to disembark the plane, rent a car, and drive the rest of the way.

The excitement of the trip, and the early drive from Dayton to Indianapolis, had caused both of us to get less than the appropriate amount of sleep. We were still communicating well. I couldn't help but think that the conversation about our future living preferences and disagreement about the ideal climate had come up when it did because we needed a good hot meal and some rest.

That was the excuse I made, anyway. It was a legitimate issue that would need to be addressed as our time together was reaching a crescendo. The only redeeming feature about our travel delay was the time zone change. As we traveled west, we gained three hours. Therefore, we would still arrive at our hotel in plenty of time to grab a nice dinner and get a good eight hours of sleep. I looked forward to that.

The pilot announced they were preparing the cabin for departure, and we should place our seats in the upright position and secure our lap trays. We happily complied as we were more than ready to reach California.

We were still holding hands as we taxied towards the runway. We were happy to leave our first serious conversation behind us, although we both knew it would follow us. There was no escaping the truth and reality of our living situation. Our physical relationship was about to end. We would soon be living in two entirely different countries. Squabbling over tropical versus wintry weather living arrangements was just the first step of many to get us to the inevitable goodbye, a goodbye I didn't want to envision.

The sound of the jet engines increased into a loud whining sound, and I could feel the power behind them. At that moment, as I thought about the coming end of the relationship, I compared it to a horrific crash or sudden death.

Our relationship was going to die soon. There was no way to work it out long term. The only thing we could do was live life to the fullest and cherish every moment together. "We've Got Tonight" by Bob Seger played in my head.

The jumbo jet accelerated as it sped down the long runway. A loud boom sounded. Craig was sitting by the window, but I immediately leaned over him and looked out and could see dark gray smoke coming from the wing. It was still snowing, so the contrast of white and gray made the imminent danger clearly visible.

The plane suddenly decelerated, but I hardly noticed it. The pilot announced we would be abandoning takeoff and heading back to the terminal. No one from the airline explained anything. It was terrifying, especially the first moments after seeing the smoke, and not being able to get out of the plane. I couldn't imagine going through that with anyone other than Craig.

Three hours later, we were finally allowed to disembark. We learned the hydraulic system had failed, and we were seconds away from the point of no return. The point of no return is the point during takeoff when the pilot cannot abandon liftoff. Without hydraulics we would surely have crashed and, carrying full tanks of fuel, exploded on impact.

After four and a half hours, with our last hour and a half spent browsing around Stapleton International Airport, the flight attendants ushered us back onto the same aircraft, which I found disturbing. I noticed our once full plane now had empty seats. Some passengers must have rented cars or changed destinations. That was not a convenient option for us. Craig and I still had a long way to go to get to our destination, so we opted to risk it. I wanted out of this miserable snowstorm. I wanted to see a sunny San Diego sky.

We arrived and took an airport shuttle to our hotel, without further incident but with a renewed and magnified appreciation for life. I was feeling more alive than ever after that experience, and I knew this vacation was going to be an epic event in my life.

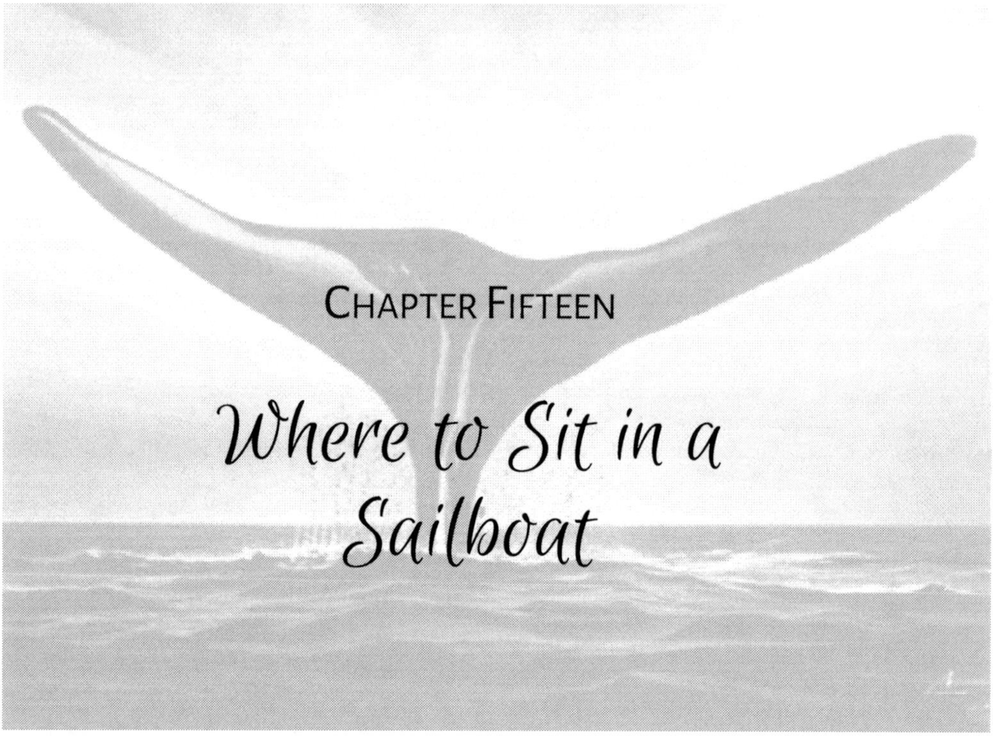

Chapter Fifteen

Where to Sit in a Sailboat

San Diego had a cool vibe. Cool breezes, clothes, and people. I immediately wanted to be like those around me. I wanted to be relaxed and easygoing, too. I needed to shake off the near-death experience from the prior day and let my frayed nerves heal. Physically, we were unscathed, but my fear of flying was now so embedded in my bones, only real death could ever erase it entirely.

The air travel portion of our trip was complete, at least until the final leg of our journey. We had opted for other modes of transportation for the next few weeks of our vacation. I was pleased and relieved I didn't have to fly again until we arrived in Chicago and after that, I might just opt to never fly again.

Healing sunlight warmed me as I basked in the light of the sun and breathed in the smell of the ocean breeze. This was heaven on earth, but I never took the company and charm of the handsome man next to me for granted. Without him, this would just be another place and any other place on earth would just be an empty place. This was just the place to revive my shaken but grateful soul.

At no other time in my life were the sun, moon, and stars so perfectly aligned for me, and I knew it. This was my time, our time, and I would commit to being present in the moment so I wouldn't miss a minute of it. I was resolved to absorb and record into my memory every moment I had with him.

The colors were brighter, sounds were clearer, smells were fresher, and the salty air tasted delicious.

We fortunately were able to catch up on our sleep and didn't have anything too exciting planned for our first full day, or so I thought. After asking around, we visited a popular taco stand and ate al fresco. As a person who had only experienced tacos from Taco Bell, this new sensation for my taste buds was mouthwateringly delicious.

The weather was barely warm, not hot. I am always chilled, so I sat with my back in the sun wearing a hooded, light-blue with pastel-yellow trim American Eagle cotton jacket I had purchased especially for this trip. The air was clear and crisp. There wasn't a cloud in the deep Maya-blue sky. I was expecting thick smog in California, but as surprising to me as a snowstorm in Denver, it was the freshest air I had ever experienced. I saw no litter along the roads leading to the restaurant, or around the outdoor eating area where we were soaking up the sun. I noticed patrons cleaned up all their trash. This place was not at all like the California I had envisioned.

Craig asked for directions to a local marina, which we happily found out was within walking distance. We had planned to call a cab to reach the marina but instead, Craig reached for my hand and we set out on foot for our first adventure, one I guessed would involve a visit to a local aquarium to see some dolphins.

"I have a special afternoon planned for us," Craig said.

"I have no doubt you do."

I felt excitement tinged with fear and anticipation as his earlier planned escapades came to the forefront of my mind.

"We're going sailing," he said.

"Parasailing?"

"No, regular sailing on a sailboat."

"I've never done that before," I said, "but I am relieved it's not parasailing."

"Maybe we can do that tomorrow," Craig said. He was looking for a reaction from me.

"Yes, that would be fun," I said. He knew I was lying.

"I suspected you were taking me to an aquarium and dolphin show. I saw a brochure for it at the hotel." Sailing alone with Craig on the ocean sounded like a ton more fun and so romantic. I had never been on any type of ship or boat on the ocean.

"I'm not sure they just let you walk up and rent sailboats, so don't be disappointed if they are already booked." Micromanaging Me was at it again.

"I already took care of that. I hope you get to see dolphins in the wild. I'm not crazy about shows with captive dolphins jumping and swimming with people on their backs," Craig said.

He smiled, that special smile of his that indicated he had something up his sleeve and something that would most definitely be a fascinating surprise to me. I suppose taking someone like me, who doesn't get out much, on a cross-country trip would take little planning. I was easy to keep entertained, but Craig's adventurous plans would arouse the interest of even a seasoned explorer. To me, they were mind-blowing adventures on a monumental scale.

I came to realize this trip was my fate. I felt safe, like I could go anywhere and do anything. I was not worried about what dangers might lie ahead in the weeks to come. I was going to embrace each moment of this trip, day by day, week by week, as if it were my last. In a way, it was.

Our relationship would end a few days after we arrived back home in Dayton. It was not something I could dwell on, or risk ruining the trip by overthinking, but it occasionally hung over me like one lonely dark cloud set smack in the middle of the clear blue sky, ready to burst, soaking only me.

When we arrived, a person, who I assumed was the marina owner or manager, greeted us and started carrying on a conversation with Craig like they were old friends. It was then that I found out, through their conversation, that Craig had been selected for the Norwegian Olympic Yachting team. His team, however, had not made the finals and therefore did not get selected to compete at the Olympics, but I was with a member of an Olympic sailing team. I found that delightfully fascinating. If I had been selected for the Olympics, I would have disclosed that by now. That was the difference between me and Craig. He was subtly awesome, and I was overtly not.

Craig had sailed for as long as he could remember. Growing up on the Norwegian coast, sailing was second nature to him. The owner of the rafting company took us over to a beautiful white twenty-seven-foot Soling sailboat. The Soling is an open keelboat that was used in the Olympics starting in 1972. It was a boat for which Craig had rigorous training. The owner of the marina had no qualms about Craig's abilities and neither did I.

I had already placed Craig on the highest pedestal, but this was like icing on a cake, good homemade icing like my mom used to make, the kind of icing where you get to lick the spoon. I wanted to eat him up and have whatever he was having. I wanted him, his spirit, presence, talents, and kindness to rub off on me.

It took about twenty minutes to get the Soling ready to sail. It's a long, slender boat that comes to a point in the front called the bow with a flat back called the stern and a carved-out hull right in the middle like a kayak, but proportionately larger. The hull opening was a soft rectangular shape with rounded edges. I hopped in first and sat right in the middle, which gave Craig a good chuckle.

"Here," he patted his hand on the left or port side of the boat, "get up out of there and sit on the side, next to me."

I blushed and laughed at myself, then hopped quickly out of the middle of the hull and moved onto the side of the sailboat next to him. I suffered internally from my own embarrassment, like a flame burning my cheeks from the inside out.

I did notice as I was climbing out of the hole, or hull I should say, Craig glanced quickly over his shoulder towards the marina to see if anyone else was watching. It might have been the only time I embarrassed him, but he tried not to let it show. He might have been concerned the owner of the marina would stop us from taking the vessel out to sea if he knew I wasn't an experienced sailor.

Coming from a sailing family in Norway, Craig admitted he had never encountered anyone with my lack of experience when it came to sailing. He now saw clear challenges with this trip, but he was not rattled by my nonsense.

"Calamity Vanity," he said. It was the first time he used my nickname. It was cute coming out of his mouth.

Craig showed me how to lock a foot inside the hull to make myself feel more secure. He sat in the rear so he could steer. I sat to his left. It felt like the boat might tip over at any moment. My back was so close to the water, I wouldn't have to lean two feet to drag a hand in the ocean.

Craig must have sensed my fear as he assured me that it would not tip. It had two large white sails. One sail attached to the front of the boat about one foot back from the bow, and the other attached to the center of the boat just in front of the opening in the hull. He explained that if he needed me to do anything with the sails, he would show me. He gave me simple tasks to do, which I memorized quickly.

I was ready to set sail. There was something about being alone on the Pacific Ocean sailing with a member of the Norwegian yachting team that made Craig even sexier and more irresistible than he already was. My life was completely in his hands, as much as my heart had been from the first moment we met.

We sailed away from the disappearing shoreline at a rapid pace. I wasn't sure how fast we were sailing, but Craig must have had the sailboat going towards its maximum speed. I had no idea a sailboat could fly like that.

"The wind is just right," Craig called out as if he were reading my mind.

It was already afternoon and I wondered and hoped Craig knew his way back to shore. As we started to turn back, Craig was busy messing with the sails, while I was leaning over the opposite side backwards because I was still certain we were going to tip at any minute. I thought that finally my weight would come in handy for something.

Getting braver and braver as the trip progressed, I leaned back further and further over the side to help Craig steer the vessel. Then I saw something floating in the water just below the surface. It was large and looked like an overturned hull of a boat. I thought someone had capsized. My mind took time to process what I was seeing. I sat upright so fast I almost tumbled back into the middle of the boat.

"Craig, look," I said as I pointed towards the water. "What is that?"

"It's a blue whale," Craig said. "They are very rare. I've never seen one."

It was a shadow at first, but it quickly glided towards us, and it ended up right next to us. It did not surface all the way, or breach, or threaten our sailboat in any way. One sudden movement of its fin or tail, and we could have capsized.

It remained partially exposed, but mostly submerged and it remained next to our sailboat. It was three times longer and much wider than our boat, yet I wasn't paralyzed with fear. I was in awe of its beauty and appreciated the miracle of seeing such a magnificent mammal in its own habitat, wild and free. It made eye contact with me and seemed to express curiosity and understanding. It was an intelligent, thinking being, and I knew I was beyond lucky to be having this type of encounter. Speechless, I fell in love with this creature.

I was absorbing every moment, every sound and every movement of the whale. We soaked up the whale's presence for the precious minutes it chose to share its home with us. We were visitors. This was the whale's world but its actions, by all indications, appeared to be most welcoming.

I'm not sure why I could not believe this was happening. Every day I was with Craig, my life was full of unique and strange experiences I could not explain. But still, I never dreamed something like this was possible.

"How could anyone want to kill these precious animals?" I asked.

"I don't believe in killing whales, but every native Norwegian descended from whalers. It's how we survived."

We then discussed Norway's long history of hunting whales, which continues to this day, a policy Craig stated he did not support. He explained what he had learned about whales and whaling. He had seen many whales, dead and alive, while growing up along a Norwegian coastline and spending many hours at sea. He knew these creatures were special and intelligent and should be protected.

I had never seen a whale and I wanted to get in the water with it, but Craig said I had to stay in the boat. The water was freezing. I didn't have a wetsuit, and I would become hypothermic—not perceived hypothermia or really cold and wet and uncomfortable like I was in the cave, but my body's organs would shut down rapidly from the shock of the cold water.

I have no idea why I felt a zealous desire to be in the water next to the whale and how I longed to touch it, but Craig advised me not to touch it. There was a type of communication going on between me and this whale, and it felt like love. The whale kept looking at me and there was emotion emanating from the whale's eye back to me and mine back to the whale.

Craig and I also got to know each other on a deeper intellectual, moral, political, and social level that day, while resting on the side of a sailboat next to a magnificent blue whale with nothing but a dark-blue, constantly moving backdrop of water surrounding us.

The whale moved slowly away from us. It had repeatedly sprayed small fumes of water from its blow holes as it was drifting alongside our boat. But this time, it submerged and resurfaced a good distance from our boat and a huge plume of water, mucus, and oil shot thirty feet in the air from the two blow holes on top of its head at one hundred miles per hour. We were just out of range to be in the line of its spray, but it was loud, unexpected, and frightening.

The spray had a strong smell of rotten fish mixed with vomit. With that, the whale was gone from sight. Craig and I both looked right and left and into the water near the boat and around the boat as far as we could see. We realized that was the whale saying goodbye to us. We never saw the whale again.

After exhausting our search around the sailboat, I gazed far out over the horizon for one last sign of the whale. I began to feel nauseous and started experiencing extreme vertigo. I was seasick. I was fine while we were traveling forward, but the passive motion of the waves tossing the sailboat had wreaked havoc on my inner ear. Embarrassed to be vomiting in front of Craig, I had little choice. I hung over the side of the boat and regurgitated the tacos and burritos we had eaten earlier.

"Please don't watch me," I said. "I'm so sorry. It's just..." I paused to puke. "I'm so sick."

"No worries. I understand. It's not my first time on a boat," he said. "One time my friend brought a girl with us on a multiple-day sailing trip. The girl was so seasick we had to keep putting suppositories up her butt to keep her alive."

It was Craig's way of reassuring me he had seen much worse than someone vomiting over the side of a sailboat.

"Do you have any?" I asked. My voice was weak, but I was no longer shy about seeking any help possible.

"Any what?" he asked.

"Suppositories," I said.

"No. I wish I did."

"I wish you did, too," I said.

I never thought I would think this way, but at that moment, I was ready for any relief from this sickness. If he had brought them, I would have dropped my drawers and welcomed the relief. Instead, we headed back towards the coast of California, but it was a long time before Craig announced he could see the shoreline.

I couldn't wait to get back to dry land. Despite my incredible encounter with the whale, I vowed to never go back on the water again, if only I could live to reach the shore. The return trip seemed like it took an entire day instead of two hours. When we arrived at the dock, it was rolling and moving too much for me, so I crawled along the pier, and rolled into a sandy inlet. I didn't move for an hour while Craig cleaned the boat and took down the sails. Craig could have left me there all night. I wouldn't have noticed he was gone. He came over and eventually convinced me to get up so we could make our way back to the hotel. I didn't want to move.

When Craig told the workers at the marina about seeing the whale, they told him it was still within the window of time when the blue whale can be spotted off the coast, but the experience we had was highly unusual. They hadn't had many reports of blue whale sightings that particular season, so we had been lucky. Any up-close contact with a blue whale was certainly something to be treasured, especially a prolonged encounter like the one Craig described to them. I missed having that conversation with the people at the marina and seeing their reactions when he told them, but it was nice hearing him relay their conversations and reactions back to me.

Someone from the marina empathized with me and offered to give us a ride. It was a much-needed and much-appreciated lift back to the hotel. Craig took care of me the best he could, giving me glasses of water to rehydrate me. Even though I had vomited in front of him for hours, he was still there with me, lying beside me, holding me, and stroking my hair. I had it all. My heart was full. I needed nothing more.

I showered and slept. When I woke, two hours later, I started feeling like my normal self. We had a late dinner at a quaint, quirky English-themed pub. The pub caused Craig to reminisce about his life back in England. He shared stories of going to uni, as he called it, and his experiences living there and for a moment I believe he slipped into a right prim British accent. I found his stories fascinating as I had never traveled outside of the U.S. And, of course, we ended the night talking about the whale again until our eyelids weighed heavy, and we could no longer remain awake.

Chapter Sixteen

Teeny Weeny Inside-Out Bikini

The next morning, the alarm in our room sounded. At first, I thought it was a fire alarm and my heart pounded. It was 5 a.m.

"Get up," Craig said. "Put on your bathing suit. I'll grab some towels."

"What?" I said, half questioning Craig's sanity. "Are we going parasailing?"

"We're going swimming," Craig said. "Not exactly swimming, we're going to run out into the water up to our necks and then run back out to wake up and get our blood flowing."

"What?" I repeated. "We can't swim in the Pacific Ocean in San Francisco. It's way too cold. Plus, did you see the No Swimming Shark Infested Water sign posted down by the pier?"

"Are you the same person who wanted to jump into the Pacific Ocean yesterday to swim with a blue whale?"

"Is this coming from the same person who said I would get hypothermia if I did?"

"You won't be in the water long enough to get hypothermia," Craig assured me, "and we'll be closer to shore today than we were yesterday. Come on, we'll be late."

He gave me the one-dimple smile he knew I couldn't resist.

I managed to roll out of bed, dig through my suitcase, and slip on the yellow two-piece bathing suit with black polka dots I purchased for the trip. I was convinced, up until that moment, I wouldn't have to wear my bathing suit due to the cooler air temperatures we had experienced since landing. I bought a pair of designer Liz Claiborne lightweight powder-blue sweats with a repeating small white royal sword design for an occasion such as this. The chilly breeze hit my bare legs, so I slipped the sweats over my yellow swimsuit as soon as I followed Craig out the door.

"I forgot my purse," I said as I turned back towards the door.

"You won't need it," Craig said. "We won't be long."

I figured I would humor Craig, run down to the pier with him, and watch him foolishly run into the frigid, high-tide, shark-infested water all by himself at 5:30 a.m. *This must be a Norwegian tradition,* I thought.

"Ocean Beach is the most dangerous beach in California with perilous rip currents," I reminded him to no avail.

"We're going to be fine," he assured me, "and you will be glad you did it."

We approached the beach and Craig slipped his shirt and pants off over his swim trunks as I just stood there watching and admiring him. It was just before daybreak but a hint of light reflecting off the ocean danced across his bare skin. He was so amazingly beautiful; he could talk me into just about anything without saying a word.

"Come on. Hurry," he said with the same smile he had used to lure me out there.

I dropped my sweats onto the sand, reached for Craig's hand, and took off running, screaming, and laughing as we headed into the fifty-six-degree water. It was bracingly cold. I experienced sensory overload. When we made it back to shore, the wind felt warm. Moments before, I was shivering in my dry swimsuit with the cold breeze from the ocean blowing my hair into my mouth. Upon exiting the water, I was dripping wet yet somehow, I felt warm.

The warm feeling didn't last long though. I started to shiver.

I reached to pull my sweats up over my wet bathing suit bottoms, but Craig handed me two towels. We wrapped them around us and lingered along the shoreline. We paused to stare out into the water as daybreak met the waves.

The darkness lost its hold as daylight dawned. A faint glow illuminated the horizon, giving life to a new day. Tourists and locals were starting to arrive on the beach, some jogging, some walking dogs, and some in wetsuits with surf boards in hand. Craig and I hugged each other to stay warm. I reached down to pick up my sweats.

Craig pointed out that I had my bathing suit bottoms on inside out the entire time and because of the bright yellow exterior pattern and the tan interior lining, it looked like I had no bottoms on whatsoever.

"When did you notice?" I asked.

"As we were leaving the hotel room."

"Why didn't you tell me before now?"

"I didn't think anyone else would be on the beach this early."

My face flushed red with embarrassment, but I was red all over already from the cold shock to my skin, so only I knew the extent of my shame.

"Oh Calamity Vanity, I love you," Craig whispered as he pulled me in close to him and gave me a kiss.

Craig had just told me he loved me, and he kissed me in a way that merged our souls as one.

I pulled away from his embrace slowly, handed him one of my towels, and signaled for him to hold it up to serve as a makeshift dressing room because I was temporarily breathless. *Two Calamity Vanities in two days,* I thought. *He really is getting to know me.*

"You might as well leave them inside out now and just put your sweatpants over them," Craig said as he held up the towel to block me.

"I have to fix this now. It's going to bug me," I said laughing.

I dropped my bikini bottoms right there on the beach and switched them around so the outside and inside were correct and slipped them back over my sandy feet and up my calves and thighs.

The towel Craig was holding was violently flapping in the wind, but he was doing his best to keep it still long enough to block me. I looked over the top of the towel and could see into the eyes of onlookers. They were wearing heavy sweats and jackets and appeared puzzled to see two people wearing only wet bathing suits standing near the shoreline of this cold, windy, dangerous beach where swimming is prohibited.

"Tourists," one lady mumbled to her dog loud enough for us to hear as she walked past us. Craig and I smiled and laughed and made faces at each other.

"See, she thinks you are crazy, too," I said.

"Not just me," Craig said. "You followed me into the water."

"You have a point," I said.

We quickly put our clothes on over our wet bathing suits and ran, hand in hand, back to the hotel.

"Hey, tourist," I called out to him as we were running. "I love you too."

I let go of his hand and ran ahead of him, and he chased me. Our adrenaline was pumping, our skin was still tingling all over from the cold shock and the wind.

"Don't you love the way you feel right now?"

"I do," I said. "I feel like a tourist who needs a warm shower." We both laughed.

"I don't think many tourists do what we did. So, are you glad you followed me and took the plunge?"

"I am. You were right. How do you know me better than I know myself?

"I just know you, Calamity Vanity. And I like what I see," Craig said.

"I like what I see, too," I said. "You seem to know how I'm going to react before I even know. I would never have done something like that without you. You've made me crazy."

Craig smiled at me.

"You've made me love you," Craig said smiling. "I love you, Vanessa."

I paused, realizing he had used the "L" word again.

"I love you, Craig."

I walked over to him, wrapped my arms around him, and let the side of my face melt into his chest.

"I know," he said giggling.

"That obvious, huh?"

"Yes," he replied as he took my face in both his hands and pulled me in for the kind of kiss that made my feet lose their bearing on the floor and my body become one with his.

We showered and went to breakfast.

"If I had a day to live over again, today would be the day," Craig said.

"If I had a day to live over again, every day since the day we met, would be the day," I said.

I thought about why he chose that day as our best day ever, but I couldn't disagree with him. It was a perfect day. I questioned whether I was really afraid of dying or just afraid of living. It was certainly not like any vacation I had ever taken with family and friends, not even Annie, and not like any I've taken since. There was something mysterious and magical about being with Craig, but I could never define exactly what it was.

Chapter Seventeen

The Golden Gate

Here we were in San Francisco, the purpose of the entire trip. This is the walk across the Golden Gate Bridge Craig predicted would happen the first day we met.

I never believed our first day on the raft would come to this moment where I would truly be standing next to Craig, gazing up at that Golden Gate Bridge. He had already set the plan in motion before we left Ohio. He had arranged for us to take a ferry ride to Sausalito and then walk across the bridge west to east. I had never been on a ferry boat. Even taking a ferry was new and exciting to me.

We passed the famous Alcatraz prison and listened as our guide told stories about it, which he obviously had repeated many times throughout the day and throughout his career, as the ferry service for which he worked began in 1820 and had carried passengers to and from Sausalito every day since. Seagulls surrounded us on the ferry and were especially attracted to me, as I was to them. I was more interested in the beautiful white birds flying all around me than Alcatraz.

We docked without incident and began our historic walk. We made a little fuss about it between ourselves as this was the pinnacle of our trip. To remember such an iconic moment, we decided to stop under each of the two towers, which span 746 feet above the sidewalk, and kiss. That way, whenever we saw pictures of the bridge in books, or in movies, we would always know, between ourselves, what that bridge meant to us, if only for a moment in time.

The meaning behind our epic walk was extremely important to both of us as each step we took on the bridge that day was a significant one. I knew when I started step number one of our much-anticipated walk there would only be one of these trips and one of these memories with my one and only Craig. I wanted this walk to last forever until the traffic noise, the constant honking, and the strong chilly wind became an annoying distraction to our epic, romantic journey. We continued walking and held hands as we walked across the bridge.

We made it to the end of the bridge, our monumental walk complete, and neither of us wanted to admit to the other what a complete disappointment it was. Finally, one of us broke the ice about the trip falling flat in comparison to our other adventures and we laughed and laughed as we literally skipped away from the bridge still hand in hand trying to find a bus or taxi to get us back to our hotel and as far away from that bridge as possible.

We spent the rest of the afternoon shopping. I bought warm sweaters at The Limited and left the store wearing the warmest one. We rode cable cars, walked up and down the steep hill of the famous street with all the pastel houses, and visited the smelly fish market. Just being with Craig was enough for me. I didn't need the bridge to solidify the way I felt about Craig, or the way Craig felt about me.

We returned to the hotel just in time to shower and dress for a nice dinner as I reflected on how symbolic our walk across the Golden Gate

Bridge actually was. We tried so hard to make more of *the walk* than it was. We set a high bar for our expectations, when normally, on our other adventures, we set out with no expectations at all. We tried to feel and capture every moment, really take in what was happening as it unfolded, and why we were there. What we overlooked was what had brought us there in the first place. Love. You can't plan magical moments, they just happen, that's what makes them magic.

Chapter Eighteen

Eternal Night Life

We had a nice meal at a restaurant with white tablecloths and a maître d'. We had gotten a lot of exercise in San Francisco that day from our walk across the bridge and then our climbs up and down the hilly streets. It was nice to sit and relax and reflect during dinner. By the end of the meal, we decided, since we had not been to a dance club since we met on the rafting trip, San Fran might just be the ideal place to add an unplanned night out dancing till dawn at a local trendy hotspot. We could sleep all day the next day and both of us loved to push our bodies to their limits, so why not dance the night away on already overworked muscles? What could go wrong?

We asked our server to suggest a good spot for music and dancing, and she graciously complied. She even called a taxi for us and told the driver our destination.

The taxi picked us up in front of the restaurant and dropped us in front of a dance club. There were no lines, but it was clearly a dance club with an illuminated sign on the exterior. It was still early for

California nightlife to be out in droves, so we figured people would arrive as the evening progressed. It was a long drive to reach the club, so going to the hotel, waiting a few hours, and then returning to the club was not our best option.

"Maybe this place will be a California version of the old Studio 54 in New York," I said, "or a place for celebs to hang out. Pretty great our waitress hooked us up using her insider connections." I could hardly contain my excitement and anticipation of what the night had in store for us.

Craig paid the driver and exited the cab. As we exited, the driver asked if we wanted him to wait and we told him no. I sensed the driver wanted to convey some information but had decided not to intervene.

We approached the door of the club and after we entered, we noticed there was something seriously unique about this place. There was a band playing. Most of the 175 seats surrounding small tables were already taken. We quickly realized, although we were dressed in attire quite suitable for a nice dinner and night on the town, our clothing was different than the attire worn by everyone else in the club.

They were all dressed like vampires, with full makeup, including the band. I was frightened.

I had to use the restroom following the long cab ride, but I had no desire to go in the restroom at this club by myself. There was a slab just in front of the stage that looked like an ideal place for human sacrifices. Did everyone in the place think dinner was served when we walked through the door?

We quickly turned to leave, but our driver had left. We were stuck. We called for another taxi after finding a pay phone on the exterior of the building. We had no coins but instead called an AT&T operator and paid for the call to the taxi company with a credit card. It took them over an hour to arrive, and I worried they might not show.

In the meantime, we tried to blend in, which was ludicrous, even with our many feeble attempts. And we tried to enjoy ourselves and make the best of it, which was clearly impossible.

With all our bravado, venting to each other, and intermittent nervous jokes and laughs about our situation, thoughts of being ritualistically murdered entered my mind repeatedly. Eventually, Craig had to relieve himself, as he could hold it no longer, so he ventured into the restroom, leaving me alone at the table. I don't know which was worse, him being alone and vulnerable in a restroom full of vampires, or me being alone and vulnerable, sitting at a table, in a room full of vampires. I still really needed to use the restroom but was too fearful to go, even though Craig made it out of the restroom unharmed.

After Craig returned, we talked about how the server who had recommended this place must be thoroughly enjoying herself. I wondered how many other tourists she had sent here as a practical joke. I had a fleeting thought about the 25 percent tip Craig had given her on an already expensive meal. That made me think of going back and saying something to her, but I had never been confrontational, and I had a feeling she would have enjoyed the drama way too much.

I was overtly grateful and relieved when our taxi arrived.

"You know what we should do? We should go back to the same restaurant in vampire makeup and thank our server for the recommendation," Craig said.

"That's a good idea and hilarious," I said. And it was a much better idea than challenging her to the fantasy boxing match I had going on in my head. Thankfully, we decided against doing anything.

"Do you want to change destinations?" the cab driver asked.

"NO," we both said aloud. That outburst allowed us to release the overabundance of nervous giddiness we had accumulated while waiting in the club for the cab to arrive. We could not stop giggling and laughing.

"Sorry," Craig said to him. "We were just joking. Please take us to the hotel." We continued to giggle but tried to keep it quiet, which almost made our laughter harder to contain.

Fortunately, I had the bladder of a young person, something I discovered, as I aged, should not be taken for granted. I was able to hold the two iced teas I drank at the restaurant for over three hours before I finally arrived at the hotel and ran directly into the lobby's restroom.

Eventually the reality of the situation was, no matter where we were or what we were doing, we were lovers in love. This was just another bizarre experience you can't plan for in a travel itinerary, one that is best remembered in the rear-view mirror.

Chapter Nineteen

Drifting Out into Space

The Space Needle is a popular landmark in Seattle with an open observation tower and was the furthest point on our trip. After leaving Seattle, we would turn and trek closer and closer to home and closer to the end of our relationship.

Like the Golden Gate Bridge, the Space Needle would forever remain a symbol of our love story. I referred to it as windows into my soul. Decades later, it would also come to symbolize something entirely different in our relationship, a turning point, a happenstance moment in time that would change everything, including my perception of everything happening around me, and leave me questioning my strong bond with Craig.

Craig and I took the elevator to the top of the Space Needle. We decided to make every single view significant in some respect. We took our time and lingered in each window, told each other something we liked about the other person, or recalled something special the other person had done for us that we would never forget, and then sealed it with a quick kiss and loving hug before moving on to look out the next window. We made a pact that every time we saw the Space Needle in magazine pictures or on television, we would know we had stood in whatever window was visible and reaffirmed our love for each other.

It was similar to what we did at the Golden Gate Bridge, but this time instead of two huge pillars, we repeated our ritual forty-eight times, one for each of the floor-to-ceiling windows. We started out in each window being serious and somber, but by the time we had our forty-eighth kiss and vow, we were acting silly.

We mostly ignored the other people surrounding us. They were just going about their hectic lives, seeming mostly concerned with keeping track of their children weaving in and out of the crowd of strangers.

We knew our love was not meant to last. If all I could take into my future was a memory in a window overlooking Seattle, then it was mine to take, and that I did. But once we finished our silly pact, we were both ready to leave.

The lines had been long as we waited for the elevators to take us up to the observation deck and they were equally long waiting to leave. In our tradition of trying physically challenging activities and being high on life, we took the 832 steps down to the ground level. I was grateful Craig didn't think of the stairs on the way up, but he later admitted he did. I think he had just decided to spare me. He wouldn't actually admit that part, or say it in that manner, but that's how I read his smile and wink after he said *he* was too tired to climb all those steps.

***

Craig and I decided to avoid further crowds and have time for some much-needed relaxation and rest in the luxury hotel suite we had splurged on for two nights, opting for an early dinner at a local Seattle fifties-style diner. We made small talk with our adorable server, who was dressed in a short pink flared skirt with a small white lace-trimmed apron with matching blouse and headband holding back her long, thick blondish hair. She moved from table to table on roller skates, which made her look seventeen, although she voluntarily told us she was twenty-two and a senior at the University of Washington. She seemed especially awestruck by Craig and quite interested in our travel adventure and how we had met.

The fifties attire and theme were a new experience for Craig. He understood it was part of American culture and history; he had just never witnessed it. He loved the burgers, onion ring baskets, and shakes she brought to our table.

At first, I thought the server might just be trying to get a good tip, but still, she was just a little more curious and friendlier than I preferred. She reminded me of the young ladies we had encountered at the rafting lodge. I was glad when we finished eating so we could get away from her. I was starting to feel uncomfortable with the way she was behaving toward Craig.

People noticed us and talked to us more than usual, no matter where we were or what time of day or night. We didn't stop being the odd couple when we left the New River Gorge. Our apparent mismatched relationship and over-the-top love vibes caused a stir everywhere we went. Our server's fascination with our story didn't feel too out of line but was a notch above the norm.

I started to get used to the attention we attracted. Mostly, I liked it. I felt famous. I wondered if we looked like a celebrity couple. Strangers noticed Craig. I wondered if some people thought Craig was an actor or athlete, and I, his manager. The latter scenario seemed more realistic than us being lovers, but they couldn't have gotten it more wrong.

I had assumed Craig was a celebrity when I first saw him, so I assumed the attention we were garnering was because everyone else was thinking the same. I had never had strangers notice me or want to strike up conversations with me when I was traveling or eating out alone, so this was different, but we enjoyed meeting new people and sharing our adventures with them.

One of Craig's appealing traits was that he was completely honest. When we arrived back at the hotel after eating dinner, he walked a mile back to the Seattle diner, in a light, but cold, Seattle rain, to pay for a soft drink the server forgot to put on our bill. I encouraged him to forget about it, assuring him the server would be okay.

I was at the point where I really didn't care about that server and was just not happy Craig was ready to trek back to that restaurant. He was worried the server's employer would dock her check for the drink even though I told him restaurants don't keep close tabs on fountain drinks. Still, he did not feel right about stiffing her for the drink. I found his honesty slightly annoying but also appealing.

"Are all Norwegian men like you? Because I think I've been living in the wrong country."

I offered to walk back to the restaurant with him. He told me to relax. Get warm. Our room had a cozy fireplace, so I took him up on his offer. I jumped into a hot shower, put on my flannel pajamas, and drank a hot chocolate by the fireplace, compliments of the hotel.

Craig returned promptly, before I even finished my hot chocolate. He did admit, when the server asked him for his address, he thought she might be flirting with him.

That irked me and my immediate thought was, *I knew it. I should have gone with him.* I thought again to myself that the server had been a little too friendly with him during our dinner. But it was a diner,

I reminded myself, with a casual fifties atmosphere where a friendly, "everyone knows everything about everybody" vibe was the norm.

Did he go back specifically to speak to her? Surely not, I reassured myself.

"Did you give her your address?"

"Yes."

I looked at Craig. I was obviously a little hurt and couldn't hide that from him.

"She told me she needed it for the credit card because it was issued in Norway, and their system couldn't process it. They couldn't bill me for the meals and had no way to get in touch with me, so she said she was relieved to see me walk through the door."

"Do you really think she needed your address to run a credit card, or did she just want your address?"

"I'm not sure. I started to leave and not give it to her, but then I thought she may be telling the truth about the card, so I turned around in the doorway, gave it to her, and left." He must have still seen a doubtful or hurt look on my face. He added, "I didn't even go into the restaurant. I never made it past their entranceway."

I believed he didn't linger, because he had returned to our room much sooner than I expected.

I put it out of my mind because we would only be in Washington State until morning and then we were off to Glacier Park, Montana. Craig would be leaving the country within weeks, so that girl was no threat to our relationship.

What man would walk a mile to pay back a restaurant for a soft drink? A man too good to be true; a kind and caring man who thought more of others than he thought of himself. I loved him even more.

Chapter Twenty

The Curling Iron

The Amtrak train slowed. Our bodies began to adjust from the motion of our trip as we slowly came to a stop. The vibrations from the train would continue in our muscles for another five to ten minutes after we exited into the brisk morning air.

Craig came prepared with a map of Montana. He had done his research. I, on the other hand, was completely lost.

"Where do we go next?"

"We have to travel along Highway 2. It is one of the most scenic highways in the world."

Craig, not being from the United States and thus sensing no danger, suggested we hitch a ride with someone to get to the drop-off point six miles further. I was nervous and cautious of strangers, but I hadn't heard of any kidnappings or terrible things happening in Glacier Park.

I had never hitchhiked in my life, but I felt like a hippie from the sixties when I stuck out my thumb. If only I had worn a flowered headband. It took only minutes before a small pickup truck stopped for us.

"You going to Glacier Park?" the driver asked.

"Yes, but if you could get us to Highway 2, that would be great," Craig said.

"I'll take you the whole way if you don't mind riding in the back. I'm going that way anyway."

"Yes, thank you," Craig said.

"Hop in," he said to me as he tossed his backpack into the bed of the truck.

I glanced inside the vehicle, but immediately noticed it had no back seat.

"Back here," Craig said. He jumped in first and offered me his hand.

We sat in the open bed of the truck. It was September and things were already getting chilly in Glacier Park. I sat in front of Craig with my back pressed against his chest. He put his arms around me to keep me warm. I rested my head on his shoulder. His chin touched the side of my cheek as I marveled at the spectacular scenery.

Craig's research was correct. This place was pristine, from the snow-covered portions of the mountains to the hidden treasures of lakes peeking through the forests. In addition to being amazing, stunning, and spectacular, it is also a frightening, narrow forty-nine-mile winding road with steep overlooks on one side and steep cliffs on the other side.

I wondered how tens of thousands of people drive across the country to see this place and then drive this stretch of highway, and never experience the view the way I was experiencing it then. There was nothing better than being snuggled up next to Craig, sitting backwards in a pickup truck, and watching the scenery unfolding behind us. Each minute offered something new to see, a lake, a mountain, a glacier, and an eagle, but no sign of bears.

I don't know which was more comforting, Craig wrapped around me keeping me warm or the views of mountains, trees, and glaciers. Falling rock signs were everywhere, so naturally, I started visualizing a falling boulder taking us out like a bowling pin and being hurled off the side of the mountain.

The truck had come to a stop, but we were only about halfway to our destination. We looked at the map. There had been a rockslide. Fifty or more rocks and boulders were blocking the highway. I thought about how close we were to the front of the line of backed-up traffic, meaning we just missed being hit by those rocks. With us being in the open bed of a pickup truck, it might not have been pretty.

While we waited for crews to arrive to remove the heavy boulders and clean up the remaining debris, other tourists got out of their cars and walked around us, and the line of cars. It was their opportunity to view the rockslide and to get a better view of the valley reaching far below us.

"You've got the best view in the house," a man commented to us as he walked his children to the side of the road to the cliff's edge, which was precariously close to the side of our truck.

"Yes," we both said at the same time in response to his comment about us having the best view.

"We should have the rocks cleared in fifteen to twenty minutes," a crew member said as he hopped out of his truck, which he parked in the now empty oncoming traffic lane next to us, "happens all the time."

"Thank you for the update," Craig said. Altogether, our trip was delayed by thirty minutes. I was anxious to get moving.

If we were going to risk our lives hitchhiking, the beauty on this stretch of highway almost made it worth taking that risk. The only thing I was missing was the truck's heater on my feet.

"This vantage point, just like you said, is the best possible way to take in this awe-inspiring landscape – this is certainly a way to travel I wouldn't have thought of," I said, "but my feet are cold."

"I have just the thing to warm your feet, but you'll have to wait until we make it to the top."

"What is it? My bare feet on your warm back?" I asked. Craig squeezed me closer.

"You'll see."

I thought since we were halfway to the top, I could last another thirty to forty-five minutes taking in the scenery, before we would curl up in a nice, warm bed in a heated room.

I continued to look for bears everywhere but didn't see a single one. From our vantage point, surely there were hundreds of bears in the wilderness surrounding us. The vast landscape reached as far as I could see and extended up into the air where the clouds and earth rarely meet.

"Looking for bears again?" Craig asked.

"You know I am."

He chuckled.

"Craig is a name whose main origin is Danish, English, and Norwegian. The English meaning is 'God of Bears.' Did you know that?" I asked.

"No, I did not know that."

"How appropriate," I added, "since I like them."

"You only like them? Not *love* them?" Craig asked.

"Oh, I *love* them."

He kissed the side of my face. I absorbed the heat from his body through my back.

Speaking of bears, Craig gave me some instructions about what not to take in my backpack, namely food. I agreed.

"In bear country I would never do that," I assured him.

Our driver dropped us off at Logan's Pass, located at the highest elevation point on Going to the Sun Road. We thanked him and offered to pay but he held his hand up and waved to us to be on our way.

I was certain we would be checking into our room, but first we joined a group of people and had coffee in the lodge. It warmed my bones. I sat closest to the stone fireplace, slipped off my shoes, and propped my feet up on the edge of the hearth. I could feel the heat from the warm stone through my socks. I was content to sit there for hours sipping a warm coffee and warming my feet.

After being served breakfast, instead of walking to the lodge's check-in desk, we exited the building with the group and followed a guide who had joined us at our table. We followed her up a wide asphalt sidewalk that gently winded back and forth as we ascended further up the mountain. The difficulty level was minimal and except for the incline, it was a leisurely walk.

I was anxious to turn back, but I politely participated in the stroll. The guide gave us a history of the park and named the scenic overlook we were now observing from the top of the paved trail we had just walked. I thought this was a nice trail with just the right amount of walking to burn off the calories from all the biscuits, gravy, scrambled eggs, bacon, toast, and grits I'd just consumed. Time for a nap.

"This is where the guided trail ends," our guide said.

Thank goodness, I thought. *Check-in time.*

"The unguided trail begins there," she said. She pointed to a narrow dirt and rock path that branched off to the right. She looked at me and Craig as she pointed Craig in the direction of the trail.

Around forty people traced their steps back as they began their journey down the winding sidewalk leading back to the lodge. I looked at Craig and he flashed that dang smile at me. I wanted to follow the rest of our group but, of course, I followed Craig. Like a hunting dog sniffing down a trail of breadcrumbs, off I went with Craig, into bear country.

We hiked for hours, occasionally stopping to rest and enjoy the view. I forgot about the lodge. I felt alive, refreshed, and revived as we casually walked at a slow pace and stopped often to view the vivid fall hues of orange, red, yellow, and green and breathe in the crisp air. We stopped occasionally to literally smell the late blooming wildflowers all around us.

In between mountain peaks, we were able to see a beautiful blue ice glacier off in the distance, although the trail we took to the awaiting chalet was not the best trail to see many glaciers. We would eventually end up on the best trail. It was breathtakingly beautiful, peaceful, and quiet except for an occasional rustling in the underbrush. The colors of greens, blues, and white snowcapped mountains were so vivid it was like seeing the world in layers not normally visible to the naked eye. It was magical. I was in love. This was the perfect place to be happy.

We made it to the chalet in six hours. I had no idea we were doing a twelve-hour trek when we started. Fortunately, I didn't get blisters. I wore great-fitting hiking boots, which was my single most important fashion choice that day.

The chalet used to put leftover food off to the side of the mountain to attract bears so guests could get a glimpse of bears eating in the wild. This worked out well until a bear grabbed a girl sleeping in a tent nearby, dragged her away, and killed her.

They later euthanized the bear and found it had an infected tooth, something that must have been terribly painful for the bear. Bears usually don't attack people. There are one or two non-lethal bear encounters on the trail per year with an estimated three hundred grizzly bears in the park. Many bears are within short range of hikers but avoid contact with humans.

Unfortunately, the park ranger explained, there had been two recent lethal bear encounters. There were warning signs everywhere about the fatal encounters saying they usually occur from feeding bears, storing food too close to campsites, bears being startled by humans, or mama bears protecting their cubs against a perceived threat.

All my life I had wanted to see a bear. Now, I had hiked eight hours to the top of Fifty Mountain and then to Glacier Park Chalet, where seasoned local hikers rumored there was still a feed pit, but it had been moved over a mile from the chalet. And still, I didn't see a single bear.

I did get to pet a deer though. The deer at the chalet are not afraid of people. They came right up to me and sniffed me. One was quite friendly and let me stroke him. He was a bit timid, so I avoided sudden movement. Some were looking for a nibble of food and wanted nothing more to do with me when they realized I didn't have any. But the one male, he wanted to be scratched and petted. He stayed near me until we finally departed.

"We can stay here for the night if you want," Craig said. "They rent tents to hikers, or we can make it back down the mountain to the cabin I rented. It has an outdoor hot tub."

The tents were just two sticks and a material not much more than a sheet crossed in an upside-down "V." We had not brought any sleeping bags. Lying on the cold, hard ground under a V-shaped sheet didn't seem appealing or private. We had to decide fast or lose daylight towards the end of our hike, so we opted to make our way back down the mountain to the cabin Craig had rented for us.

I was dreaming of the hot tub at the end of the trek. Craig had said he had something to warm my cold feet during that open ride in the truck that morning; we just had to get to the top of the mountain to get to it. It was a private hot tub in the middle of the woods, on the side of the mountain. It would be worth the wait. Just the thought of sitting up to my neck in the bubbling warm water with Craig after such a long trek made the hike back down the mountain seem worth it.

"We should make it to the cabin by 7:30 p.m., so it should still be light. It will take less time to go downhill than it did to hike uphill. It will be easier going down as well."

I was sold on the idea of hiking down to our cabin, but we both agreed we needed to eat first. I went inside and bought peanut butter and cheese crackers at the chalet, one pack for me and one pack for Craig. I slipped those into my backpack because Craig had already ordered both of us a meal and had taken a seat on a white plastic chair at a small, round, wobbly metal table as he waited for our food to be prepared. I joined him at the table carrying two lemonades.

We hydrated well with water and started drinking a second lemonade as we waited. The employee making our meal lived at the chalet for the entire summer. He only traveled back down the mountain at the end of each season. He served as a cook, a host, an overnight clerk, and occasionally a medic and forest ranger. He chatted with us as we scarfed down the cheeseburgers and fries he had brought to our table. Everything tasted mouthwateringly delicious, and the lemonade was better than cake and ice cream.

I noted how much better everything tasted when I was parched. It was either thirst and hunger causing the increased sensations in my taste buds or that I had finally slowed down long enough to notice things to which I normally paid no attention.

We began our descent down the mountain.

We were about three miles down the trail from the chalet when I pulled out my butane-powered curling iron from my backpack as a joke to show Craig. I clicked the button on it until I heard the butane ignite to show him how it worked. I told him I was disappointed we didn't camp as I had planned to wake up in the morning and curl my hair with it.

We had this joke about my hair when I first committed to taking this trip. Craig said I would have to survive a camping and hiking trip around the country without fixing my hair. I knew better and when I saw the butane curling iron at a department store in downtown Dayton, I devised a plan. I had never seen one before. Perfect. I bought it immediately. You fire it up like a cigarette lighter and it heats up fast so you can curl your hair anywhere.

I knew it would just be fun to use it in front of Craig and make him laugh. Laughs aside, it was a handy gadget to have on a trip. It was lightweight. No electrical cord was needed, so it was the perfect travel curling iron because big permed and curled hair was still all the rage.

Craig just shook his head and smiled.

"That is so you," he said. "I can't believe you hauled it all the way up the mountain just to make me laugh at you. I meant laugh with you." His proficiency of the English language was good, but at times, small mistakes got him into trouble.

"Oh, you are lucky you changed that sentence," I said jabbing towards him with the hot curling iron like it was a *Star Wars* lightsaber.

Already having my backpack open, I saw the peanut butter and cheese crackers I bought earlier.

"I bought peanut butter and cheese crackers at the chalet, one pack for you, and one pack for me in case we get hungry," I said.

Craig's smile changed, and his face and voice showed his immediate concern.

"You weren't supposed to bring food on the trail, remember? It can attract bears."

"I haven't seen any bears, have you?" I asked with disappointment in my tone.

"Maybe you have noticed how loudly I've been talking as we walk around the bends in the trail," he said.

"I hadn't noticed until you just said something."

"I want them to know we are coming so as not to startle any bear that might be crossing our path. I've been talking non-stop and louder than necessary, on purpose," Craig said.

"Should we eat the crackers now?" I asked.

"If there are bears around, they will already be able to smell us and they will smell peanut butter regardless of whether they are open and they will still smell the wrappers even if we ingest the crackers," he said.

We were puzzled about what we should do next. We didn't want to eat again so soon after the meal at the chalet, and we didn't want to discard the crackers or the wrappers as that was strictly against park rules. It causes bears to associate food even more with hikers, which could be deadly for future hikers.

Craig realized I was feeling distressed about my mistake. I had never seen him concerned before or even slightly miffed at me.

"It's not your fault," Craig said. "I've just been thinking it would have been better if we stayed at the chalet and traveled in the morning.

It's the bears' feeding time and there will be many bears foraging for food. They mostly sleep during the day. I know better than to take you down a mountain pass in the evening. It is my fault. Let's just keep going and keep talking, and make our presence known."

"Yes, let's do that," I said louder than necessary for Craig to hear me, not out of anger but as a warning to any encroaching bears.

"Hey, bear, we are here. Hey, bear, we are coming," I said louder than necessary.

I experienced a new excitement that rose inside of me at just the possibility of seeing a bear. I had gotten us into a fix this time, but still there were no bears to be seen.

Until there was.

Moments later, a large bear was on a hill just to our right as we came around an L-shaped bend in the trail. It was uphill from us about fifteen feet and as he slowly stood up on his back feet, he appeared to be more than six feet tall.

Paralyzing fear set into every inch of my being. I was finally getting to see a bear, but as other people had warned me, you really don't want to see one, when you finally do. Things happened quickly.

"Keep walking slowly," Craig said.

I wanted to take his advice, but my legs weren't getting the message. The bear sniffed the air, to the left and to the right. We walked backwards facing the bear. Craig had somehow managed to hold onto my backpack and steady me as we walked backwards together.

"It's a grizzly bear. Don't run. Play dead, if necessary," Craig said.

I don't know how he managed to speak or how I managed to comprehend his instructions. But he said it with a snarl and a low, guttural sound filled with determination I had never witnessed coming from him. I felt safe, and peace came over me momentarily.

The bear lowered himself slowly to all fours and I was so relieved he was going to walk away, but then he turned and started to walk towards us. We kept walking backwards down the trail, but the bear slowly made his way down the hill, almost comically sliding on his rear to reach the trail. For a moment, it was like being in a zoo, watching an animal do something silly like scratching its butt on a rock, but then you realize there is no barrier between you and the magnificent deadly beast.

All my love for bears was quickly fading as I feared this might be my last moment on earth. I wanted and needed this animal to just turn and walk away. He did not.

He didn't charge. He just clumsily lumbered towards us, sometimes stopping, sometimes sniffing the air again. Then he would lower his head and move closer to us. Within moments, the bear was right upon me and sniffing me and I'm not sure if it was five seconds, or a minute, because in moments of intense fear such as this, time loses all importance and measurability.

Craig was right next to me, but the bear was more interested in me. I tried to drop my backpack to put it between myself and the bear, but as I let the backpack slide from one shoulder, I realized I still had the butane-powered curling iron in my hand. It was still powered on and scalding hot.

I held it in front of my face and neck as it was my only protection. I hoped the bear didn't knock it out of my hand. My grip around the handle with my right hand and the plastic tip on the end with my left hand was white-knuckle firm, but I was shaking uncontrollably. The bear sniffed it for several seconds keeping his nose inches away from it.

I could smell him. I had heard bears have a strong, foul body odor, and indeed, he did. He smelled terrible. He leaned closer, bumping the curling iron with his nose. He backed off quickly for a split second and again, I thought he was going to turn and run. He growled a growl so loud and powerful it shook the ground beneath my feet. I wanted to drop the curling iron and run but my legs wouldn't move. I held fast to the only weapon I had.

He lunged at me with his mouth wide open and his huge paws spread out and wide, displaying claws as long as my fingers. His mouth was inches from my face. I don't know where I found the strength, courage, or wisdom, but I jammed the hot curling iron sideways into the bear's mouth as far back as I could as he opened his mouth and clamped down onto the hot iron.

The bear's mouth crunched down on the curling iron. I love animals and would never hurt them, but this was truly life or death, and I had to use what I could to protect myself. I heard a sizzle as the superheated metal contacted the bear's wet tongue. The bear made a loud sound, a shriek or moan combined; a sound I had never heard and hopefully will never hear again. I let go of the mangled curling iron, still backing away from the bear. For a moment, I believed the bear was going to become angry and lunge at me again and maul me to pieces. I realized I had dropped the curling iron. I thought this was it.

Instead, the bear retreated. He ran up the hill on all fours and into the woods shaking his head side to side like he had been sprayed by a skunk. What a sight that was, seeing the back end of the bear retreating into those woods. We continued to walk backwards as fast as we could and then we turned and ran fast and far until I couldn't catch my breath.

It all happened so fast; it was hard to comprehend it had happened at all. We came face to face with a grizzly bear, and a hot curling iron I brought as a gag ended up saving our lives. There were no marks on either one of us. How I didn't get swatted and torn apart by at least one of his claws, I did not know. How I didn't burn my hands on the curling iron, I did not know.

There was a curling iron lying half a mile back on the trail, but we didn't go back to pick it up. We just stopped long enough to catch our breath and then we ran until we were completely winded.

Later, when we switched from running to walking, while still breathing heavily and trembling, we wondered aloud what the next hiker would think when they saw that crunched-up curling iron. We walked at a breakneck pace fueled by adrenaline and made louder than normal conversation as we approached our destination.

The last half-mile of our trip jetted off from the main trail as a narrow pathway. I started to get concerned when the sun began to set. I knew it would be harder to see the map Craig needed to reference to find the trail as the trees blocked the remaining daylight, but we made it to our destination without further bear encounters or other frightening incidents.

We didn't pass anyone going towards the chalet, so we had been the last hikers on the mountain that evening. We talked about how, if either one of us had been wounded, how hard it would have been to get down the mountain to seek help. That is when the reality set in of what could have happened. The fear came to rest in our already chilled bones.

The cabin had all the comforts of home. It had a hot indoor shower and soft down-filled comforters on a king-size bed with a rustic wood frame. It had plump brown leather chairs with an old western theme throughout. Craig had rented this cabin to surprise me. I looked around the cozy cabin and knew why we hadn't checked into a room at the noisy, crowded lodge that morning. This was perfect.

Once again, Craig had given me something I would never have experienced on my own. If I had traveled without him, I would have checked into the lodge, walked with the guide to the starting point of the trail, turned around with the other guests, and headed back to the lodge. From there, I would have checked into my room and napped until lunchtime. By dinner, I would have been bored out of my mind and looking for a way to return home before the end of my planned vacation. That was my usual pattern; the one the old me had practically set into stone. This was the new and improved me, though, setting new standards and hiking up to them.

We put on our bathing suits and headed straight to the hot tub. I looked right and left and behind myself for bears as we jogged to the tub. We folded back the four-inch-thick thermal vinyl lid and sat it next to a tree. Inside, we found a cooler filled with ice floating inside with chilled wine and plastic wine glasses and a corkscrew. We never saw a single soul that night to thank them, but kudos to whoever set up our room because they had thought of everything.

Craig and I talked and talked about the bear. I peered deep into the woods and scanned the tree line regularly to make sure there wasn't another bear just outside the hot tub waiting to grab us. I noticed Craig was doing the same thing. It was dark all around us with little moonlight. I knew there were bears nearby and I didn't want to run into another one between the tub and the cabin. As soon as we exited the water, we ran back hand in hand as fast as we could. My heart was pumping fast as Craig closed and locked the door behind us. Our skin was wrinkled like prunes. We had stayed in the tub for so long because we were afraid to get out and run to the cabin.

We both tossed and turned but remained wide awake until midnight as we tried to wind down from our adventure.

While we were in the hot tub, I decided the relaxation the wine brought was worth the tradeoff of a headache the following morning. I was wrong. I was sore from head to toe from the hike, the run, and the bear encounter. The combination of the wine relaxing my nerves, the hot water warming my bones, and vibrating jets easing my sore muscles was the perfect topping to a day I'll never forget, but the hangover I had from the wine made me sluggish for days.

My relationship with Craig didn't have days to waste on feeling ill or under the weather. I should have passed on the wine, but sometimes I just never learn.

What an adventure. Nothing will ever compare. The entire experience of fending off a grizzly bear occupied my thoughts for the rest of the trip and has entered my mind hundreds of times since.

Over the years, I fretted a bit about burning the bear's mouth with the curling iron, but I had little choice and I'm sure the bear healed just fine. I tell myself maybe he or she got just enough burn to think twice about sniffing the next human that crossed his path, and that in the long run keeping him away from hikers would keep him alive longer in the park.

A month after our bear encounter, in October of 1989, a female bear attacked a hiker in the same general area of the trail where we had our bear encounter, and a sixty-two-year-old woman fended it off with a pair of binoculars as it attacked her husband. They both survived. The bear, however, did not. The park rangers located the bear hours after the attack and euthanized it. I was sad for the bear. I hoped it was not my bear, or my fault, for hiking with peanut butter and cheese crackers.

Chapter Twenty-One

A Strong Wind on a Gray Day

The journey that we embarked on in Glacier Park had been a whirlwind of life-altering adventure, beauty, and love. But as we returned to the Amtrak train station to head towards Chicago, it felt as though our journey had come full circle.

We arrived in Chicago, the Windy City, the following day. From there, we would fly back to Indianapolis to pick up my vehicle and drive the rest of the way home to Dayton.

On the train ride, my head rarely left Craig's shoulder and my hand remained in his. The Windy City awaited us eagerly with its towering structures and bustling streets. Once we arrived, we visited some tourist destinations such as the Sears Tower.

Although we had experienced so much, there was still a feeling of incompleteness that lingered in the air. But the beauty of the city and the warmth of Craig's embrace soon lifted my spirits. As we strolled along the crowded streets and took in the sights and sounds of this vibrant place, I couldn't help but feel grateful for this incredible journey.

We were really surprised to get nearly blown off our feet while walking around the city and realized people were not joking about the strong wind. At times, I felt a thick, lingering sadness in the air, and I believed the wind was smacking me right in the face with a purpose.

With a stunning view of Lake Michigan, we spent most of our time in our cozy hotel room, holding each other and taking in the beauty of the glittering lights of the city twinkling outside. It felt like we were the only two people in the world. Time seemed to stand still, yet the hands on the clock moved steadily forward as we inched closer to our destiny with each passing moment.

Despite the distractions of being in a new destination, the reality of Craig's departure and the subsequent end of our relationship, fast approaching, weighed heavily on both of our minds. We held each other tighter, took long walks arm in arm, and our glances at each other turned into prolonged periods of eye contact where no words were spoken, but volumes were being said. We didn't mention the impending doom, but it hung over our heads like the nuclear gray cloud cover that blanketed the city.

***

We departed two days later from Chicago O'Hare Airport and landed in Indianapolis. We picked up my car. Secretly, I wished my car had been stolen so we would get delayed another night, but there it was, sitting right where we had left it. We arrived back in Dayton and stayed at his apartment one last time.

"I would like to stay my last night at your parents' house so I can meet them," Craig said after packing his belongings. "Do you think they would mind?"

"They will be happy to meet you."

I made the arrangements. Right up to the end this guy just keeps melting my heart and making me smile.

My parents met Craig and they saw all the goodness in him that I saw. In the brief time they spent with him, he stole their hearts, too. I thought at least if I can't eat, sleep, or function after he leaves, they'll be more understanding of my pain. They would realize what I had, how special he was, and be able to comfort me with a perspective they wouldn't have had if they had never met him. Maybe that was Craig's plan all along. He always had a plan and somehow, even throughout all our risky adventures, I believed he always had my best interest at heart. It was the perfect, albeit painful, ending to our adventure.

Chapter Twenty-Two

The Tearful Goodbye

We drove to the airport in Cincinnati, which is located across the Ohio River in Kentucky, just over an hour's drive from my parents' house in Dayton. Craig suggested en route that I should not park in the parking garage and go in with him, but instead I should drop him in front of the terminal. I agreed by only nodding. We didn't speak again during the drive, but we locked hands as soon as we got into the car and never let go until the last inevitable moment.

Words were of no comfort and therefore useless to us. Tears started streaming down my face as we approached the terminal. I knew I couldn't enter the airport. I wouldn't want to cause a scene. Craig was right. It would be easier for both of us to say our goodbyes in private so I could sit in my car for as long as I needed to regain my composure before driving home.

We arrived and Craig got his suitcase. I walked around to his side of the car in a zombie-like state. What was about to happen to us was too difficult for me to fully comprehend. We held each other and sobbed. Our hearts were broken.

"You should write a book about this," Craig whispered.

"Maybe I will," I somehow managed to say.

I looked into his eyes for the last time and saw tears streaming down his face.

"Send me a copy when you do."

I nodded, no longer able to speak. The pain I was experiencing upon his departure was more than I believed I could bear.

We decided to part company as "in love" as lovers could ever be, and it was my idea we should not ruin it with regular everyday life communications. We froze our love in time and space so it would live on, long after our goodbye, long after our youth faded.

It was a love that would continue long after we were gone from this earth.

In a sense, it was an experiment I drummed up to see if we could make a love that strong last for all time. We sealed our pact with one final kiss and embrace.

I was a strong woman. I could conquer this permanent separation but only if I knew our love was not in vain. The decision to part as lovers at the highest point of our romance was a matter of survival. I knew there were no workable options or other decisions that could be made to keep this relationship going.

The only plan of action I could think of to keep myself alive without him was knowing he would always love me. No matter where he was in the world, no matter what he was doing, or who he was with, he would always love me.

He held me, neither of us wanting to be the first to let go, but we eventually did and just like that, he was gone. I knew I would never see him again, but I would carry the memories inside my head and live with him inside my heart forever.

Chapter Twenty-Three

Is This Seat Taken

Craig's plan to meet my parents had been a good plan and just what I needed. My mom cried with me for days as she held me and worried herself over me. She and I both knew what I had lost, and what I had gained. The one thing about which my mom and I both agreed was I would never be the same. The experiences changed me in ways I could never have imagined.

I would be better than before I met Craig. I had finally matured. It was long overdue. I would eventually live again, and I would live a better life than I had envisioned prior to meeting him. I was determined to recover from this and carry the warmth of his love with me, throughout my life. That was what Craig would have wanted and expected me to do, to continue with life, more joyful than before, and be successful at it.

In 1990, four months after Craig's departure, I interviewed for an accounting position in Southern Pines, North Carolina and considered relocating to a small town (population 118 according to the census) with the name ironically being New River, North Carolina. New River had a sentimental ring to it, and I wondered if it was a sign of some sort. The name of the nearby city and its proximity to my potential employment was weighing heavily in my decision-making process.

I had been searching for a place where it was warm, and where I could find work. I decided if I wasn't going to follow my love to Norway, where there are sixty-three inches of snowfall per year and the average daily temperature is below zero, I would at least move away from snow altogether. The annual snowfall is seventeen inches in Dayton, which was seventeen inches more than I deemed necessary for a happy existence.

After researching states with warmer climates throughout the United States, and four trips to interview and explore housing possibilities, I committed to the North Carolina relocation. The plan included securing a temporary condominium until I could find a home to purchase with a barn on a parcel of land where I could keep a horse.

I was determined to go on living and fulfill the promise I made to myself to get back into horses. As Winston S. Churchill said so eloquently, "There is something about the outside of a horse that is good for the inside of a man." The only thing in Mr. Churchill's quote I would change is the word "man."

A relationship with a good horse pays dividends that cannot be measured or counted by any person, and I knew about counting and tabulating debits and credits and dividends. Since I was an accountant, and a resolute one who put my work first and foremost, work was not difficult for me to find. But I planned to work to live from that day forward, not live to work any longer.

I rented a room from a young man named Brian Young. He had black hair and was 6'2" tall. We met on a Trans World Airlines flight during one of my return ventures from a house-hunting trip.

Fortunately for me, Brian didn't remain a stranger for long. He was polite and kind with a big sense of humor that almost matched mine. I learned many pleasant things about him as I got to know him.

At the time of our initial meeting, he was wearing a cast, almost a full body cast, or the closest thing to one I've ever seen. It looked comical at first, although looking back, admittedly not funny at all, as he had problems getting down the plane's narrow aisle and I thought this surely couldn't be real. Who breaks their entire body?

"Is this seat taken?" he asked upon approach.

I was sitting in the middle, with an empty seat next to the window and another empty seat next to the aisle. I could tell he needed every inch of the middle seat and the aisle seat for his arms, because they couldn't fold against his chest due to the cast.

"I'll move over next to the window," I said.

"Thank you. I'm Brian," he said. "Forgive me for not shaking your hand."

It made me smile. I wondered why he had not selected a seat in an empty middle row, because the plane had many vacant seats. I also knew from the way he introduced himself, this wasn't going to be a quiet flight. He wanted to chat. I didn't mind. I welcomed the distraction from the three things I try to avoid: takeoff, flying, and landing.

"What happened to you?"

"I was in the military and had been practicing static line jumps for the 82nd Airborne when my parachute only partially opened. I hit the ground hard, breaking many bones, mostly in my upper body."

Of course I just met a guy who had been injured on an airplane during a skydiving jump. Is there something about me? Should I ask to exit this aircraft immediately and rent a car to drive the rest of the trip? Should I warn him to do the same? My luck with aircraft and things that fly, in general, hadn't exactly had fairy tale endings.

I spent the next ten minutes sharing my crazy flying stories with my now captive audience.

"So, I'm traveling with lady luck," he giggled nervously.

"Calamity Vanity, my friends call me." I proceeded to explain the calamity portion of my name.

"Are you going to Charlotte?" he asked.

"I'm going on to Dayton from Charlotte. I came down looking for an apartment. I interviewed with an accounting firm in Southern Pines, North Carolina. They offered me the job and now I have to decide if that is really where I want to live."

"I live in Pinehurst, just outside Southern Pines. I just bought a two-bedroom, two-bath condo. Construction was just completed last week. Maybe you could be my roommate."

I had committed to not rooming with anyone ever again, but especially a stranger I met on an airplane. In addition to his cast, Brian was wearing a cowboy hat, which is not something you see every day. That hat, along with the immobility of his arms and neck, made him appear to be the most harmless man I'd ever met.

"Not so fast, Cowboy, we just met," I reminded him.

"Well, I would have to ask my mom first," Brian said.

"How old are you?"

"Twenty-five. But I went to an all-boys high school and military college, and I would have to make sure rooming with a woman is okay with my mom."

I was now thirty-one, and aside from wondering what it was that had me attracting the attention of yet another twenty-five-year-old, I intuitively knew I could trust Brian. I appreciated the respect he had for his mother when he said he needed to ask her if she minded if he roomed with me. Little did I know we would soon become best friends forever, long before BFF was an endearing acronym.

Within days of meeting Brian, I accepted the position as a certified public accountant in Southern Pines.

Brian and I had exchanged numbers at Charlotte Douglas International Airport. As promised, I kept Brian informed of my job- and house-hunting decisions. Two months later, Brian was preparing to return home from an extended convalescent stay at his mom's house in Virginia.

I had already given notice to my current firm, packed, rented a storage unit in Southern Pines, and moved to a furnished one-bedroom apartment in the nearby city of Aberdeen. My firm had agreed to let me stay in the apartment for forty-five days while I searched for a place to live.

Before my time ended at my company furnished apartment, I spoke to Brian to coordinate our next meeting. Brian's offer to rent a room in his new condominium seemed more enticing than ever after looking around my new town for a place. By now, I had spoken on the phone to Brian a couple of times and confirmed with his mom that he was a legitimately nice guy, an Army officer who was transitioning out of the military due to his injuries.

"What a coincidence you had a seat next to me on the plane and you needed a roommate, just as I was moving to the area," I said.

"Oh," Brian hesitated, "I didn't have a ticket for that seat. I just saw you and I wanted to talk to you. It helped pass time on the flight, didn't it? I'm glad I did."

"You dog," I said. "Roommates only, right," I said.

"I promise," Brian said.

"Okay, when can I meet your mom?" I asked.

***

Brian's Mom, Carol Young, flew home with Brian to get him settled and I agreed to meet Brian and Carol at Brian's new condo. Brian had transitioned into a flexible cast but was still wearing a rigid plastic neck brace and his head was adorned with another cowboy hat.

He was moving slowly and deliberately as he hung his cowboy hat on the hat rack mounted on the wall near the front door before joining us at the kitchen table. I noted, even without a body cast, he still seemed quite harmless to me.

Carol was forty-six, a family physician, and we bonded quickly, which according to Brian was quite unusual, as she had never liked any female she ever met, at least if Brian was somehow involved with her. Carol's husband had been a test pilot for the United States Air Force and had died during a test flight when Brian was only two years old. Carol had never remarried.

Maybe Carol sensed Brian and I were in the "only friends" zone, and she probably knew an older, responsible, professional female might be just what Brian needed while he was healing.

We began eating a delicious meal Carol had prepared with gnocchi and tomato sauce made from fresh tomatoes, orange bell pepper, onions, and cream cheese. I love to cook, so my interest was genuine as I watched her prepare it, making mental notes of the ingredients.

"What's up with the cowboy hat Brian?" I asked.

"We own two horses," Carol replied on Brian's behalf, noticing Brian had just taken a bite of food and was struggling to answer.

"I trained horses, until my parachute accident," he said.

Brian had answered after covering his mouth politely and swallowing. I not only noticed but liked that he had manners.

"What kind of horses?"

"All kinds," Brian said. "I train horses for other people. Most are either spooky, spirited, misunderstood, or all three. They sometimes come to me with issues that need to be ridden out or corrected. Most are nice horses; some just fell into the wrong untrained hands at some point in their lives. I also work with veterinarians to determine if there is an underlying physical condition contributing to their behavior. I've trained Quarter Horses, Arabians, and Paints but lately, I've been taking on more clientele who own warmbloods. Southern Pines and Pinehurst are a hub for the dressage discipline."

"I own two half-Arabians and show in the sport horse classes at the Arabian Horse Association–sanctioned shows," Carol added. "Brian keeps them in show condition for me while I'm working in Virginia."

"Mom prefers Arabians," Brian said rolling his eyes.

"You stop that Brian," Carol scolded him. "Arabians are sweet people pleasers. They care about their owners."

"Carol, have you ever showed at the Horse Complex in Lexington, Virginia?" I asked.

"Yes, how do you know about that facility?"

"I have friends who show there."

"I'm impressed," Brian said.

"Small world," Carol added.

"Besides the weather, the horse community and convenience to competitions was the reason I chose the job in Southern Pines," I said.

What I didn't tell them was I was getting another horse. I needed another horse. I needed an after-work distraction to keep my mind off Craig. The exercise, time outdoors, and mental aspect would also help me sleep each night.

"Where do you board your horses?" I asked.

"New River. Mom owns a farm there. We have people running it. I bought this condo closer to town so I could heal and go back and forth to the hospital for treatment. I'm going to keep this condo as an investment property after I get better. Then I'll get back to working horses at the farm. It may be a year before I can ride again," Brian said.

I could see Brian was in pain, not physical pain, but emotional pain at the possibility of not being able to ride again. I remained silent so he could continue.

"Horses are my life, so I'm not going to stop riding regardless of what the doctor said. Mom thought it would be best for me to be in this condo and away from the farm because she knows if I'm at the farm, I'll be tempted to do things too soon and possibly hurt myself even worse than I am now. Logistically, it's also hard to maneuver at the farm in this cast and neck brace."

Carol looked worried when Brian said he was going to ride again regardless of what the doctors said. Brian caught the look on his mom's face. He paused and took a deep breath, obviously letting the reality of his situation sink in for a moment. His mother continued staring at him with concern and compassion.

"New River is where I initially planned to move just before I met you," I said.

"Why did you want to live in New River? Do you know someone there?"

"I really like the name," I said.

Brian looked at me like that may be the dumbest reason I could have come up with, but my answer made him smile, a genuine wide smile.

"I can't believe that is your reason for choosing a place to live, but what I really can't believe is that you admitted it. I think we're going to get along fine. I like you," Brian said.

"Southern Pines is host to championship dressage and eventing competitions and that also played a large part in my decision-making process and it's also an easy commute to competitions in Aiken, South Carolina," I said. "I am an equestrian, Brian. I ride. If you need help working your horses, maybe I'll be able to help until you're back on your feet."

He focused on me as if his ears had at first tricked him and then he perked up and paid attention to me. He looked at me and then over at his mom. Carol had a look somewhere between confused delight and astonishment on her face.

"My first horse was a half Arabian/half Saddlebred named Mayberry. I lived on his back. I once jumped over a picnic table bareback, but I was only fourteen at the time. I still did it, so it counts," I smiled.

Brian seemed pleased. He was smiling and looking back and forth between me and his mom.

"Do I know how to pick 'em or what, Mom?"

I told Brian and Carol I had drifted away from riding horses for the previous eight years, due to work and school, but I had always been the most content with horses as part of my daily life. I enjoyed riding and working with them, including groundwork, round penning, long lining, lunging, showing, or exercising them under saddle.

"Take me to the stables this weekend and introduce me to your horses. You can watch me ride and if you like my riding style and the way I communicate with them, I'll exercise them for you, until you heal."

"You got a deal," Brian said. Carol smiled at Brian, and he smiled back at her.

***

I agreed to rent the room from Brian and made a call to a local moving company to have my bedroom furniture delivered from my storage unit.

That was the beginning of not only our long and beautiful friendship but also our farm partnership. Within months, I moved out of Brian's condo in Pinehurst and into a stylishly decorated modern guest house on Carol's farm in New River. I began managing the daily operations of the farm and overseeing the employees and lesson program and, of course, managing their financial records.

I kept my job at the CPA firm because the farm part was quite manageable. I lived on site and enjoyed being around the horses, so it didn't feel like work at all. If I felt like lunging a horse at 9 p.m., I just flipped on the lights in the round pen and I did just that.

Little did I know when I coined the term "so it counts" that day after describing my picnic table jump on Mayberry, it would become a regular part of our satirical repertoire. Brian and I always jokingly had to add "so it counts" or "it counted" to the back-and-forth banter we had in the future, especially when it came to Brian's lengthy list of dates including comical notes, which he kept on an Excel spreadsheet.

He would say, "Uh we only kissed, so it didn't count."

I would quickly add under my breath just loud enough for him to hear me, "Oh, it counted."

Brian was popular with the ladies but had trouble making permanent commitments because he always thought a better match for him might be just around the next corner. Years later, I told him I was glad to be just his friend.

"I certainly wouldn't want to be a part of your stupid list," I said one evening as he was working on his desktop computer in the corner of his living room.

"Oh, but you are."

He flashed his silly grin. I lunged towards his computer to get a look at his infamous list just as he pressed the save and exit keys and made his screen go dark.

Chapter Twenty-Four

Farm Acquisition

By 1993, Brian and I had started to make a name for ourselves on the horse show circuit with our successful, but above all compassionate, training methods. We understood that, alongside reliable results, it was important to improve the lives of horses and of their owners and riders, too.

Our hard work paid off beyond our expectations; so much so, we decided to form an official business corporation between us after combining my background in accounting and business with our knowledge of horses and training as well. That's when things got even better. Not only did we become prosperous entrepreneurs who proceeded to purchase neighboring parcels of land by his mom's original farmstead once they arose, but we managed to remain friends, which was equally important.

There was a special bond between Brian, his mom Carol, and their neighbor Sam Rogers in New River. They were like family. Sam had always turned to Carol first for help with minor sprains, aches, and ailments to avoid a visit to his own physician in town. Brian was always willing to lend Sam a hand or help him with storm cleanup after a hurricane or mow his pastures for him when Sam's hired helper couldn't make it to work. It was no surprise when Sam contacted Carol first to see if she or Brian were interested in buying his land. Sam felt especially comfortable entrusting them to preserve his property in all its natural glory over any potential monetary gain.

"Sam, Vanity would love to purchase her own parcel of land if you would consider it. I feel confident she would not sell it to a developer who would turn it into a cookie cutter subdivision," Carol said.

"I adore Vanity," Sam replied. "Mention it to her and let's set up a meeting."

The price on vacant farmland in the area around Southern Pines, in the early nineties, was quite low per acre, but developers were starting to come in from out of town and buy parcels of farmland. New subdivisions and shopping centers were popping up all around and starting to reach out further into the outlying areas like New River.

We were grateful to have a neighbor who thought of us first, and I was grateful for having the wherewithal to purchase Sam's parcel when he offered it to me. Land in New River would later become sought-after prime real estate. The value accelerated when New River was listed in a national magazine as one of the safest places to live in America. New River could have lived without the attention. I wanted our quiet community to stay small and hidden from most of humanity's modern vices.

Developers would have to wait for our corner of New River because, try as they might, these parcels weren't for sale then and they aren't for sale now. As of this writing, thirty years later, the parcels are still home to some of the best horse grazing lands in the county.

Many of the perimeter acres were allowed to naturally reforest and are reserved as a wildlife sanctuary for trail rides only.

***

In 1995, Brian and I built our barns first, then a shared covered riding arena right in the center of our two parcels, then built two residences, one centered on each of the two properties. We fenced around the perimeter of all three properties, so we jointly owned 165 acres.

"Do you want to put in an intercom system in our two houses?" Brian asked.

"Is that possible?"

"It is. My friend sells them. I can get him to install it."

"How does it work?"

"Once installed, I can press a button and I can talk, and you can hear me and then you press the button, and you can talk, and I can hear you."

"Isn't that what a phone is for?"

"I thought it would be neat to be able to communicate with you like we used to when we were roommates. You know how we could just walk out into the living room and get into each other's business," Brian said.

"That's sweet."

Brian looked embarrassed.

"Yes, Brian, I think it will be fun. When I see you come home with a date, I can press the intercom button and say, 'Hi, honey I'm home,' and then watch your date run out the front door."

"Maybe it wasn't one of my better ideas," Brian said, now second guessing his original enthusiasm.

"Oh, no, I insist on having it installed."

"Think not."

"Think so."

We had it installed so I guess I won, or maybe Brian just manipulated that conversation to his advantage so we both won. For the first week we used it to annoy each other every hour on the hour, often just pushing the button and giggling and not saying anything, but after the first week, we hardly used it.

I still felt more comfortable in that big house all by myself knowing there was a way to get Brian's attention quickly with the touch of a button, should I ever need him. Later, we expanded it to the barns so we could use the intercom to communicate with each other in either house from either barn. We used that several times during animal emergencies. On a farm, those dreaded emergencies occur more often than one would think and often, time is of the essence in getting proper help to the animal in order to influence a positive outcome.

Brian always let me name the baby horses called foals, with the exception of NR Wild Card. In 2000, Brian was on foal watch around midnight with some of his buddies. That's what you do when a soon-to-be mother horse called a dam is about to give birth. You watch her until she starts to give birth and you know when that is because the babies two front feet will start to emerge. Sometimes, foal watch lasts for hours and sometimes it lasts for weeks. The guys were playing poker when Wild Card's dam went into labor. That night, I could have taken my turn sleeping on a nearby couch, but I couldn't resist catching up on my sleep in my own bed. Besides, I knew there were enough hands around to deliver the foal safely. Even though it's exciting when the new foal arrives, I decided sleep was more important. They didn't need me.

When the foal's legs and nose appeared just outside the opening of the birth canal, Brian had the best cards of the entire evening in his hand. The guys stopped playing cards just long enough to press the intercom button to wake me, over the intercom, to please come and deliver the foal.

"You guys are pathetic," I replied.

I guess they all thought they were going to finish their hand immediately, but I started barking orders for towels and I needed man muscles to help get the foal on its feet so it could start nursing.

The guys soon went back to finishing their poker game, which Brian won.

"That intercom just paid for itself," Brian said gathering up his friends' money. Brian had a sarcastic wit I really loved, even when it was aimed at me.

"I knew I should have never agreed to that thing," I said.

I just shook my head at Brian, but I was secretly happy I hadn't missed the delivery of the foal. There was no place I would rather have been at that moment than right there in the barn, covered with placenta and other birthing gunk, all of it wet and slimy, including the foal itself.

"Welcome to the world, Wild Card. I hope you turn out to be as good as the hand I just had," Brian said. That name just stuck, and Wild Card lived up to his name. He was feisty but always my favorite horse on the property; the horse I rode around the farm's perimeter to check fences and the one I rode most often for another twenty-three years.

Chapter Twenty-Five

Aubrey

Aubrey Targaczewski was an excellent addition to our farm and training facility. I met her in 2015 when she was twenty-three years old. She had recently moved to North Carolina with a horse and was looking to board him. She had been keeping her horse at her friend's farm until she could find a place for him. I showed her around the facilities and clicked with her from day one. She was a West Point graduate, recently married to a man named Steve, who was one year and one grade ahead of her. Steve had attended helicopter training for thirty-two weeks in Ft. Rucker, Alabama and Aubrey chose the same career path.

Once they were working in their established careers, they got orders to Ft. Bragg, now known as Fort Liberty Army Base. Aubrey, an equestrian from an early age, purchased a premium registered Westfalen warmblood named Spartacus. He was also known by his barn name "Barney" to all that loved and cared for him. Aubrey and Barney competed successfully at the Prix St. George level in dressage, which is a phenomenal accomplishment.

Aubrey worked her own horse, then started working my horses, then the horses of our other boarders, and eventually the horses we were paid to train for other people. She started hanging around the barn, slowly at first, but over the years, she became a permanent fixture at our facility. Aubrey, although she was a military helicopter pilot during the day, lived close enough to visit the barn in the evenings after work and had eight weeks leave every year and most weekends free.

Steve flew Blackhawk helicopters for work and bought a fixed wing single engine Cessna for himself. Steve's hobby was flying, while Aubrey's hobby was horses. Aubrey loved to fly helicopters and when she later made the rank of Captain, she piloted a helicopter across the entire United States on two occasions, once flying solo.

In every minute of her spare time, she rode horses. Aubrey loved to ride horses as much as I did, and she was better at it. She had a nice seat and hands and the communication ability to get a horse to collect into a nice frame and go forward freely with minimal effort. It's a gift you're either born with or not, and Aubrey was born with it.

Occasionally, Steve would grace us with his presence at the barn. He occasionally rode Smokey, called a husband's horse, which was a trustworthy old gelding who wouldn't hurt a fly and didn't like to go fast, especially with someone on his back. One of our boarders had purchased Smokey on a whim and found she had little time for horses with her busy career, so she gifted Smokey to Aubrey, for Steve.

That's a common tactic horsewomen do to get two horses; we say we got the second one for our partner. Usually, as was the case with Steve, he wasn't amused because he just saw that as two board payment bills each month instead of one. Aubrey, knowing Steve wouldn't ride Smokey often, always had a second mount available for her friends from work or for herself when her horse, Spartacus, needed rest from a minor injury or a missing shoe.

Steve preferred to do flyovers in his Cessna while we were riding, rather than riding himself. We enjoyed waving to him during his fly-overs and he provided us with aerial farm photos for our website.

Aubrey and Steve became like family to me, Brian, and Carol. We were lucky to have Aubrey, as military orders for a married couple rarely keep them in the same state for more than three years. We enjoyed every precious year we had with them riding, training, and showing horses.

In 2016, Aubrey helped me set up a non-profit organization call Dog Days of Summer. We raised money and donated it to our local shelter to spay and neuter shelter pets.

My mom, age eighty-six, died that same year from a heart attack and my dad three months later, age eighty-eight, from a stroke, although it seemed like he just gave up and died from a broken heart after Mom died. It was a tough year overall. I sold their house, which had been my childhood home, and used the money my parents left me to take the non-profit to a new level. They would have been proud of me for using their funds for such an important endeavor, and helping animals continued to help me heal.

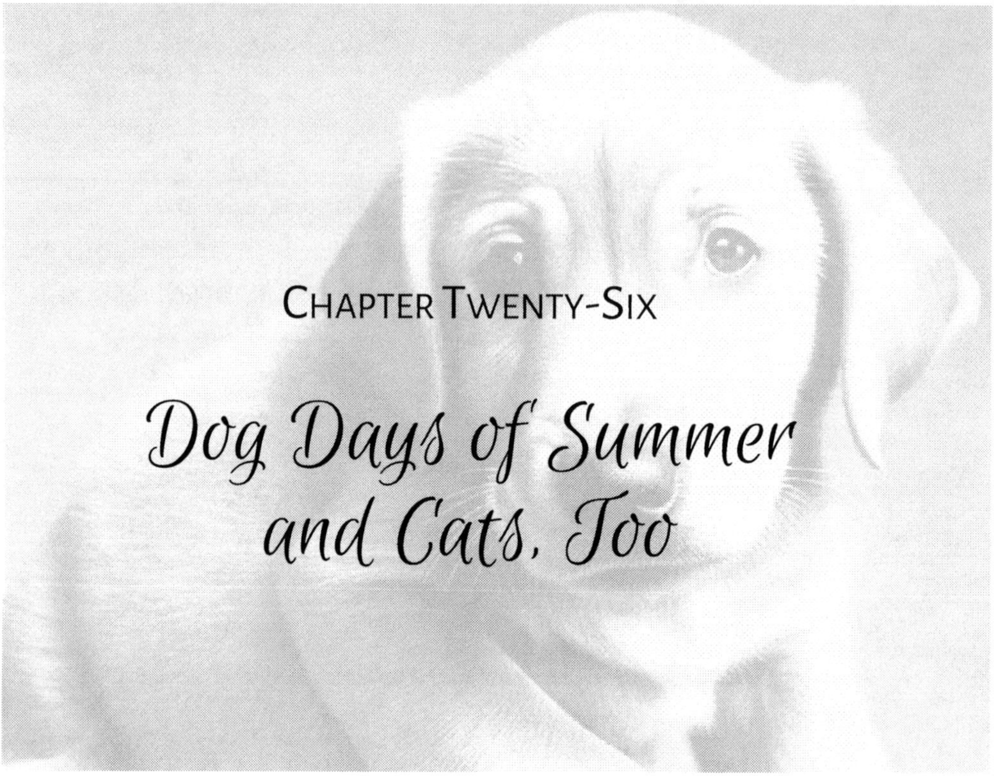

Chapter Twenty-Six

Dog Days of Summer and Cats, Too

Aubrey, Carol, and I were all animal lovers and animal advocates. It's yet one more thing we had in common. My mom and dad's legacy inspired me to start the Dogs Days of Summer non-profit spay and neuter clinic, with my friends Aubrey and Carol. After losing my parents, I decided rather than just raising funds and donating those funds to our local shelter, I would build a permanent low-cost spay and neuter clinic on my parcel of land.

We had a small parcel surveyed and situated the clinic with road frontage so the public would have easy parking access to the clinic. With the help of local businesses and the one local radio station offering us free advertising, we were able to secure enough funds and volunteers to get it up and running.

Aubrey was instrumental in securing most of our donations and hired our employees as she was charming and intelligent and had a natural ability to organize people and projects. She had made a lot of friends at the local Army base who were glad to help her with such a worthwhile project.

The highest cost was hiring veterinarians, who worked tirelessly despite much lower wages than they would make running their own practices. To me, they were the heroes of this story. Everyone who participated in running the clinic said it was a labor of love.

Equally important to our operation, we had volunteer drivers who would pick up animals from high-kill shelters in surrounding counties, drive them to our clinic, and then take them to a no-kill shelter, neutered or spayed and ready for adoption.

We opened the clinic in the summer of 2016, and it was an overwhelming success. In 2012, Carol had officially retired and sold her medical practice in Virginia and permanently moved into her residence at the farm, so she was able to dedicate much of her free time to running the clinic, much like she did when she was running her practice in Virginia. She was an integral part of the organization and I believe it gave her a new purpose, which she embraced.

In the first ninety days, our clinic spayed and neutered over one hundred animals, all of which were adopted out to their, hopefully, forever homes. It was fulfilling to know we were making a difference every single day by helping these animals live better lives.

My parents would have been proud this venture helped give so many animals the chance at a life they deserve without their constant cycle of reproduction refilling the shelters to capacity. We were able to reduce one shelter's kill rate from 90 percent when we started to 45 percent by 2018. We are now working to get that number as close to 0 percent as possible.

***

One day Carol and I were working in the clinic on the same day, which was a rarity of sorts, along with Becky, one of the many dedicated volunteers at Dogs Days of Summer. Aubrey brought in what she thought was a feral cat she had trapped with food and a cage at Fort Liberty. The orange tabby was partially visible under the cover Aubrey had placed over the cage to quiet and calm the feline, but she was still making quite a fuss and meowing in a loud, aggressive manner.

Meowing at undesirably loud volumes is a typical behavior among cats faced with sudden cage confinement but this cat's cries sounded especially shrill and heart wrenching. We assumed she was just afraid. We reassured ourselves, knowing this program was doing far more good than harm, this frightened cat would, in a matter of days, be spayed and hopefully placed in a loving home.

Katie Roberts, D.V.M., the clinic's primary veterinarian, lifted the cover and opened the cage. Just as she was about to reach in and sedate the cat, it bit and scratched her arm just above the thick gloves she was wearing as it shot out of the cage, jumped off the stainless-steel table, and ran across the room.

"Oh no," Dr. Roberts exclaimed. She had a startled look on her face and was looking at her own now bleeding arm.

"What's going on?" Aubrey asked. I entered the room right behind Aubrey, but I hadn't closed the door. The tabby scratched Aubrey's leg with its back claw as it whizzed past us. This all occurred within a matter of seconds.

"We have an emergency. I think this cat has rabies!" Dr. Roberts exclaimed.

"What should we do?" Carol asked. She had come rushing into the room to help.

"Everyone grab a blanket," Aubrey ordered. "We have to toss the blankets over the cat in order to subdue it and to protect ourselves."

We quickly moved into action. While Carol ran off to fetch our supply of surplus blankets, I drew a strong sedative into a syringe for Dr. Roberts to use on the cat. Dr. Roberts and Aubrey tried to locate where the animal was hiding inside the building.

It didn't take long.

"He ran through the blanket. He got away. He scratched me again," Aubrey called out from the lobby in a high-pitched volume with a few choice words to boot. She was clutching her leg.

"He ran that way," Aubrey said pointing.

The cat then pounced onto my leg with its claws, scratching me all the way through my pants, digging in with all four feet as it darted up my side and arm like I was a tree. It kicked off me leaping through the air just before it landed and ran into the first open door it could find, knocking all the supplies off the counter in the surgery room.

"I can see him. He's right over there," I said pointing. "He's ready to pounce again and he's got foamy saliva dripping from his mouth."

The cat wasted no time as it jumped on me again, hissing, and swatting at me. I tried to jump aside but the cat was on me, biting and scratching like a crazed maniac.

With blankets outstretched, Aubrey and Becky were onto me, knocking me off my feet, but swiftly wrapped their blankets around the cat, who let go of me as he tried to escape out the corner of one of the blankets.

"We got him, Vanity," Aubrey said.

"Oh, thank goodness you got him," I said.

"Are you okay?" Aubrey asked.

"I'm fine. Shaken a bit, scratched and bleeding, but fine. You all okay?"

"Yes, just scratched and bleeding," Aubrey said.

"Bit and scratched but fine," Dr. Roberts added.

They handed the blanket bundle with the cat securely inside to Dr. Roberts, who administered the sedative through the blanket.

Soon the cat was sleeping peacefully but the ordeal was far from over. It had managed to break the skin on three of us during its escape.

Carol, having spent most of her life in family medicine, advised us to immediately wash our wounds with soap and water and informed us we would all need rabies shots, including her and Becky, who had no noticeable scratches. Carol checked us all over and doctored our wounds.

"There is saliva from the cat all around the office. Becky and I will be in there cleaning for days. I would just feel better if we all go now and get the rabies vaccines," Carol said, and we all agreed.

Dr. Roberts, Becky, Carol, Aubrey, and I all traveled together to a local hospital that conveniently had a doctor's office on the first floor. We received an initial dose of the vaccine and had to each have four additional doses over the next two weeks.

Aubrey and Becky experienced nausea and vomiting shortly after they received their vaccine. I broke out in hives after my third shot, but Carol and Dr. Roberts just got sore arms at the vaccination site. Fortunately, I just broke out on my stomach, and it only lasted a day, and I had no side effects from shot number four or five, except a sore arm.

A necropsy performed at North Carolina State College of Veterinary Medicine revealed the tabby did have rabies and would have died an agonizingly painful death and exposed other animals to the incurable, viral brain disease. Based on the outward signs we saw, including the animal's behavior, we all pretty much knew the outcome.

We were animal lovers, so we didn't blame the cat; we knew her aggressive behavior was caused by the virus.

I think each of us worried, even after getting the vaccines, that we would contract the disease but were reassured no one has ever contracted rabies after receiving the vaccines. Still, I awakened drenched in nervous sweat for a few nights afterwards and googled symptoms of rabies. I didn't feel completely out of the woods for about six months.

Aubrey apologized for days about bringing that cat into the clinic. We encouraged her to continue her work in animal rescue. It was an important program, and she was making a difference. What happened in our office was a rare occurrence that would, most likely, never happen again.

As a result of our experience, we added free animal rabies vaccinations to anyone who wanted to bring a pet to our clinic and that service, supported solely by donors, continues to this day.

"I'm glad you brought the tabby into the clinic instead of me because Calamity would have become permanently attached to my name. I would have never lived it down," I told Aubrey.

"You're right. I'm getting to be more like you every day," Aubrey said.

That made me smile.

The clinic remains a permanent fixture in our town and a legacy to my parents. I never ran out of things to do there. If I got bored at the farm, I would ride the golf cart over to the clinic, and as soon as I walked through the door, someone would put me to work doing something. It brought great joy and a sense of accomplishment to my life. It started out to be all about the animals but ended up being equally about the generous people who tirelessly volunteered.

Chapter Twenty-Seven

How the Heck Do You Get Down There

Carol came over one evening in 2018 and told me she was going to give a speech at a conference in Washington D.C. about a paper she had published in a medical journal. Her speech was about autism and her belief it was somehow connected to what we call Neonatal Maladjustment Syndrome (NMS) in newborn horses and calves. I had read her paper about the subject, and it was fascinating. She invited me to join her.

She suggested I shop or do touristy things during the day while she was at the conference. I asked her if I could bring Aubrey because Steve, Aubrey's husband, was on a temporary duty training exercise with the military for three weeks. It was what we called TDY or, sometimes, "being in the field."

Carol thought it was a great idea and said she didn't mind at all if Aubrey came along so I would have someone to hang with during the day, and I suggested she invite Brian as well. We had reliable employees at the time who could care for the farm for a few days.

Carol called the hotel to add an extra room. I would room with Aubrey and Brian with Carol. Brian drove us in his SUV, and we had a pleasant trip.

The first morning, I woke up and discovered Aubrey was no longer in my room. I assumed she had gone down to the lounge for coffee.

I took the elevator down to the first floor, but I didn't see her in the lounge, so I walked over to the lobby and took my place in one of the three lines that had formed. I had always wanted to visit the Smithsonian but had no idea how to get there, so I decided to ask one of the hotel clerks for directions.

"Good morning, may I help you?" the clerk said.

"Do you know the best way to get to the Smithsonian?" I asked.

"Which one?"

"I didn't know there was more than one," I said as I was immediately embarrassed.

She looked at me, amused.

"How many are there?" I asked.

"Seventeen here in D.C.," she replied.

I heard a few chuckles from those in line behind me.

"If I make it to one of them, can I walk to the rest?

"You'll have to do some walking, but yes."

"Then any one of them is fine. Can I drive my car there?"

"I wouldn't recommend it, take the metro."

I assumed the metro was a bus. I noted a bus stop sign through the glass window of the hotel's lobby in plain view of where I was standing.

I pointed to the sign and said, "Do you know what time the bus leaves for the Smithsonian and is that the bus that goes directly there?"

"No, it's a subway," she replied. "It's underground."

"I had no idea there was a subway system anywhere except New York City," I admitted.

I heard more chuckles from those around me and the clerk just stood behind the counter silently staring at me like she had just met her first neanderthal or something.

"Where would it pick me up?" I asked.

"It's underground," she repeated slowly as if her saying it slower the second time would tell me how to get there.

I heard a synchronized burst of laughter from the people in the lobby as I looked down at the floor and asked, "How do I get down there?"

I then glanced at a doorway fifteen feet to my left and momentarily thought I had solved the riddle. The clerk spotted me sizing up the doorway as I took one step towards it. She said, "That's a coat closet."

She emphasized the word "coat."

The people around me began roaring with laughter.

Aubrey and Brian had just made their way down to the lobby to find me while Carol was still getting ready in the room. They caught the end of the conversation I was having with the clerk and heard all the laughter.

The clerk handed me a map of the Smithsonian museums like she wanted me to take the map and move on, but I began looking at it while still holding up the line.

"Whatever you do, don't hold up that map and act the way you are now while riding the subway. It will make you an easy target," she leaned in and quietly said to me.

Great, now I'm going to get mugged.

"Calamity," Brian said. He appeared to be as embarrassed as I was because his face and the tops of his ears were red, and he rarely ever called me Calamity.

"We got this," Aubrey said to the clerk.

"We'll make sure she gets there," Brian said.

There were smiles and nods as Aubrey took me arm in arm and walked me through the lobby out the revolving glass doors. I jokingly commented to Aubrey about how all those nice people were laughing with me, and not AT me.

"Yeah, something like that, Calamity," Aubrey said smiling.

I finally got a Calamity out of Brian and Aubrey! I must have done something really funny.

Pointing, Aubrey explained to me we would walk two blocks that way and then go down a large set of concrete steps that lead underground and there we would catch the train.

"I assume there is a sign then that says SUBWAY?"

"No worries, Vanity. You won't miss the large sign with an arrow that points to the stairs. And we'll be with you. Why didn't you wait for us?"

"I was just excited. I came down looking for you, then grabbed a bagel and coffee and thought I would just save us all some time by asking directions. I think I will laugh about this for years."

"You're not the only one. I think the people in that lobby will laugh about this for years, too. It was hilarious. I don't think Brian and I will ever forget that conversation. I'm sorry we missed the first part, but you can tell us about that on the train," Aubrey said.

"Where's Brian?" I asked.

"He went to grab a coffee and some fruit. He'll join us any minute."

"Okay, one more thing. Do we have to pull a cable to let the driver know when we want to get off the train?" I asked Aubrey.

"No, they will announce stops. We will hear Arlington announced, and soon after that we will hear Smithsonian."

"Arlington? Like the cemetery Arlington?"

"Yes, that's where my uncle is buried," she replied, "my mom's brother. I plan to make a visit there tomorrow if you want to come with me."

"Yes, so you've been here before, I mean there?"

"I visited his grave once while I was at West Point. My uncle died in a military helicopter accident before I was born. He's the reason I became a pilot."

"I'd be honored to join you," I said.

I had always been cautious about telling my stories of airplane accidents to Aubrey and Steve because one, I kept my past mostly to myself and two, they were both pilots, but the irony of going to visit the grave of yet another person who died far too young and in a tragic air accident would undoubtedly stir deep emotions in me. I would have to try hard to keep my feelings in check, but I imagine at Arlington seeing row after row of white headstones, I might not be the only one shedding tears.

On a different note, if there was ever a time where I truly felt I was channeling my mother, it was during the conversation I had with the hotel clerk. My mom used to publicly embarrass me and my dad on a regular basis, acting just like I did at the counter. It made me miss my mom so very much. I truly had become just like my mother as we were always laughing with her and not AT her.

Chapter Twenty-Eight

A Chance Encounter

One evening in July of 2019, although exhausted from working on the farm all day, I reluctantly got up off my comfy couch and responded to a knock on my front door.

"I've been trying to call you. You might want to meet Aubrey's parents," Jessica said. Jessica was one of our horse owners who kept her horse at our farm for training.

I invited her to step inside the foyer.

"They are out in the barn. Aubrey was looking for you," she said.

"Thank you. I'll be right there. I do want to meet them. I think I left my phone in the feed room. No, I didn't, here it is," I said spotting it on the counter. "I had the volume turned down accidentally."

"Tell her I'll be there in five minutes."

"Okay," Jessica said turning to leave.

"Thank you again, Jessica," I said.

I hurried into the bathroom, looked in the mirror, sighed at the sight of my unkempt self, fixed my hair the best I could on such short notice, and applied some light-rose lip balm to my lips. Lipstick did little to disguise that I was covered with hay dust and horse dander all over my hair and clothes.

I decided to change my shirt at the last minute to a lightweight blouse that looked a little more professional and was definitely cleaner. I didn't have to impress Aubrey's parents, but I was rough looking and just felt the need to freshen up before meeting them.

I wanted to tell them Aubrey meant the world to me and thank them for raising such a helpful, ambitious daughter.

I walked from the house to the barn along a concrete driveway. My macaws were playing in their large outdoor flight aviary. They called out in my direction the words mom, momma, hello, and apple, and one just made a shrill baby horse whinny sound. My bird learned to make that sound when I weaned a six-month-old foal, from its dam, in a fenced area next to my birds.

The result was the foal called for its dam for the first few hours of the separation and my bird mimicked the sound. My bird repeated that high-pitched baby horse whinny every day for over twenty years.

Roosting time is 5:30 and my birds do not like it when I'm late. They let me know by getting loud if I forget to bring them inside to their large indoor cages, on schedule, where they relax and watch baby learning shows on Netflix and sing-along channels on their own flat-screen TV until 8 or 9 p.m. Then it's lights out and they rest quietly until 8 or 9 a.m. the following morning.

I started to divert back towards the birds, to please them and silence them because their voices carry for a good half mile when they are angry, but I realized I needed to head directly to the barn to avoid missing my guests.

I was pulled in two directions as usual. Rest on a farm is evasive. Just when I felt ready to kick back, put up my feet, and relax, something would change. Something would beckon me. I would shift gears, and then off I would go to do the next chore or greet the next guest. In this case, it was guests from Washington State, Aubrey's parents. I buzzed past the squawking, talking birds and towards the entrance to the barn.

I walked into the modern barn with its fourteen-foot-wide concrete long aisles and its decorative inlaid bricks, which purposely coordinated to the brick on the main residence. It wasn't a big red kind of barn you see on a dairy farm, but a modern barn built especially for horses. Some were high dollar horses, and some were low dollar auction block horses, who just got lucky for finding their way to this loving farm. I cared for all of them, and about all of them, equally.

I saw three people standing in the aisle in front of the hot-and-cold-water wash rack. The wash rack was used for bathing horses for a show or cooling them down after a sweltering summer workout.

The evening sun was shining through the stall windows to my left as I approached. I couldn't make out the faces of my guests, but I heard them talking.

"Hello," I called out still some distance away. "I'm Vanessa. Nice to meet you," I said as I sped up and finalized my approach.

"Hello, nice to meet you. I've heard so much about you," Aubrey's mother, Leah said. "I'm Leah."

"Hello," Aubrey's dad said as he reached out to shake my hand.

How impolite, I thought to myself. He didn't introduce himself and a man is not supposed to reach out to shake a woman's hand unless she presented her hand first. Doesn't he know that? My critical, snobby thoughts were cut short as I reached for his hand and realized I had heard a familiar voice.

My eyes met Craig's eyes for the first time since our tearful goodbye at Cincinnati International Airport in 1989, thirty years prior. Shock, surprise, joy, and a rush of adrenaline overwhelmed me, all at once.

I wondered if Aubrey or Leah could see the blood pumping through the artery on my neck.

That smile. It was that smile again. He took my hand and briefly held it, long enough for me to know he knew it was me, but not long enough for anyone else to notice how long he held my hand.

Not only was I shocked to see him standing in the aisle of my barn, but I was stunned when I realized my beloved Aubrey was his daughter. The daughter I was supposed to have. The child who was meant for me.

No wonder I was so drawn to her from the moment we met. She carries the DNA of my only true love. But then I quickly worried, what would happen if she ever found out? Would this ruin my relationship with her? I wasn't willing to risk it. There was no sense in spilling this secret. I had held it this long; I could hold it longer. I must remain calm. I must remain quiet.

I barely spoke. I didn't thank them, as I had planned, for being Aubrey's parents. My mouth would not work. My brain was racing. My breath was labored. I pretended like I was winded. It was only half pretend because I really couldn't catch my breath, but I wanted them to think it was because I had been running all over the farm and just needed a minute. I made my way to the closest bench and sat quietly for a moment.

I realized I should get up and move because surely Leah would engage me in conversation soon. Conversation was something I could not muster at that moment, not with Leah, at least not right then or even in the foreseeable future.

There was something familiar about her, I thought; but of course, Leah would look familiar, she's Aubrey's mom and Aubrey resembles her. Staring at Aubrey for the first time next to Craig, the resemblance was so clear. Why had I not seen it before?

Craig's eyes did not leave me. Once again, he looked at me and did not look away as if we had been transported back to 1989, on that warm sunny day in New River, West Virginia.

I was polite but short and guarded with my words. I wanted to touch him. I wanted to hold him and kiss him, but of course, I could not.

I listened while my guests made small talk, but he and I never spoke. We didn't have to use words to communicate. I realize we were both going through the exact same emotions at the same time, once again. It was like a thousand-piece jigsaw puzzle had just assembled itself in a matter of seconds.

All too soon Leah had taken ahold of Craig's arm and let him know it was time to leave. Aubrey had to report for flight duty the next day at zero dark thirty at Fort Liberty Army Base and they needed a good night's sleep before Aubrey dropped them at the airport.

They were leaving. It was for the best. What would I have done or said if he had stayed another minute, another hour, or another day? I couldn't have contained myself for another five minutes or disguised my happiness.

Tears of joy welled up inside of me but remained just below the surface. They were ready to spill over like a pot of boiling water on a stove, but I knew they would scorch every surface they touched. I held them back with all my might.

How could no one read into this or feel these vibrations? Surely the air was different. I could feel it.

Aubrey and Leah were caught up in their own worlds, oblivious to the magic happening right in front of their eyes. Thank goodness they did not know. I hadn't felt this way since Craig and I last embraced.

Love and loss so powerful it could move the air around me and shake a tree. Emotions powerful enough to make me nearly levitate, but unnoticeable to even those closest to me. That was the turmoil happening inside my heart at the very moment I realized it was Craig.

"The End of the World" by Skeeter Davis was softly playing in the background on the barn's radio, drowned out only by the sounds of several angry birds. Even that song playing at that exact moment was completely unusual and strange.

"It was nice to finally meet you. Aubrey is quite fond of you," Leah said.

I couldn't even muster a verbal response. Just a smile and a nod of thanks to Leah. They walked down the long aisle and out of the barn onto the large concrete parking pad and got into Aubrey's black Sierra pickup truck. Craig and I followed slowly. I lingered beside Craig as we walked. He looked over at me the entire way to the end of the barn.

Leah needed a little boost to get into the tall truck, but Craig was on the opposite side of the vehicle and didn't seem to notice in time to assist her. Leah managed to pull herself in using the grab bar inside the passenger door. Craig gave me a lingering glance and smile as he made sure he was the last one to enter the vehicle.

He sat in the rear seat on the driver's side behind Aubrey. I had to make sure my reaction to his smile was contained and locked away in my mind and heart. I had to bury my emotions because everyone in the truck was now facing me as they lifted their hands for a final wave.

After they left, I leaned against the concrete block barn wall, just inside the aisle, and my weak legs gave way as I slid into a sitting position. I remained frozen in place for some time. I was filled with joy and shed tears of happiness. I tried to understand and absorb the ramifications of what had just occurred. Aubrey was Craig's daughter. That thought swirled in my head like a merry-go-round. I felt dizzy and lightheaded. I leaned my back and head against the cool block wall and welcomed its support.

I thought back to the conversation Annie and I had driving home from the rafting trip and how we had hashed and rehashed every angle and aspect of every conversation and nuance from the trip.

"I have to call Annie," I said aloud with no one around to hear me.

I needed to tell her what had just happened. Annie had moved to Texas years earlier and taken a job as a paralegal, but we still talked as if she lived next door and no time had passed. *Wait until she hears this story. She is not going to believe it.* I realized I didn't have my phone with me, so I slowly stood up and headed to the house to call her.

Just as I located and reached for my cell phone in the kitchen where I left it, it rang. It startled me a bit. I was already on shaky ground from the events that had occurred in my barn a half hour earlier. I could see it was Aubrey. My heart sank. Had she noticed something was going on between me and her father?

Aubrey rarely called me, especially after leaving the barn. She usually messaged me if she wanted me to turn her horses out, or bring her horses in, or add supplements to their feed. Did Craig tell her?

"Hello?"

"Vanity, I have a favor to ask of you," Aubrey said.

"Yes, of course."

My voice was quivering from the unfolding events.

"Are you alright?"

"Yes, why?"

I assumed right then Craig had told her about us.

"You just sounded funny when you answered the phone."

"I'm fine," I said.

"Would you drive my parents to the airport in the morning? Work called and asked me to come in two hours earlier. If I take them that early, my parents will have to wait at the airport for four hours, in the middle of the night, before their plane leaves."

"Of course," I said.

I couldn't believe I had just agreed to drive Craig and his wife to the airport.

"Can you pick them up at 5:15 a.m.? I'll owe you big time."

"You won't owe me anything. Glad to do it."

Somehow, I managed to say that to Aubrey ever so casually like it was no big deal. It was the only deal. It was the biggest deal in my entire life since the day I met Craig on that raft.

I was relieved to know Aubrey didn't suspect anything, but I went into an internal meltdown realizing I was going to see Craig again.

Chapter Twenty-Nine

The Second Goodbye

At 2 a.m., I was still awake. I spent hours deciding what to wear, then changed my mind and picked out something completely different. I had two and a half hours before I had to leave. After the phone call from Aubrey, I completely forgot to call Annie and instead I went into panic mode.

After agreeing to drive Aubrey's parents to the airport, I paced around the room accomplishing absolutely nothing for the next hour. I had long conversations with myself and rehearsed exactly what I would say to Craig during the half-hour car ride to the airport.

My birds were my friends, advisors, and only audience. They listened intently as I rambled on and on and told them all about Craig and our great love affair. They relished the extra attention they were getting, or maybe they just thought I had gone stark raving mad and dared not interrupt. Regardless, I appreciated that they lent me an attentive ear without rendering judgment or advice.

I wanted to shower, fix my hair, and apply makeup for my meeting with Leah and Craig, but I knew it would look odd if I were completely manicured at such an early morning hour. If this were a normal situation, driving my friend's parents to the airport, I would barely crawl out of bed, grab a diet Pepsi or a cup of coffee, throw on some jogging pants and a sloppy T-shirt, and off I would go.

It would still be dark. I realized no matter what I did to make myself look refreshed, I was still going to look exhausted. I hadn't slept a wink since we parted company the previous evening.

My mind was racing, but coffee this morning was most definitely at the top of my agenda. Coffee sometimes makes me nervous and shaky. I opted for decaf so I wouldn't need to use the restroom halfway to the airport. *What is it about this guy that makes my digestive system churn?* Some things never change. Why is it that all the good things—like our youthful looks and memory—leave us, and all the dreadful things—like irritable bowel syndrome—remain with us for life.

I opted to make my now strawberry-red hair with blonde highlights look nice, washed, blow dried, and flat ironed straight in my now shoulder-length bob. I added a light dab of makeup and some light lip gloss and normal clothes that wouldn't give the impression I stayed up all night deciding what to wear. Although Craig would still know me well enough to realize I had.

Brushed teeth, used mouthwash, and chewed gum. Considered taking mints. Definitely gum. I was too nervous to eat and needed the added protection gum could provide in a closed car with Craig, especially at such an early morning hour with an empty, sour stomach and no sleep. Wore a light jacket, the one that bragged about one of my recent horse accomplishments, yes that jacket would be fine, the one with USEF, which stands for United States Equestrian Federation with horse of the year on the sleeve. Perfect.

Keys in hand and off I went. Closed the door, set the house alarm, locked the door, and walked to my car. *Where are my car keys?* I could not find my keys. The house door was already locked and so was my car door. What did I do with my keys? Oh no. I always did this.

No worries. I had a key hidden in a special place in the hay loft, but that meant I had to climb into the hay loft and locate the Realtor-type lock box to retrieve my hidden house key.

I tried to climb the flat concrete block wall like a rock climber without a belay. Then I remembered there was a ladder in the shed. I ran to the shed. The shed was usually locked, but this time it wasn't. That was the only thing going my way at this early-morning hour.

It was dark outside and there was no electricity in the shed. I had always meant to connect it, but just kept putting other projects ahead of it. I was certain there were snakes hiding somewhere in the dark corners, curled up in pieces of equipment as I had so often found during the day. I braved the dark, timidly felt around with my hands, hoping on my life I didn't disturb a sleeping copperhead while locating the ladder.

I was out of breath by the time I dragged the twelve-foot ladder into the barn so I could prop it up against the stall wall and climb into the loft. The problem with that plan was the stall had a horse in it. I put a halter on the horse, like a harness on a dog, and moved the horse to the crosstie grooming bay, in the center of the barn, across from the wash rack.

I dragged the ladder into the stall and climbed up and over the edge of the loft, but I hadn't considered the recent hay delivery blocking all access to the loft and my key box.

I had an arduous task to complete because the hay was packed in so tightly, I could hardly budge the first bale, but I somehow summoned all my strength and wiggled it side to side so I could free it and get a passageway started. I tossed twelve fifty-five-pound bales of hay down into the stall, one by one, until I had removed enough bales to squeeze my way through the six hundred remaining bales of hay. Finally, I located the key box.

It was dark in the loft and even though we had lights and electricity in the stalls, it didn't illuminate the loft, or the tunnel I had just bored through hay. Although I had managed to reach the key box, there wasn't enough light for me to see the code numbers to open it. I didn't have my phone with me.

I climbed back down the ladder, found my phone, and climbed back up. Using the flashlight app, I opened the box, got the house key, ran to the house, and found my car keys on the steps to the garage. I had dropped them while setting the house alarm with my pinky finger while trying not to drop my purse and coffee. I set the alarm again and headed hastily to my car. I was finally ready to leave. I was covered with a thick layer of the dust that always settles on hay stored in horse barns, but there was little I could do to change that now.

I jumped into the car, put my foot on the brake, and pressed the ignition switch. I was heading towards the farm's security gate when I realized I had left Aubrey's horse tied in the crosstie stall. I backed my vehicle down the long, winding concrete driveway as fast as I could all the way to the barn.

Fortunately, my vehicle had a backup camera. I still missed some of the curves and rutted the grass in places along both sides of the driveway. I quickly pulled the ladder out of the stall. I walked the horse to his stall, over, around and through the maze of hay bales. The horse took it in stride. Me, not so much. I became winded due to physical exertion and lack of sleep. I rarely sweat or overheat, but I started sweating.

I hopped back into my car and drove like an Indy 500 driver until I got to the wrought-iron security gate, which I noticed for the first time was the slowest-opening gate I had ever seen. I looked at my watch, then my vehicle's GPS screen, which I was trying to program as I waited for the gate to open. I had just enough time to get there. I wouldn't be early but was thankful Craig and Leah wouldn't miss their flight.

I looked over and saw anxiety in the passenger seat next to me; the same anxiety that caused me to have a sleepless night. I never leave home without her.

During all the commotion I had just created for myself with the key fiasco, I had temporarily stopped dwelling on the fact I was about to spend thirty minutes in the confined space of my vehicle with the love of my life. A life that had never been the same since the day we said goodbye. The ironic parallel of another airport goodbye with the same person, thirty years later, was not lost on me. A panic attack nearly paralyzed me with fear.

I focused on just calmly and quietly taking Craig and Leah to the airport. She was his wife. Those words. Thinking of him having a wife made me sad. I should have married him, not her. When I was truthful with myself, I had always wanted him to be happy. I was not experiencing feelings of jealousy, just shock at how a coincidence like this could even happen.

I calculated if it had been an exact thirty years, but I came up with twenty-nine years, ten months, and I couldn't remember the days, but I thought seven, and hours I had to wing it, but I attempted the calculation repeatedly, in my mind, while driving to Aubrey's. None of it was precise except the years.

Before I had time to think any further, I arrived at Aubrey's house. Craig and Leah walked towards my car, each pulling a suitcase. Two additional suitcases sat on the front porch steps. I stepped out of the car after popping open the hatch of my SUV to help them load their suitcases.

I assumed Craig would not let me pick one up and put it into the vehicle, and I assumed correctly. I did, however, pull one piece of luggage from the front door of the house and handed it off to Craig. His hand sat atop my hand for a moment, then he reached up to brush hay out of my hair, which was made visible by the streetlight under which we were standing. I thought for a moment we were going to kiss.

"You are covered with hay and cobwebs," Craig said with a smile. "Did you sleep in the barn?"

His question broke the silence. I turned red and broke into a huge grin, but it was dark so no one could tell. We hopped into the car. Leah instructed Craig to sit in the front as he needed more legroom than she did. Their suitcases had left a smaller than anticipated space in the one remaining unfolded back seat, and I had forgotten to remove some of my personal items from the vehicle to give them more room.

I wasn't sure if Craig sitting next to me was going to make the drive easier or harder. I longed to reach over and hold his hand. Craig and I had never traveled anywhere together without interlocking our fingers. I grasped the steering wheel firmly with both of my hands so as not to tempt fate.

I relayed a detailed version of the story of losing my keys, climbing into the barn loft, and how I almost caused them to miss their flight. Leah and Craig both chuckled and even I found humor in it as I rehashed the event. Sharing that story eased some of the tension I was feeling on that awkward ride to the airport.

Craig would understand the reasons behind my morning's fiasco far better than Leah. I suspected Craig had not slept well either and, like me, longed for a moment with just the two of us. I also had time to gather my thoughts and words to tell them how much I cared for their daughter and what a help she had been to me over the years. I did that, mostly, for Craig.

I was not sure if Aubrey had ever explained to Craig how close our relationship was. Aubrey certainly couldn't have explained to Craig how deep my emotional connection to her was, because she wasn't aware of it. Until the previous evening, when I realized Craig was Aubrey's father, I had not understood why I was so drawn to Aubrey as soon as I met her.

I loved her like I had given birth to her myself. This was my only chance to make my fondness for Aubrey known to Craig. I was certain Craig would share my thoughts and have a deep understanding of what I was communicating, even if the two of us would never have an opportunity to discuss it further.

Craig communicated with me by looking at me while I spoke. I was able to look into his eyes during periodic stops at stop signs and red lights. I could tell he was grasping the bizarre coincidence of my relationship with his daughter, in addition to the coincidence of the two of us meeting again. I was glad I had someone next to me, once again, who understood me on a level beyond spoken words.

We waited in a slow-moving, lengthy line of vehicles approaching the drop-off spot at the terminal.

"Are you from Norway?" I asked Leah.

"No, American, I'm from Washington State."

"How did you meet Craig?"

I noticed Craig squirm a bit.

Leah hesitated as if she was trying to think of where to begin or how to explain.

"Craig was on vacation, and I was working as a server in a restaurant in Seattle," Leah said.

Leah's answer didn't fully explain why they were together. She continued, maybe because her explanation was met with silence.

"I closed out a meal ticket without noticing I did not charge him for an item he ordered. An hour later, he returned to settle his tab. He wanted to make things right."

"Did you live in Washington at the time, Craig?" I asked with a quiet, trembling voice, already knowing the answer. Craig didn't know what to say, so he didn't say anything. There was an awkward silence before Leah answered.

"He lived in Norway. Craig and his friend came to the restaurant and told me about the cross-country trip they were taking. I didn't know whether he had come back to hit on me, or he was just a nice guy. I determined he was just a nice guy and one of the best-looking guys I had ever seen, so as he was walking out, I asked for his address. We wrote back and forth occasionally and a few summers later, I visited him in Norway."

I wondered how many summers a few summers were. I surmised it was the following summer.

"What happened to his girlfriend?" I asked Leah, looking directly at Craig to let him know I had just figured out he married a girl he met while he was on vacation with me.

I hoped the trembling, higher pitch of my voice wouldn't reveal my stress level to Leah. I didn't care if Craig heard it. Craig looked at me with the kindest, but strangest, expression I had ever seen. I looked away quickly and waited for Leah to answer. I knew if I spoke, my voice would crack, and I would burst into tears.

It was a very weird question, I'll admit. In any other circumstance, I would never pry, or ask someone I hardly knew a question like that, but, in this scenario, I couldn't resist. Was the love of my life a two-timer? Had he really met his wife on our vacation? It was still such a shock to me; I hashed it over in my mind like a question instead of a fact. But I knew what I heard.

Maybe because Leah was taken by surprise by the unusually personal nature of my question, she shared her memories from the restaurant that day, as if they happened yesterday.

"They broke up at the end of their vacation," Leah said.

Silence filled the air.

Leah playfully poked Craig in the shoulders with both of her hands. I presumed Craig just hoped she wouldn't say anything further to hurt my feelings. But she did.

"Their entire relationship was strange. She was really odd, older than him, and a bit overweight."

"Leah," Craig said sharply to shut down Leah's conversation. More silence.

"I believe he has pined for her ever since and just got stuck with me, but I'm glad he gave me his address." It seemed like an attempt on Leah's part to finish her conversation on a positive note since she could obviously tell by the tone of Craig's voice she had somehow gone too far.

"She tricked me, actually. She said she needed my address to run the credit card because it was issued in Norway, and I believed her," Craig said. There was no playing or laughing or jabbing now. Just a serious sentence from Craig that reassured me he was not a player.

I assumed Leah could sense Craig didn't like the way the conversation had gone and that he was bothered by it. If only Leah knew the real reason for Craig's dismay was because the odd, older, formerly overweight woman whom Craig had never really gotten over, was sitting right next to him. Leah would have turned fifty shades of red had she realized the truth.

Then I wondered if he *had* told her about us. It was possible, since they had been in a long-term relationship, he may have told her everything after they left the barn last night and she just wanted to see if I would react. I convinced myself later that wasn't the case because I couldn't see Craig staying married to someone who was cruel. If she knew who I was and said the things she did, well, I wouldn't want to picture him in a relationship with a person like that. I was rooting for her still. She had my Craig, and he deserved the best.

I pulled over to the curb to unload my passengers and their suitcases.

"We made it," I said.

"Sorry about carrying on like that. I'm not usually chatty," Leah said.

"No worries," I said. I gave Leah a quick, reassuring glance, hoping the car would still be too dark for her to see the tears that had welled up in my eyes and were anxious to overflow.

"I probably shouldn't have asked such a personal question. It was nice to meet you...again..." I said with the word "again" barely audible and trailing off under my breath.

If Leah heard it, she probably thought I said it because we had met the previous night. But, in reality, we had met thirty years earlier, in a restaurant in Seattle, Washington.

To avoid grasping Craig's arm so he would have to remain seated next to me, I reached down and pressed the radio button. I turned the volume to low, so the sound was barely audible. "West End Girls" by Pet Shop Boys was playing. It was one of my favorite songs. I wanted to turn it up to drown out the sounds of my sobs, but instead I mustered up the courage to exit the vehicle and help them with their luggage. I didn't want to appear rude by sitting in the car and not saying goodbye to either one of them.

My heart was all over the place. Happy, yet sad, devastatingly hurt, but slightly uplifted by Craig's last comments and to hear he'd never fully gotten over me. Leah and Craig grabbed a suitcase and headed towards the baggage handler, who had already engaged Leah in pre-flight check-in conversation.

"Has the bag been out of your possession?" the baggage handler asked.

Craig returned to get the last two bags from the back of my SUV. Leah was already heading towards the revolving glass door and gave me one last wave before turning her back towards us.

"I'll catch up to you at the ticket counter after I check these two bags," Craig said. Leah turned, nodded, and gave a thumbs up, and hurried through the door, possibly just wanting to put all the awkward car conversation three thousand miles behind her.

Craig stood next to me. He was on my right side as he leaned over and kissed me on my right cheek. I was looking directly into the back of my vehicle because I knew if I looked into his eyes, I would begin to sob, just as I had thirty years earlier at the airport in Cincinnati.

The circumstances and feelings were too similar for me to process or hold inside any longer. I tried not to blink. I tried to hold back the tears, but they flowed down my cheeks.

Craig held my right hand with his left hand as he used only his right hand to pull the two remaining pieces of luggage from the vehicle, one at a time, and placed them on the sidewalk next to him. He never let go of my hand. There was so much love flowing between us through our fingertips, I wondered if either of us would ever be able to break free.

Craig leaned in to kiss me again on the cheek when he realized I was crying. My tears turned into sobs. I turned to face him and fell into his arms with my face buried in his chest. He wrapped his arms around me and held me in a long, loving embrace that could send the brightest light into even the darkest of souls.

No words needed to be spoken, but in his still fabulously familiar Norwegian accent, he whispered in my ear, "I have not forgotten. I still love you, Vanessa."

Time stood still as we held each other for a full minute. No other words were spoken. I let go first. He backed away and wiped the free-flowing tears from his own eyes. He continued to walk backwards staring at me while he pulled the suitcases to his place in the queue. With tears still streaming down my face, I managed to smile at him, to let him know even through something like this, I was still happy, and I still loved him.

He returned my smile through his tears, but this time, it was a broken-hearted, "I'm sorry you had to hear all that," sad smile. I wanted to run to him and never let him go. I broke eye contact with him, walked around the side of my car, got in, and drove out of sight.

I pulled over a half mile later, my head resting on the steering wheel, and I cried, a good, long cry. I had just started to drive home when I noticed a plane that had recently lifted off the runway and was gaining altitude, getting ready to cross, still quite low over the highway. The Fayetteville Regional Airport was small with relatively few flights leaving or arriving, so I surmised it was Craig's plane.

It was still early morning; there were no cars around me. I quickly got out of my car and stood next to it. I looked up at the windows of the airplane and hoped it was Craig's side of the plane. He always liked window seats. I put my hand in the air, and I waved. I hoped he saw me. Somehow, I just knew he did.

Chapter Thirty

Truth Be Told

I knew this was going to take a lot of processing. Was I mad at him for meeting his future wife on our vacation? No, I was not. Yes, I was. I was obviously conflicted and knew processing this was going to take some time.

All those years I felt a little guilty for being jealous, or feeling like something was up or out of alignment, because he returned to that restaurant in Seattle, and there you have it, justification that intuition is real. I knew deep inside when that inner voice was telling me something didn't feel quite right, it wasn't.

I had my chance to go to Norway with him. I could have. Leah gave him the child he really wanted. That was something I could not give him, and I never told him that was the reason I did not get on a plane and find him or do anything to stop him or delay him from leaving. I was unable to bear children.

I was born with a congenital birth defect called Mayer-Rokitansky-Küster-Hauser (MRKH) syndrome. I was born without a uterus and without a kidney. Since I have working ovaries, today invitro fertilization (IVF) with a surrogate would have been a viable solution, but back then, it wasn't common or even something I was aware was a possibility. I was raised knowing I would not have children and I became accepting of that so early in life, it didn't occur to the younger me to mourn the loss of children I never expected to have.

Craig was not aware of my condition. I decided I would never give Craig a choice. Instead, I let him leave and although saying goodbye to him was the saddest thing that had ever happened to me, there was a small sense of relief my secret would remain just that, a secret.

I didn't have the guts to give Craig the chance to reject me because of my revelation or commit to a life with me that would not fulfill his dreams to be a father.

From day one, I convinced myself I was not worthy of him. I felt defective and ashamed as I had let our love continue for far too long due to my own selfishness. It was just a summer love, I repeated to myself just so I could justify concealing the truth and continuing the relationship, although I knew better. Our relationship had become too serious for me to keep from sharing such a life-altering fact with him. I just couldn't muster the courage to tell him.

I almost blurted out the truth one night while he was lying in bed next to me, naming our two yet to be conceived children, one boy's name and one girl's name. I didn't sleep well that night as my secret haunted my thoughts.

Quiet tears flowed onto my pillow once he turned out the lights, and only after I was certain he was asleep. The only way out of the lie was to let him go so he would never be the wiser. For some reason, I thought it would be easier to let him go than to be truthful, but the price I paid for that decision affected everything that happened to me from that day forward.

Chapter Thirty-One

Break These Chains

The day after I dropped Craig and Leah off at the airport, I lounged around the house contemplating and rehashing life's recent events. I heard Craig's voice repeatedly saying those words, "I have not forgotten. I still love you, Vanessa."

For days overlapping into weeks, my thoughts continued to replay those words. His soothing voice is something I had longed to hear for three decades but thought I would never hear again. His voice had seared into the essence of who I was and became woven into every strand of my DNA.

I also replayed Leah's voice in my head. I struggled to come to terms with all I had learned. Our chance encounter had revealed three important things to me about Craig. One, he met his wife while he was vacationing with me; two, he was Aubrey's father; and three, he still loved me.

Up until the car ride to the airport, I had been frozen in time. I had, for years, been going about my daily activities, chores, career, animals, and a little bit of family, as if everything were normal. But nothing had ever been normal since our first goodbye, and any sense of a routine facade I had created for myself vanished after our second goodbye at the airport in 2019.

I had formulated many questions in my mind, not excluding, once again, questions about my self-worth. Was I not good enough, after all? Why did he choose Leah? Should I have followed Craig to Greece when he first left? Hard to do when I was afraid to fly, didn't have a source of income there, and didn't even have a passport. Why didn't I write to him as Leah had? Why did he never return for me? I even wondered if that creepy, cold hand pressing on my back at Mammoth Cave had been some type of message or warning signal that things weren't all they seemed. I dismissed that thought pretty quickly.

I went through a range of emotions from being happy he still loved me, to wondering how that was even possible, seeing he was now married to Leah. Yet I knew exactly how that was possible. No man on earth had ever replaced him in my heart, not physically or emotionally, and I knew he must feel the same.

I wanted to go to him, find him, and talk to him one more time. I wanted to call Leah and be angry with her if only to let her know that I knew what had happened and tell her who I really was. These thoughts entered my mind only briefly. They would come and go while I was driving, trying to sleep, or shopping for groceries.

I was never truly angry with Leah or Craig, just upset and hurt. I made the choice not to go with Craig and for good reasons. Leah had nothing to do with it. My logical mind guided me through the questions I had and provided me with all the answers I needed.

Still, I wanted to question Craig about how long it was after he returned to Norway, from college in England, that he met up with Leah. Did they see each other while he was still in school in Bath? Did he communicate with her while he was an exchange student in Greece before he even made it back to the University? When exactly did he get together with Leah and start dating her?

I wanted to know, but at the same time I realized it wouldn't make any difference and I knew I didn't have any right to question him. Ultimately, believing our breakup was my decision allowed me to talk myself off the proverbial cliff.

Craig had, right in front of several beautiful women, chosen me, so I did not believe he would ever meet his future wife while he was traveling with me. He had me, heart and soul, and I had myself convinced myself Craig felt the same. Thoughts and feelings were flooding my senses once again. I realized I hadn't felt much of anything since he left the first time.

During any given hour of the day, for months after our second airport goodbye, I rationalized every set of circumstances. Fortunately, I was like steel on the outside and relied heavily on my horses and accounting job to keep me focused on issues other than Craig.

I also had Annie. Only Annie would let me vent for hours without acting one bit tired of me. Only Annie knew me well enough to know what seeing Craig again had stirred in my soul.

I also thought of Aubrey, the beautiful daughter they raised. When I thought of her, any residual, negative feelings I had for Leah vanished. Leah had given life to Aubrey. Aubrey was perfect. I knew deep inside I had done the right thing by letting Craig go.

Seeing Craig again worked up all kinds of energy in me. I cleaned the house to let off steam. I dusted, waxed, vacuumed, and mopped. I cleaned blinds and light fixtures, changed light bulbs, and scrubbed shower doors. I suppose I was trying to wash and rinse away my emotions. I just couldn't be still. It was a productive period in my life where I transformed negative energy into something positive, instead of trying to drown it out with alcohol or sedatives. It may have been easier to do, but for me, it would have been much less effective.

The second goodbye was my get out of jail free card. It was a key that opened a door for me. I was free. I was hurting still, but free. Years have a way of masking pain like a Band-Aid over an open wound. Prior to our chance reunion, I had sentenced myself to life. I wasn't locked up behind bars, but instead had created my own personal dungeon.

My body had been free to move about for thirty years, but my emotions, the core of my being, had been locked inside a dark, damp basement where no visitors were permitted past restricted visiting hours. I had become my own guard and warden. Our encounter ripped the Band-Aid off my feelings. I faced the light of day and began to heal.

I had years ahead of me to live a much fuller life. I had wasted enough time. I considered the possibility of meeting someone new. Before the chance encounter, I never thought I could ever be with anyone else, and I didn't consider the possibility of it. Was our meeting in the barn really a coincidence or something more spiritual, to set me free, perhaps?

My positive spirit, the part of me that initially attracted Craig, resurfaced. It didn't take time. The dungeon door swung open. I had put myself into that box, and Craig had swooped in and unknowingly unlocked the door. I could breathe fresh air again.

I was alive and I was grateful to be alive. I knew I could share the remaining years of my life with someone who loved life as much as I did. I was my loving self once again.

The cleaning therapy I put myself through kept giving me the same thought. There was someone else out there for me. I knew I would meet someone and have a longer, deeper connection than I did with Craig. It would be better because my next relationship would last. I was no longer stuck in 1989, surviving on memories, memories that now were based on additional information.

Eventually, I achieved some kind of inner peace and came to terms with our second goodbye.

Chapter Thirty-Two

Support from Friends

Eighteen years earlier, in 2001, after knowing Carol and Brian for over a decade, I had told them all about my love affair with Craig and explained to them I had just never been interested in dating anyone else after him. They had no idea the effect his love had on my life up to that point until I shared that story with them. Afterwards, they stopped trying to introduce me to people and arranging blind dates.

In August of 2019, I decided over dinner to tell Carol and Brian about meeting Craig again and tell them the entire coincidental barn reunion story. I was on my way to healing but still needed support from my friends.

"Do you remember when I told you about Craig, the guy from Norway, and how I have never dated anyone after him?"

"Yes," Carol said.

"Yeesss," Brian said dragging out the word because he knew me well enough to know something juicy was about to be served next to the salmon on his plate.

"My Craig from Norway is Aubrey's dad."

SILENCE filled the air.

The look on Brian's face when I revealed that Craig was Aubrey's dad was priceless. And Carol nearly spit her wine through her nose when I got to the part about being reintroduced to him in my barn.

"Are you Aubrey's mom?" Brian asked confused.

"No, Brian, Aubrey has a mom."

Carol shook her head at me apologetically and then looked at Brian with a "come on, Brian, get with the program" look.

"All that education money I spent on him," Carol quipped.

"Aubrey's dad and I dated, more than dated. Remember my story about moving here to get away from the memories and why I'm so jacked up when it comes to dating anyone."

"Vanity, I met Aubrey's dad while he was here," Brian said. "He's still a really handsome guy."

"Yes, Brian, he is, but thanks for reminding me how hot he still is."

"He is," Brian said.

"Yes, and he's married to Aubrey's mom and guess what, she met him while he was on vacation with me."

"What? NO WAY! How?" Brian said.

"Yes way."

"No way," Brian said again.

"Brian," Carol said as she reached out and held both our hands momentarily, "let Vanity tell us what happened."

After they both got over the initial shock, they loved the part about Aubrey asking me to drive them to the airport. It was a fun night telling them the story. They both loved it.

They had mostly rhetorical questions, as did I, because they knew, as did I, there were no known answers for these types of coincidences. How does something that bizarre happen? Who knows? At least, this time, I had two comrades on the hamster wheel with me, spinning questions with answers that led only into an endless circle.

"You know that counted, right, Vanity? It really, really counted," Brian said.

"Put that on your spreadsheet," I said.

"This incident is going to be a whole new column with its very own heading," Brian said. We laughed so hard and just shook our heads in disbelief. "I don't want to hear anything more about my list, when you slept with Aubrey's dad," Brian added.

"It didn't happen in that order, Brian, but you can spin this tale any way you wish."

I loved Brian. He was like a brother to me, only worse.

Telling Carol and Brian was the right choice. They could now compassionately embrace the unbelievable situation I found myself in with full understanding of what I was experiencing. We became even closer. They supported my efforts to start drafting the book Craig had encouraged me to write when he left thirty years ago. They thought Craig's idea to get all that adventure-filled living and loving down on paper was a good one.

"Start writing the book, it will help you heal," Carol said.

"I will, Carol. That's a good idea." And I did.

Carol and Brian were my biggest supporters and cheerleaders. Their unwavering friendship gave me purpose and focus and was an aide to my continued survival and mental health. I was a strong person, but even strong people need someone to lean on, now and then. Strong people learn to be flexible when life throws a curve ball, to lean and bend, and learn. "Strong people lean" was my motto. Fortunately, I had wonderful people to support me whenever I leaned too far.

Annie was also there for me and had always been there for me. She took time to visit me from Texas. I hadn't had any alcohol, by choice, for as long as I could remember, but this day, Annie and I split a bottle of wine as soon as Annie arrived. I poured out my soul to her as she poured wine into my glass.

Annie's the friend where I didn't ever have to hold anything back. We had our laughs, too. It wasn't all doom and gloom looking into that bottom of a wine glass. We had our giggles as we rehashed memories from the rafting trip, the bus ride, the car ride home, and that first night together with her listening to us, which I had managed to embarrassingly block from my mind, before Annie admitted it was something she could never completely block from hers.

We also laughed again about me thinking she hired Craig as a male escort. And we repeatedly talked about the encounter in the barn, the ride to the airport with Leah calling me weird and fat, while not realizing it was me.

More than a little tipsy, Annie nicknamed the barn incident "close encounters of the weird kind." For some reason, we thought that was the funniest catch phrase Annie had ever coined and the funniest thing I had ever heard and spent hours saying it and laughing while eventually lying on our backs on the hardwood floor looking up at the ceiling, giggling.

I spent the next day looking for aspirin. Lesson learned, once again.

A few days later, we had dinner with Carol and Brian. Annie had a wicked sense of humor, and I should have known she was up to something when she pulled out a bag of special mints.

"Let's all have an after-dinner mint," she suggested.

Annie tossed a hard candy into her mouth, then handed one to me, Carol, and Brian. I didn't really want one since I was already full from dinner but took one anyway to be polite.

"They have a soft cherry center, so bite into them," Annie continued, a strange smile crossing her face.

I looked around and saw everyone else seemed to be enjoying their mint. As soon as I bit into mine, I knew it was one of Annie's practical jokes. Of course, mine was the only one in the bag that had a rotted fish–tasting gel in the center. I didn't get sick, but the taste lingered for hours. Annie admitted she didn't know it was going to taste as bad as it did, and although she flip-flopped between apologizing and winking at me for the rest of the evening, I believed she was sorry for doing that to me.

I was concerned, but didn't share my concern that night with Annie, about how Carol and Brian were going to react to such an immature joke taking place at their dinner table. Carol could be a bit more formal than the rest of us. She was getting ready for her seventy-fifth birthday party and that was another reason Annie had come to visit.

The next morning, I realized Annie wasn't in her room in our guest cabin when I knocked to let her know I was making breakfast. As I was walking back to the house, I saw Annie sneaking out Brian's front door and heading across the pasture in the golf cart back to her room. Amused, I surmised Brian must have not been too upset with Annie over the breath mint stunt the previous night.

Around noon, I walked past Brian, his spurs clickety clankin' in the concrete aisle of the barn. He was walking his newest horse, Heza Wild One, out into the arena. He looked tired, like he hadn't gotten much sleep.

"That definitely counted," I called out to him.

He stopped walking; his shoulders hunched over and his head dropped, as if he were a child who had just gotten caught stealing a cookie from a cookie jar. He turned his head to the side just enough to reveal a huge smile and red face.

"It definitely counted," he said agreeing with me. He walked away mumbling something.

"Ironic, you chose to ride Heza Wild One today, too," I added. He turned towards me, eyes looking down to the ground, still smiling from ear to ear and shaking his head left to right.

"I have no comment," he said.

No further comment necessary. Brian seemed quite pleased with himself.

***

Not to be outdone by Annie's practical joke, I gave Annie enough time to freshen up and make her way over to the main house.

"Let's call a truce," I told her in my most sentimental voice. "Let's have some Irish mocha mint coffee and make peace. Let's sit on the porch and celebrate our sisterhood. No more practical jokes, just sincere love and appreciation for one another."

Annie looked at me suspiciously.

"It's only hot chocolate with mint flavoring. I promise."

We sipped the minty hot chocolate from our matching mugs, which said "Friends Are Special" on them. I told her how much she meant to me. She softened, got sentimental, and I thought I caught a glimpse of a tear welling up in the corner of her eye.

"There is something sticking up in the middle of this cup. What is that?" she asked as she started to dump it out over the front porch rail.

"Don't pour it out, just keep drinking. I didn't put anything in it. It's part of the cup," I said.

She cautiously swallowed larger gulps until she could see a middle finger sticking up at her, which had been molded right into the center of the mug. We laughed hysterically as we shared tears of laughter.

"I really thought you were being sentimental for a change," Annie said.

"That was what I thought about your after-dinner mint," I said.

I couldn't stop there and let her off the hook for sleeping with Brian.

"Did y'all have a nice time last night?" I asked.

"What?" she said innocently. "What do you mean?"

I looked at her in a way that told her I already knew.

"Want to hear all about it?" she said as she realized I must have spotted her leaving Brian's house earlier that morning.

"No."

I knew she was going to tell me anyway. I grabbed pillows off the porch swing to cover my ears, but I could still hear her going into more detail than necessary as we both cackled like chickens in a hen house.

"Come on," I said, "we have to help get things set up for Carol's party tonight."

Chapter Thirty-Three

Eben

In October of 2019, Carol hired caterers for her seventy-fifth birthday party. Carol, although retired for seven years, had stayed in touch with many of her former colleagues and had accumulated a lifetime of good friends, so we expected over one hundred guests. Annie, Brian, and I didn't have to do a lot, but we knew where everything was kept and where Carol wanted the tables and chairs. We supervised the moving of furniture into a temporary, mobile storage unit the caterer had provided to make sure nothing got damaged. No surprise, Brian kept an inventory of the relocated items on his laptop spreadsheet.

Fortunately, Carol was looking out for me and had sensed my recent isolation and was ready to step in and intervene when she invited Eben Burke to the party. Carol initially made it out to be a random introduction, but later admitted she had been brewing the match in the back of her mind for years.

"Vanity," Carol said, "I would like to introduce you to my dear friend Eben Burke."

"Nice to meet you," I said. I extended my hand. Eben reciprocated my handshake as he leaned in and gave me a brief hug, which caught me pleasantly off-guard. He was tall and handsome, I noted. I was still trying to process why I felt like falling into a complete stranger's arms when our conversation began. But, right away, everything felt natural like I had known him for years.

"Did you come down for Carol's birthday party?" I asked. It was pretty obvious he had but I had to start somewhere.

"That and house hunting," he replied.

"House hunting?"

"I just accepted a job with a local hospital and secured a remote teaching position at UNC Chapel Hill. Teaching is something I have always wanted to do."

"Are you a nurse?" I asked.

Carol was eavesdropping on our conversation, so she piped in to help.

"Eben will be Radiologist-in-Chief at Moore Regional Hospital and teaching radiology classes for UNC. Eben and I worked together years ago in Virginia. He's a good catch, Vanity, and he'll be living near us." Carol said.

"Oh my, sorry about that," Eben said. I noticed he had an accent and I liked it. "Shame on you, Carol," he added.

"It's not like the two of you are spring chickens, you need to get on with it," Carol responded.

"I'm speechless," I stammered. "I've never seen this side of Carol."

"She must have had a rum and Coke," Eben said.

"Who, Carol? I've never seen her drink a drop."

"Well, she is drinking rum and Coke tonight," Eben said smiling.

"For a moment there, Carol's tone sounded exactly like my mom, telling us we were no longer spring chickens. This was something my mom would have said. It made me miss her."

"My mom didn't have a filter either," Eben said.

We both laughed. "Too funny. Carol successfully made a great life for herself and for Brian, too. She's seventy-five, so she can have a cocktail or two tonight to celebrate. To Carol," I said as I held up a Diet Coke.

"To Carol," the guests in the immediate vicinity responded as they held up their glasses.

"Carol and I were colleagues back in Virginia when I first started practicing radiology. She took me under her wing. I enjoyed eating lunch with her and hearing about her cases and discussing mine with her as well. Two heads, you know."

"Better than one," I added.

"You're already finishing my sentences. Maybe Carol is right about us."

"Maybe Carol forgot to tell you she's known me for almost thirty years, and I've never dated anyone."

"She told me," Eben said. "I actually find that intriguing."

I wanted him to keep talking so I could listen to him. Eben was originally from London, England. Even though he had lived in the United States for thirty-four years, he still retained his British accent.

Eben went on to explain he knew Carol had family in New River, which was near his new hospital. He had met Brian on three previous occasions when Brian visited his mother, but Eben had never met me. Eben, being a widower and empty nester, had longed for a warmer climate since being named Radiologist-in-Chief at the hospital in Virginia near the clinic Carol owned before she retired. When a colleague referred him for the new position in Southern Pines, he knew it was the right move at the right time. He was looking forward to mild winters.

Carol liked everything about Eben and had mentioned to him she often wished she had a daughter to introduce to Eben. Once she met me, she started formulating a matchmaking plan in her head, but could never work out the logistics of getting the two of us in the same state. With the news Eben had recently shared about his move, Carol's plan was coming to fruition.

Before long, Carol's wheels were spinning and she was thinking of a way to get Eben to stay with Brian at our farm while he was house hunting in Southern Pines. By this time, Brian and I had been living in separate residences on the farm for decades and I had resigned from the CPA firm and opened my own firm, building my office on a corner piece of land on my property.

"Are you a horse trainer?"

"I'm a CPA, that's my office on the far corner of the property. You drove past it as you turned into the farm."

Basic getting to know each other conversation continued until the party ended. Occasionally, Steve, Brian, Annie, Carol, and Aubrey all made their rounds and briefly and individually joined in our conversation, but Eben and I didn't break away and mingle with anyone else but each other the entire evening. I noticed that no matter who came up to us to chat, they didn't stay long and kept leaving Eben and me to ourselves.

Everyone later admitted they were in on Carol's matchmaker plan all along and that was why everyone just made rounds long enough to keep checks on how my conversation with Eben was going. Annie and Brian were noticeably absent throughout most of the evening. I don't even want to know what the two of them were doing.

Before I knew it, three hours had passed. It was almost 11 p.m. I was enjoying Eben's company tremendously and didn't want the night to end, but Eben called it a night as he had traveled that day and was getting tired.

Somewhere towards the end of the evening, Brian and Annie reappeared. Brian and Carol approached, as I realized Eben was staying at Brian's house. Annie was mingling with the few remaining guests. She could entertain anyone she'd just met. Her personality was contagious.

"Let me cook breakfast for everyone in the morning," I said.

"Deal," Brian said.

"I can take us all out to eat," Eben offered.

"Vanity's a great cook," Carol said directly to Eben. "You'll love it."

"Breakfast isn't a great litmus test, Carol," I replied smiling at her. "I'll be back in the morning, about 8:30."

Annie and I took the golf cart back over to my place.

"Well?" Annie questioned me.

"Well, what?" I replied playing coy.

"You know what. Do you like him?" Annie was smiling. I noticed her hair was tousled like she had been romping around earlier with Brian, so I thought of turning the tables and directing the conversation back to her night's events, but I changed my mind.

"Who?" I asked, not able to keep a silly smile from enveloping my entire face.

"I knew it," she exclaimed. "Oh my god, you have a boyfriend."

"I talked to someone for three hours at a party," I corrected her.

"And you're making him breakfast in the morning."

"Not the same thing," I said.

"Is so."

"Not so."

"We'll see," she said.

In a weird way, I hoped Annie was right about Eben. Maybe it was time for me to have a boyfriend. *Is that what you would call it at my age?* I wondered.

***

My attraction to Eben grew, over several months, beyond the sound of his voice. Our hobbies and interests were different, but we were both open to learning new things, and we fell in love.

There is something mystical about falling in love. It's impossible for strangers to avert their glances because they want what you've got, even if they can't quite figure out what that is. At least that was the aura I was giving off to everyone around me shortly after I met Eben Burke.

Eben had already been married and had a family. His wife died in a car accident when his three children were in primary school. He hired a full-time childcare worker to care for his children while he was at work. He dedicated every minute of his free time to his children, attending their plays, games, and recitals until they each graduated from college and became self-sufficient, productive adults. He often shared news about his children—what they were doing, where they were living and working—and he proudly boasted about their accomplishments.

I didn't see it as bragging. I saw him as a good father who raised his children well, a father who deeply cared about his children. That made Eben even more attractive to me.

Since I didn't have children of my own, Eben's children didn't have to compete for my attention. I meshed perfectly into their adult choreographed world with their father.

I disclosed my secret about not being able to have children because of MRKH syndrome, in one of my first dinner dates with Eben. My affliction didn't matter to Eben at all, other than since he was a doctor, he was aware of my rare condition but hadn't ever seen a patient with MRKH. He was glad my only remaining kidney was working like a charm. We were well past childbearing age, but it was still a relief to know this burden I had carried throughout my life was finally out in the open and a non-issue.

"I waited for decades after my wife died for our children to grow up and graduate before I pursued any type of relationship. I didn't want to complicate their lives with any more than they had already been through. I guess I just wasn't ready myself either and used my children as an excuse to be alone."

He paused and we smiled at each other.

"Being a physician, you just can't imagine the things I see and hear. The sexually transmitted diseases alone had me afraid to date for an entire decade, so it's refreshing to meet someone who hasn't been..." Eben struggled to find the right word.

"Promiscuous," I said.

"Yes, I guess that's the right word. I was trying not to sound like an old-fashioned prude," he said.

"Your British accent and use of the Queen's English does that for you, no matter which words you use," I said.

"You're not the first person who has mentioned I sound like a pompous ass."

"That's not what I said."

"Good, because I'm not one. I like you, Calamity Vanity, even though you just dragged your arm through the spaghetti sauce and now you have red sauce all over your lovely white sleeve."

"I knew I shouldn't have worn a white blouse with floppy sleeves to a spaghetti dinner. Don't say I didn't warn you. I earned the name Calamity Vanity. It wasn't an inherited title."

The excitement in the air quickly turned into shock and confusion as water started spraying all over us and the restaurant. The servers seemed aloof, as if the drenching deluge were a common occurrence. We exchanged glances, wondering if we were the only ones witnessing the chaos unraveling around us. We had just received our orders, but alas, my appetite would have to wait since my food had become waterlogged and inedible. Eben and I glanced at each other, confirming that the situation had become unsalvageable. It wasn't the dinner we had in mind, but it made for an unforgettable evening.

Our dinner plans had been ruined by a mishap with the sprinkler system. A manager followed us outside and explained what had gone wrong. The new system had either an incorrect setting or was too sensitive to the smoke coming from the grill. Without the proper training, the staff had been unable to turn off the sprinklers, causing the restaurant to flood. Though help was on the way, it was clear our meal was beyond saving. The manager was apologetic and offered us a free meal if we returned another day. Despite the disappointing turn of events, Eben and I decided we would take him up on that offer.

Eben and I were thoroughly soaked thanks to our hesitation in evacuating.

"Want to go to my place, put on sweats, order a pizza, and watch a movie?" he asked.

"Yes, sounds like a good backup plan."

Eben loaned me a pair of sweatpants, a sweatshirt, and a pair of his socks. Eben's condo was neat and clean, yet cozy. Brian and Carol had let Eben rent Brian's condo in Pinehurst while he was looking for a place to buy.

"I used to live here," I said to Eben and then I explained how I met Brian on the plane.

I was warm and comfortable as we sat next to each other on his big, soft couch. I had a blanket over my legs and was sitting with my feet tucked underneath me, leaning against Eben's shoulder. We ate pizza, started to watch a movie, and ended my thirty-year dry spell. That was the beginning of my new life and love.

Our physical attraction quickly blossomed into a meaningful relationship and within six months, I wanted to spend all my free time with him.

Eben grew up on a horse farm in England, but he wasn't a horse person himself. He knew about them. He knew they were a tremendous amount of work. He knew how to put a halter on them and how to walk them, but his mother was the rider in their family. She was the horse person.

Horses are either in your bones when you are born, or they're not. If they are, the love and passion for them never leaves you. I had strayed away from horses at various times in my life, but the longing for them was always there, just below the surface. You cannot make a child become a horse person and you cannot make a child who was born a horse person abandon their dream.

No matter what the cost or sacrifices of owning horses, the flies, or the constant pursuit to eliminate the flies, or cleaning the urine-soaked, ammonia-smelling stalls, if you are a horse person, it's a labor of love. It is arduous work and there are days it takes everything you have to get the work done and complete all the chores, but the result is worth every dollar spent and every ounce of sweat.

My horses brought Eben warm family memories, like he had come home after a long, hard journey. He was welcomed by my friends, too, most of whom were either shocked or thrown slightly off guard to see me so giddy. No one had ever witnessed my silly behavior and interest in new hobbies; Eben's hobbies to be more specific such as nature walks, identifying frogs, rock collecting and polishing, and gardening.

"I heard Vanity retired, sold her business, and is studying frogs now," they would say to each other in gossip circles.

"I think she was abducted by aliens and implanted with a new personality," one said. "She giggles all the time, even when no one said anything funny."

"I heard her talking about growing her own vegetables," said another.

Brian and Carol said the neighbors kept them in the loop of these small-town rumor ramblings. I understood I became the main topic of conversations at the only diner in town, which served a daily breakfast to half our town's population. It made me smile. I was happy to be a part of our close-knit town, and everyone was happy for me. I had found love again, although most people just believed I had found love period. They just didn't know the "again" part.

Chapter Thirty-Four

Rock Collecting

My relationship with Eben remained strong as we grew closer and spent more time together. He was busy with his new job but worked remotely most of the time due to Covid lockdowns. He took me to dinner, once a week at first before the lockdowns, then I started cooking for him, either at his place or mine. We sheltered in place at the farm for most of the lockdown.

In April of 2020, Eben invited me, Carol, and Brian to go on a nature walk with him while he did some rock collecting. It was a good, safe way to get out of the house and spend time outdoors, and Eben had never asked all three of us to join him on one of his walks, so we all agreed.

Less than a half mile into the woods, at a nearby nature reserve, Eben bent down near a stream and appeared to be looking at a beautiful rock he had found.

"Look at this Vanessa," he exclaimed. "Black diamonds."

He certainly got my attention and the first thing I thought was how lucky he was to find something valuable on such a short jaunt. He was still kneeling on the ground as I approached to see what he was so excited to show me.

He was holding a ring. He looked into my eyes.

"Vanessa, will you marry me?" he said.

I quickly answered, "Yes, YES."

I looked at the ring. The center stone of my new ring was a huge square yellow diamond surrounded by two rows of diamonds, one row of light diamonds and one row of black diamonds. The wedding band, which he showed me later, matched the ring and had two more rows of diamonds. It was beautiful. Eben had good taste. His selection was ideal. How he managed to find a store open so he could purchase it, I have no idea.

I assumed Carol had helped Eben with the ring selection because she had an idea of what I liked.

"Did Carol help you choose this ring?"

"No," Eben said shaking his head.

"Brian and I had no part in this. We didn't know about any of this until he just proposed, but we couldn't be happier for the two of you," Carol said. "Love the way you proposed, Eben. Thanks for including us."

"You're responsible for bringing us together. It wouldn't have been the same without you and Brian," Eben said.

"I agree," I said. "It was perfect."

"As for the ring, I picked it myself. I told you I was a rock collector, remember?" he said jokingly.

"A very good one, too," I said. "I love this ring. I love you, Eben. Yes, yes, yes, I will marry you."

"You both are good people and you've both waited such a long time to find each other," Brian said with tears in his eyes. Tears of joy.

I had the biggest smile possible while holding Eben's forearm and presenting Eben to Brian like the ultimate prize that he was.

"Hey, Brian, does this count?"

"It definitely counts," Brian said with a huge grin. By this time, Carol and Eben had been subject to the "does it count" joke between me and Brian so many times, they needed no further explanation.

"I can't wait to tell Annie," I said.

"Call her now, I don't mind," Eben said.

"I left my phone in the car."

Brian had his phone, so he got Annie on video chat, and I showed her the ring and told her all about Eben's proposal as we walked back to the car.

Annie made sure I remembered she had predicted this outcome the night of the party.

"You were right," I conceded. She was happy for me. I was happy. I was in love.

Eben had dreamed of a big church wedding with all his friends and family from around the United States, Germany, Switzerland, and Holland in attendance, but it wasn't possible due to ongoing Covid travel restrictions. Instead, we opted to apply remotely for our wedding license and got married with only a minister and two witnesses present, all of us wearing masks. We were still just as married, but I know Eben would have loved for his children to be there. We vowed to have a huge wedding reception and fly in all our friends as soon as the threat from the virus was contained.

Any initial thoughts Eben may have had about me moving away from the farm were out of the question, but fortunately Eben had no qualms about moving in with me, especially since he hadn't found a property to purchase of his own yet. Brian and Carol had no problem with him ending his lease on the condo as they knew it would rent within days of Eben vacating it.

Eben started to enjoy working with the horses in his free time, walking them to and from their stalls, grooming them, and occasionally cleaning their stalls for me when an employee couldn't make it. Keeping good employees during Covid was another issue entirely, but we were fortunate we usually had at least one, sometimes two people around to help.

Eben and I both agreed the barn chores were good exercise and therapeutic, and in the open air you could move about freely without risking being contaminated or spreading the virus; something horse people already knew. Cleaning the barn clears your head. Of course, that could be due to the ammonia smell, but it seriously made me feel refreshed and alive. It gave me time to think and formulate solutions to all the world's problems. Unfortunately, I was always so exhausted after shoveling manure, I would get sleepy halfway through a hot shower, and put off solving the world's problems as soon as my head hit the pillow.

It was a well-earned sleep, and an earned sleep is the best kind.

Chapter Thirty-Five

Mont Blanc

One month after Eben and I got married in July of 2020, Aubrey called, crying, to tell me Craig had been climbing Mont Blanc in the Alps when a chunk of ice and rock broke away from the mountain sending an avalanche down what they call the Death Couloir.

Three of Craig's climbing companions died. Craig was airlifted to a hospital. He had hit his head hard on the side of the mountain as he tumbled down with the barrage of falling ice and rock debris. He had also been struck multiple times by the debris, bruising tissue, and breaking bones throughout his body. He somehow managed to get pushed out the side of the avalanche by its powerful force, tossed up into the air, and landed on a large rock shelf on his back. His climbing companions had become trapped towards the middle of the slide as they tumbled down the Couloir, and they were pummeled to death by high-velocity boulders.

There were climbers at various locations on the mountain that day and more than one climber caught the accident on film. In one video, you can see what looks like a rock or piece of debris being tossed in the air and it later became known that was Craig's seemingly lifeless body, identified as such because of where he landed and from where he was rescued.

Although Craig was wearing a helmet, he had suffered irreversible damage leaving him unable to walk or speak. He was able to swallow but had to be hand fed soft foods only. He could open and close his eyes but didn't appear to be aware of his surroundings.

When I heard the news, I immediately wanted to rush to his side. I wanted to care for him and nurse him, but Leah was still his wife, and I was newly married to Eben. I contemplated telling Aubrey and Eben everything so I could see Craig, but knew that wouldn't be fair to her, her mom, or Eben.

Leah and Craig had abruptly moved back to Norway just after they returned home to Washington State. I was unaware of the reasonings behind their move, or if our reunion in the barn had anything to do with it. I didn't know why it would be connected, but they didn't mention they were moving back to Norway during the car ride, or to Aubrey during their visit.

Hearing Craig was seriously injured was the most difficult news I had heard in a long time, but I had to react appropriately when Aubrey gave me the news. I had to hold in my emotions and try to comfort her the same as I would any other friend whose father had been injured in a terrible accident. I wanted to scream and cry and see him, but I couldn't.

The agony of knowing Craig was injured and not having a way to do anything to help him was more painful than our first and second goodbyes combined. I wanted hourly updates, but even asking Aubrey for daily updates seemed odd, so I cautiously asked her for updates when she visited the barn, and it tore my insides to shreds when she only had distressing news.

The days following Craig's accident were the closest I ever came to telling Aubrey the entire story. I was feeling a persistent dread. I wasn't hungry, and I trembled, a lot. At first, there was always some hope, but within a week, Craig's prognosis was grim. The best the doctors could hope for was he would live, but they doubted he would walk or communicate ever again.

I hoped, upon hearing that he would be trapped in a lifeless body forever, he would die soon and in his sleep. He was only fifty-six years old. I would not want a soul with such a zest for life to live an immobile life. I knew he wouldn't want that either. Unfortunately, that is exactly what happened and every day, it pained me. My own health deteriorated. Knowing Craig was in a long-term care facility was almost too much for my broken heart to bear.

Chapter Thirty-Six

COVID-19

In January of 2021, Eben was still doing most of his work, reviewing and interpreting CT scans, remotely. He only reported in person to the hospital one day a week due to the pandemic, and for most of 2020, they asked him not to come to the hospital at all.

The lockdown restrictions we were subjected to because of Covid didn't affect me as much as others. I had always remained on the farm to care for the animals, so I wasn't a regular commuter. I worked with the horses, groomed them, rode them, and trained them, and the farm needed someone to be onsite twenty-four hours a day, seven days a week to watch over the animals and property. More often than not, that someone was me.

Just because the restrictions didn't affect me as much as others, I didn't mean to suggest Covid didn't affect our business. It did. Our clients couldn't visit their horses; our employees couldn't come to work; and we couldn't pick up feed. It was a difficult time, but we managed along with everyone in the world. We weren't alone in the struggle.

After the Covid restrictions were reduced slightly, I could pick up supplies for the farm and make quick jaunts to the feed store. Brian and I worked out a system where he covered for me, and I covered for him. That system worked out well except when we both came down with strep throat at the same time. What a miserable week that was. At first, we both feared we had Covid and everyone around us feared the same, but Brian and I both tested negative.

Neither of us could keep up with the chores that week and our only employee was too new to the farm to be effective. Eben filled in for us and avoided getting sick. He also managed to keep his work with the hospital and the online classes he was teaching at the university via Zoom going.

Eben and I were still blissfully happy together. Our heads, however, weren't so far into the clouds that we didn't realize the Covid pandemic was getting worse, not better. This was a concern for both of us. Brian and Carol, and all our dearest friends, were concerned, not only for themselves, but for us in return, and everyone else they loved.

It was a concern for the entire world. Never had I seen city streets so deserted, so quiet, and never have I been as afraid as when I got the call that Annie, my closest friend and instigator of my rafting trip relationship with Craig, was in the hospital on a ventilator with Covid.

I could not call her. I could not rush to her bedside. I could only agonize and imagine what she endured. I read through our last text messages and looked at the calendar to see what day she sent me her last text and what day she had read mine. I wanted to see proof that just two weeks prior, she was fine and sending and receiving messages.

Surely, she would be okay. Her last message to me was "sounds great, something to look forward to when this is over" in response to our plans to get together as soon as the pandemic restrictions were lifted. Three days before the text, I spoke to Annie. She wasn't concerned about getting Covid, because she was working from home and didn't have to be around anyone. She assured me she was hunkered down in her home, like everyone else, and would get through it.

I wanted to tell her to drink lots of hot water and gargle with salt water like I read on the internet, but I couldn't speak to her. I just had to wait. I called the hospital so many times, even though I tried to stop myself. I knew they were short staffed and busy with all the Covid cases. I tried to get Eben to circumvent the system and call doctor to doctor to get me inside information on Annie, but the hospital was so inundated with sick patients, Eben didn't feel good about even bothering the few doctors they had showing up for work. He tried, but they didn't tell Eben anything more than they told me, and they didn't have a doctor available to come to the phone when he called. We just thanked them and disconnected the call.

Even though the nurses were going through all that mess and protocol, and having to wear masks and hazmat suits, they were kind and helpful every time I called. They cared. They understood what it was like to have a loved one on a ventilator.

Annie and I were friends long before the rafting trip, but we were really more like sisters. Like me, Annie's parents had passed and Annie had no siblings. Annie did marry and had three children, starting five years after the rafting trip, two boys and a girl. She had gotten a divorce three years after her last child was born because her husband had met another woman at his work, whom he later married and divorced. He participated in parenting throughout the children's lives and paid child support. He had maintained a decent relationship with Annie, given the circumstances, but after their children became adults, they no longer communicated. He lived thousands of miles away from Annie, so he wasn't going to be an active part of her support team.

Annie's daughter, Beth, had grown up to be a veterinarian; her oldest son became a police officer; and her youngest son an accountant, like me. I spoke to Annie's daughter every other day while Annie was hospitalized. She felt as helpless as I did. All three of Annie's children were trapped in their respective houses like the rest of us. They were told they could not visit their mother in the intensive care unit. It was difficult for me to hear, but even more difficult for them.

After fifteen days on the ventilator, Annie started to show signs of improvement. The hospital, after video conferencing with Annie's children, formulated a plan to remove the breathing tube. They explained, as we were unable to witness any of this in person, that the doctor would turn off and remove the ventilator and Annie would wake up on her own—hours, days, or weeks later, or maybe not at all. It would usually take about twenty-four hours for the sedation drugs used to keep the patient from fighting against the ventilator, to leave her system.

We waited. The hospital allowed Annie's children to watch via live feed, and they added me into the live feed just as they pulled the ventilator from Annie's throat. If Annie had remained any longer on that ventilator, they would have had to make choices about cutting a hole in Annie's throat called a tracheotomy and putting a trach tube directly into her lungs. Everyone agreed it would be best to wean her off the ventilator before it got to that.

As the tube was removed, she jerked around suddenly as if she had been startled by something. She was in obvious distress, and that, in turn, frightened me. Once the tube was removed, seconds later, she was peaceful again, but in a drug-induced coma. We all got to tell her we loved her, and I hoped she thought we were right beside her and could hear us.

The call ended with the nurses promising to update us either way and to keep us updated regularly. I cried myself to sleep and slept with my phone. Eben held me in his arms more often than usual that week.

I wanted Eben, as a doctor, to make things all better or tell me they would be, but with Covid, he was no help. Doctors were not immune and had no power over it. They were hoping to avoid its wrath, same as everyone. I was glad I chose accounting and horse training. I didn't envy Eben or anyone working in the health care profession; all were much braver than I, just for going to work.

I woke to the familiar Verizon ring tone, the standard one that comes with a new phone. Awakening from a groggy early-morning sleep, I rubbed my bleary eyes as my hand fumbled for my phone, which was ringing insistently. I saw it was the hospital's number. I tried to answer it before the last ring. I missed the call.

Fear overwhelmed me. Did Annie die during the night? I called her daughter, but her phone rang and rang and then went to voice mail. I tried to call her son, but I couldn't spell his name correctly because my hands were shaking as I tried to pull him up in my contacts list.

I called the hospital, but I wasn't paying attention to the voice-activated prompts and got thank you for your call goodbye. I called again as I concentrated on staying focused and pressing the right buttons. I was about to get through to the ICU when I received an incoming call from Annie's daughter Beth. Beth was crying. I braced myself for the news.

"Vanessa."

"Yes?"

"Mom is awake. She can't talk yet, but she gave me a thumbs up on live feed this morning. She's going to make it."

Relief flooded my senses. I fell back into my pillow sobbing thankful tears of joy.

I wanted to book a flight so I could get to Annie's side ASAP, which is what I would normally have done in any other set of circumstances, but I couldn't. I had to remain sheltered at home, waiting for further news. Beth called daily for the next four days. On day five, they decided to release Annie. Beth didn't wait. She had hopped into her car and driven the thousand-mile journey, stopping only three times for gas. She told me she packed enough food in a cooler so she wouldn't have to buy snacks or fast food along the way, and took face masks, hand sanitizer wipes and gel, and disposable nitrile gloves to touch the gas pumps. She had also stocked her car with all her pantry items and cleaning supplies before she left for Texas.

Beth waited in her car to pick up Annie at the hospital entrance since visitors were still not allowed to come inside. She called to let them know she was outside and a person with a hazmat suit wheeled Annie through the automatic doors and helped her get into Beth's car.

Although weak, Annie commented, "Breathing outdoor air and seeing the sunshine is the best feeling in the world."

Beth took Annie home and prepared her mom's house the best she could without being able to go to the store to get additional food and supplies. It was the best Beth could do for Annie's recuperation since being exposed to Annie herself meant she needed to isolate herself from everyone for fourteen days. She ordered food from an online delivery service and opted for contactless delivery, although, according to Annie, her appetite had not returned to normal, and she had no sense of smell.

Beth didn't want her mom to be alone for the first month after being released from the hospital, so she took a family leave of absence from her job and planned to shelter in place with her mom. I was grateful Annie would have Beth to look after her. It gave me a sense of peace.

Annie's trip home from the hospital was uneventful. Annie herself, though weak and hoarse from the intubation and sore throat she either had from the tube or from Covid, called me every other day. It was good to hear her voice. We talked about how she dodged a bullet. She didn't have a thorough recollection of her hospital stay. She remembered being so ill she believed she was going to die. She remembered hearing the nurses talk to her, but mostly about her, while she was in a coma, but she couldn't respond no matter how hard she tried.

She was unaware of the fear her family and I were going through at the thought of losing her. She was grateful she made it out the other side of Covid and was hopeful she would now be immune and could get back to a normal life, sooner than those of us who hadn't experienced Covid's wrath. I didn't envy her journey but thought what a relief it would be for her to know she had survived the dreaded and feared disease and would possibly have less chance of a recurrence.

***

Eighteen days after Annie was released from the hospital, Beth found her lying on the floor, face up, next to her bed. Beth hadn't heard a sound.

Annie was gone. Sobbing, Beth called 911 first, and then called me to tell me Annie was stiff and cold already, and her eyes were fixed and dilated. Beth knew she was dead. We barely spoke until the ambulance arrived. Our shared grief, through our tears and despair, was all the communication possible, or necessary, at the time.

An autopsy revealed Annie had a massive stroke, most likely an after-effect of having Covid. Strokes are ten times more likely within the first three days of diagnosis, but still possible in the weeks after discharge, a fact that took all of us by surprise.

We both thought Annie was going to be fine. Neither of us would ever get past her loss without feeling a great deal of pain, guilt, and thoughts of shoulda, coulda, woulda, all the while knowing there was nothing we really could have done, and no way we really could have known. Beth had Annie cremated and kept her ashes for a more appropriate time when we could get together, with Beth's brothers, to spread Annie's ashes off South Padre Island in the Gulf of Mexico, which had become Annie's favorite vacation spot after she moved to Texas.

Chapter Thirty-Seven

Empty Nest

In February of 2022, the inevitable did happen and Aubrey, at age thirty, received military orders to move to Fort Rucker, Alabama. Immediately following, Steve also received orders to move to New York. It's common for the Army to split up married couples and send them to serve in different states, as there are many factors at play in the decision-making process to send officers to one location or another.

Many times, I couldn't help thinking about Aubrey. Her bright smile, her infectious laugh, and her surprisingly insightful advice made her impossible not to adore. But, as the days went on, I realized that my affection for her extended beyond just friendship. I thought of her as family, and I loved her like a daughter. It was her father who had captured my heart years ago, and that relationship had only deepened the feelings I had for his daughter. However, I knew revealing this truth to Aubrey could threaten our friendship and damage the beautiful bond we had built over the past seven years. The weight of my secret was suffocating, and I knew I had to find a way to tell her without causing harm. I always knew I would eventually tell her; I just didn't know how or when.

I didn't want to live a lie, seeing her every day, while not revealing the truth. The longer I was around Aubrey, the harder it was for me not to tell her. I tried to act the same when I was around her but sometimes, I stared at her too long trying to distinguish which features my Craig had passed on to her and which features she had inherited from Leah.

Aubrey knew me well enough by then to know something was amiss. I hoped she thought I was just getting old and off my rocker a bit. I stared off into space when she caught a glimpse of me staring at her. She may have thought a touch of dementia had overcome me and that was for the best, although the ego part of me wanted to tell Aubrey. In a way, I was relieved Aubrey was moving to another state before I blurted out the truth.

While Aubrey was an experienced Army officer, she knew living on her own would be hard even with her training. The months leading up to their separation seemed like an eternity of paperwork, meetings, and waiting as they went through all the necessary steps before finally accepting their assignment. Aubrey, Carol, Brian, Eben, and I were all elated when Steve was able at the last minute to get his orders to New York changed to Ft. Rucker so they wouldn't have to live apart.

The day came when we said our goodbyes to Aubrey and Steve; it felt strange having no idea if, or when, we would ever meet again. Long-distance moves have a way of permanently separating people. While good intentions abound and plans to get together are shared in abundance near the beginning, the longer people are apart, the harder it is to find the time and resources to interrupt their daily lives to go and visit, even someone they love. It takes a significant amount of determination to stay in touch, and that often falls by the wayside.

Despite our sadness at parting ways, there was still that initial sincere hope we would see each other again.

Aubrey and Steve found an amazing boarding facility with a large, illuminated, ventilated indoor arena, much like ours for Smokey and Spartacus. As soon as they arrived in Alabama, they purchased their first home. We were relieved to know they made it to their destination safely and, most importantly, they were together.

It is common for horse owners to buy and sell horses multiple times in a ten-year period, but I was happy Aubrey kept the same two the entire time she boarded with us. I get attached to them even though they aren't mine.

Horses can have productive careers from three years old to twenty-six, give or take a few years. Smokey and Spartacus were twenty-three and fifteen, respectively, when they left my farm and still had many good riding years left, although Smokey's remaining years leaned towards being a good lesson horse for beginning riders.

Smokey was what I call a million-dollar horse because of his ability and patience to allow young riders to make mistakes under saddle without bucking, rearing, or bolting. He allowed the student to learn balance, and to develop soft hands and a good seat. A trained, calm, older horse like Smokey allows a riding instructor to teach basic riding skills to students and doesn't get overly responsive to rider aids such as squeezing of the legs and jarring of the hands in the horse's mouth, or the heaviness of the rider's seat during a downward post.

It's a lucky child who gets introduced early to a been there, done that horse for lessons or long, quiet trail rides, or to be their first mounts at lower-level dressage shows. Good horsemanship comes from building the rider's confidence and balance, and no better horse for that task than Smokey.

I was happy for Aubrey, who was moving forward with her life and career, yet I was reeling from the loss of having her and her horses around the farm every day, feeling sorrowful pain, loneliness, and emptiness like what my empty nester friends had described to me when their children go off to college for their freshman year.

I had repeatedly and so casually brushed off the distress of my friends, with a "get over it" attitude and comments like "you should be glad your adult children are finally out of the house and living on their own so you can rediscover your own interests and hobbies." Suddenly, I felt all their pain, and carried a burden of guilt for my previous thoughtless comments as I could finally relate to the magnitude of their losses.

Chapter Thirty-Eight

The Call

In March of 2022, one month after Aubrey and Steve moved, I noticed Eben sitting in a chair in the living room putting his sock on with a gadget he brought home from the hospital.

"What is that?"

"My back hurts again. I can't bend over to put on my own sock today. It started getting worse last week, so I brought this home from the hospital. We give them out to our patients all the time. They work well."

Eben proceeded to demonstrate how he threaded his sock around it, then used the handles to put the sock over his toes and pull up his sock. This scenario stopped me in my tracks. My heart skipped a beat and my pulse raced. I looked at him and immediately bent over and assisted him in putting on his socks.

"You are too young to need a gadget to put on your socks. You, *doctor*, need to go to *a doctor* and have them x-ray your back."

"I've had multiple x-rays. I scheduled myself for an MRI tomorrow."

"Good, it hurts me to see you in pain. It's about time you find out exactly what's wrong with your back. I hope you don't need back surgery, but if that is what you need to feel better long term, you might want to consider it," I said.

"If the results show I need back surgery, I'm inclined to schedule it and be done with it, after a day in pain like I've had today."

Eben rubbed both his back and his abdomen. It concerned me. I believed it was just a strained muscle, but I was glad he was going to get it thoroughly checked.

"Maybe your back is hurting from all those Zoom classes you are teaching. Most of your work over the last two years has had you confined to that desk chair in your office. If you were teaching in a regular classroom setting, you would be teaching from a standing position and would be moving around a lot more. We should at least buy you another chair; one that is more comfortable or ergonomically designed."

"I agree. I have been sitting too many hours in front of a computer."

Eben had tried physical therapy, cortisone injections, ibuprofen, gabapentin, acetaminophen, aspirin, and two other prescription-strength arthritis pain relievers with short-term, but no long-term, relief.

Eben's routine blood work had always come back within completely normal ranges, and palpitations of his back revealed nothing that could be pinpointed, such as a bulging disc. Eben was a workaholic, and when not working for the hospital or teaching, he was always on the tractor, fixing fences, or walking horses. He had adapted well to farm life during our nearly three years of marriage, but

I thought the work was getting to be too much for him and he should delegate more to our younger, fitter employees.

My phone rang.

It was Eben. He was on his way home from the hospital after getting his MRI.

There are times in life when we receive calls that convey news our brains are not capable of processing and our hearts refuse to accept. For moments, days, and weeks afterward, we continue to register, process, and even try to rewrite or ignore the meaning and impact those first words have on us.

"There is a mass on my pancreas."

"What? Back up," I said as Eben glossed over the words and started to tell me something unrelated and unimportant about the mild narrowing of the spinal column in his back.

"Back up to the mass part. What mass? Tell me exactly what they said. Slowly this time."

"They found a mass on my pancreas," he repeated.

"What kind of mass? What exactly did they say?"

"That was all they said."

"Who are they? Did you not read your own report?"

"It was my co-worker Dr. Bryant and his team. I haven't seen the report myself yet."

He meant his associate Jerry, as in Dr. Jerry Bryant. Again, I felt relieved knowing Jerry would be handling Eben's case. I knew Eben would receive the best care possible so Eben would be fine.

"Can you go now and get a copy of the report and CD?"

"Yes, I will get it tomorrow," Eben said.

"No, now. Can you go now and get a copy of the CD with the MRI on it and the full report? You are a radiologist. Surely, you already know what it is. Please take a picture of the report as soon as they hand it to you and text it to me. I want to see exactly how they describe the mass and I'm going to google it, if you don't tell me."

"I can just pull it up on my computer when I get home. I don't have to get a physical copy or a CD. I have another appointment already to get a second MRI on my abdomen. The first MRI only shows a part of the tumor, so I don't know how large it really is. Since I ordered the MRI for my lower back only, it only caught a portion of it on the images."

"Oh, so now it's a tumor. When is your appointment?" I asked.

"Two weeks."

"Two weeks? Can't you pull strings and get it tomorrow? You work there, for God's sake!"

I spoke faster and louder and with more profanity than was necessary. My emotions were now taking over and getting the best of me. I'd lost Annie, had found out about Craig's accident just twenty months prior, and couldn't stand seeing another person I loved dying, injured, or ill.

"I'll see what I can do, honey. I love you. Try not to worry. I'll come straight home," Eben said.

Eben came home thirty minutes later and printed a copy of the report off his computer. I didn't need to google it because Eben was a radiologist. But I still did. Eben knew as soon as he had received the report what it was. The report had confirmed his suspicion. He had adenocarcinoma of the pancreatic duct.

The second MRI confirmed he had stage IV pancreatic cancer with a tumor 4.9 cm. I spent until the wee hours of several mornings researching everything I could find, looking for a cure or any way out of this situation. I searched for something reassuring like, "oh it's not that bad," or "everything is going to be alright," to no avail. I would then crawl into bed and curl up against Eben's back and sob, as quietly as I could, in order not to disturb him. Several nights, Eben rolled over and cried openly with me.

His diagnosis and prognosis were not information Eben readily wanted to share with me. I think he had delayed getting an MRI because he didn't want to confirm what he already suspected. His back pain was more likely connected to the narrowing of his spinal column and not related to the pancreatic cancer, but his abdominal pain and indigestion were directly connected, which he had been ignoring and keeping to himself for far too long. In Eben's defense, pancreatic cancer is a vicious disease that often goes undetected until it has reached advanced stages. Unfortunately, the symptoms of this cancer can be vague and easily misinterpreted by even the most competent professionals.

After his diagnosis, Eben still downplayed the seriousness of his illness as he tried to process and accept the finality of it himself. The Big Dread overwhelmed me. There were days when I felt my heart would burst or I held back tears, or I shook inside and sometimes visibly. I wanted to hold Eben and make everything right.

That horrible call. The one we all think about now and then and know could happen to any one of us at any given time. The call that comes with shocking news, but no one knows when or how, or if, it will come, but when it does, it transports our lives in a direction we would never dare think about or envision. The call we all believe will happen only to someone else, not us.

We loved each other. No other person stood by me and supported me like Eben. No other man had stayed by my side as my lover and my friend.

Eben was only sixty-two years old. I wanted to spend the rest of my life with this man. I wanted us to live together into our nineties. I wanted us to be healthy and fit long after our ages said we should relax in our easy chairs. I needed to shake the feeling of hopelessness that had taken over my psyche. I wanted to fight this thing and win. I wanted to keep this man. He was all I had and even more, he was all I wanted.

I searched for answers I wanted to hear, but they eluded me.

"Space Oddity" by David Bowie went through my head over and over for weeks.

***

Eben's three adult children and mother visited and spent several weeks and weekends with us over the next six months. My feelings stabilized. Family is a good distraction. I was grateful to have them around. I appreciated the constant stream of visitors because they kept Eben occupied. Eben needed them. I just needed Eben. I was also grateful I still had my health and that I still had Eben. That was something I didn't take for granted, not even for a day.

Everyone at the hospital, a hospital with a state-of-the-art research facility, where half the staff knew and admired my husband, would surely be able to make him better, right? The thing about cancer is, it doesn't care who you know or who knows you or what you do for a living.

It was all up to timing now, nothing more, nothing less. I could pray. People told me they prayed for us, and I appreciated their prayers, but I had used up all my own prayers long before this happened.

Prayer is a powerful thing, and for those of us who have experienced its miraculous healing touch, it's undeniable. And even though I wanted to pray for Eben's survival, I couldn't bring myself to do it because the very act of praying for his life was an admission that he might not make it. And that was a place of complete darkness and loneliness where I wasn't willing to go.

We were just getting into the flow, the flow of our senior adult lives together. Our retirement was just around the corner. Eben had planned to work for another five years, but I had already taken the necessary steps to retire. The sale of my firm had been negotiated and signed and I was ready to hand over my accounting business to a new generation. Instead of basking in the glory of a life well lived, I waited for the inevitable destruction to come my way.

It was time to enjoy the fruits of our labor, not time to fight a terrible disease. We had a long-term plan to live life to the fullest and with that one call, it turned into a daily plan. We weren't day-to-day people, but there is a lesson to be learned by living in the moment and appreciating every minute of it. We did just that, but Eben's disease loomed over our heads like a dark cloud, thicker than the cloud cover in Chicago on that blustery day back in 1989. Every day I woke up just a little closer to a finish line I never wanted to reach.

***

Eben died the day after Thanksgiving in 2022. I had always disliked the entire winter holiday season, especially the commercial aspect of Christmas, and losing Eben just gave me another reason to crawl into bed and stay there with the blankets pulled up over my eyes until spring birds started chirping and flowers started blooming. I don't remember eating, bathing, cleaning, riding horses, or breathing. I did some more writing mostly because I could do that in my pajamas and without a shower. I eventually did some praying, albeit too little, too late. Good thing breathing was automatic, or I wouldn't have done it.

I pictured Eben in the arms of his first and real true love, the mother of his children. I pictured him happy and at peace with her. I wasn't the least bit jealous. I hoped she was there to greet him and take our Eben home.

The song "How Do I Live" by Trisha Yearwood played like an endless loop in my mind.

Chapter Thirty-Nine

Part II – The Last Ride

There's a certain mystery to the kind of love and passion Vanity experienced. I'm not sure if love is a purely spiritual or physical event, or a combination of the two. It's like a hurricane, whose center is calm and blissful. As long as two people remained centered, away from the turbulent world spinning violently around them, they could remain in love and unharmed.

But emotion on that level often spawns tornadoes, which can pick you up and transport you to places you would never otherwise experience. Then it either gently or painfully hard sets you down in a completely different location with an entirely different frame of mind than you had originally.

We don't fall in love. We rise up into its vortex. Though the journey is incredible, and the view indescribable, the landing can be painful, sometimes deadly.

Sadly, for Vanity, it was the latter.

On the first warm days after Eben died, with a hint of summer just on the horizon, Vanity was just getting back to living again, visiting with the horses in the pastures and barns. She saddled a horse whenever staying in the house and going through Eben's belongings got too unbearably sad. She rode around the arena for short bursts at a time. Horses were always Vanity's rock. They grounded her to what was real and gave her a reason to go outdoors and soak up the sun. Riding couldn't change the past, but it allowed her to get lost in the moment and temporarily forget about losing Eben and Annie, and about Craig still lying unresponsive in a nursing facility in Norway. She loved Eben and was mourning his loss, but nothing could compare to the passion she felt for Craig and the longing she still had to be by his side.

One night, after a particularly long and satisfying ride on her old, dependable horse Wild Card, Vanity went to sleep with an unusual sense of peace and overall deep sense of accomplishment with her life's achievements.

She never woke up.

Chapter Forty

Part III – The Will

In March of 2023, Aubrey got a call from a number she didn't recognize and almost sent it directly into voice mail. She was, however, expecting a call from someone at her company's headquarters and didn't know the area code they would be calling from, so she accepted the call at the last minute. Instead of being a work issue, she was surprised when the caller identified himself as an attorney in New River and said he needed to meet with her, in person, as soon as possible.

The attorney then shared the news that her long-time mentor and friend, Vanessa "Vanity" VanBuren, had died in her sleep of a suspected heart attack. Vanessa had left something important for Aubrey in her will and it could only be conveyed to Aubrey in person.

He further explained Vanessa had requested, upon Vanessa's death, for the attorney to contact Aubrey immediately and ask her to help Brian with all the animals and to carry out Vanessa's final wishes. He added he hoped she would be able to make arrangements to come to

New River. He gave Aubrey his phone number and asked her to call him to schedule a time to meet.

Aubrey was saddened, of course, and deeply curious. She called Brian immediately, a call she dreaded and couldn't believe she had to make, to give Brian her condolences. Brian told Aubrey he didn't know what the attorney wanted with her, although he later had to apologize to Aubrey because he did already know.

"I bet she left me her cats," Aubrey said.

"Better you than me," Brian said.

Aubrey didn't wait for her company headquarters to call her back after she left a voice mail, instead she walked into her commander's office and requested immediate family leave.

Aubrey wasn't exactly Vanessa's biological family, but after she explained the situation to her commander, she approved Vanessa's leave. She was lucky, she thought. If they had been in a training phase, or in the field, or deployed, she would never have been able to get away on short notice, but she never took leave or vacation days, so she had accumulated almost four months of leave. Surely, she wouldn't need more than three days to settle whatever issue this was.

She decided to leave that evening and arrived in New River the next morning. She called the attorney and he suggested she come to his office at noon. Aubrey slept and showered inside Vanessa's house, then fed Vanessa's three cats, four macaws, and five dogs, and had breakfast with Brian, who told her Carol had been in Arizona all week visiting friends but would be home that afternoon.

Brian and Aubrey talked about Vanessa non-stop as they were trying to come to terms with it in their own ways. They enjoyed each other's company the best they could while dealing with the new reality that Vanessa was really gone. Brian was taking it especially hard.

Vanessa had been the sister he never had. He was glad Aubrey was there to dispel the eerie quiet that had blanketed the farm that morning.

At 11:40 a.m., it was time for Aubrey to take the fifteen-minute drive to the attorney's office. Aubrey invited Brian to ride along with her, but he said he had to take care of all his animals and horses and Vanessa's horses, so he would stay behind anxiously waiting to hear what the attorney had to say. Brian, in his moments of grief, almost told Aubrey the story about Vanessa and her dad but had decided to wait until Aubrey returned from the attorney's office.

The drive into town was a pleasant one, mostly back roads with little to no traffic, and there was so much on Aubrey's mind, the drive ended quicker than Aubrey had anticipated. She realized she had been daydreaming for most of the drive when she found herself in front of a small brick building with a large parking area next to it and "Charles Bauer, Esquire" on the sign.

Aubrey entered the building and was immediately greeted by Mr. Bauer's legal assistant. Aubrey sat down and reached over to pick up a magazine but was stopped by the assistant's voice before her hand reached it.

"Mr. Bauer will see you now. Follow me, please," she said.

Aubrey thought to herself how nice small towns can be with little traffic, empty waiting rooms, and fast, personalized service.

"Ms. Targaczewski," Mr. Bauer said.

"Aubrey is fine," as she extended her right hand for a firm handshake, one she had learned from years in the military.

"Aubrey, I'm terribly sorry I had to deliver the news about Vanessa over the telephone. Vanessa told me so much about you. It's an honor to meet you. I feel like I know you, although I'm sure you aren't aware of what I'm about to tell you."

Aubrey nodded, confused. Why would this person feel like he knew her, she wondered. As fast as that thought entered her mind, Mr. Bauer explained.

"Ms. Targaczewski," Mr. Bauer said.

"Aubrey," she said, "please call me Aubrey."

"Aubrey, you are the sole heir named in Vanessa's will."

Mr. Bauer paused and looked at her and allowed her a moment to take in the enormity of that statement.

"What? What does that mean? Why?" she asked.

Her emotions had boiled up to the surface earlier that morning as she settled into the rhythm of the farm and had spent her first night ever inside Vanity's house without Vanity buzzing all around doing morning chores. This news was overwhelming for her.

"Let me go over the facts of her estate and if you have any questions, please let me know. I have a list of assets typed for you here," Mr. Bauer said.

He handed Aubrey the list. He read each item and the estimated value from the house, the acreage, the barns, the Dog Days of Summer animal rescue facility building, the 501C non-profit corporation, furnishings, tractors, mowers, vehicles, horses, bank accounts, life insurance, and the office building on the corner lot being leased by the CPA who purchased Vanessa's accounting business.

The property was paid off free and clear and Vanessa had no debt, so it was an incomprehensible amount to Aubrey as she stared at the list of assets. She wondered how Vanity had amassed such a fortune, but then realized Vanity worked all the time, didn't have children, rarely took vacations, and must have purchased the life insurance when she was quite young to afford the premiums.

Mr. Bauer allowed Aubrey some time to absorb what he was telling her and then asked, "Do you have any questions?"

"What about Eben's children? Two boys and a girl, I think. Adults now, I know, but won't they expect to be left something from their father's estate?"

"Ms. VanBuren already discussed that with me and left me something to read to you," Mr. Bauer replied as he fumbled through the papers on his desk and found the note. "Ah, here it is, she thought of everything, you know. Do you mind if I read it to you?" he asked Aubrey.

"Please do," she replied.

***

Mr. Bauer began reading, *"Aubrey, I choose you as my sole heir, not only because of the information you will learn while reading a book I left for you, but also because you have a genuine, loving heart. You have always exhibited kindness towards me and the animals in my care. You are also intelligent, educated, and business savvy. You are the only person I can count on to run such a complex training facility in my absence. I hope this note finds you retired and me much older, as I wouldn't want to interrupt your Army career, but I finished the book and haven't been feeling well or like myself lately and decided there was no time like the present to set these plans in stone. Brian has everything he needs financially and will be inheriting Carol's farm when Carol passes. Brian supported my decision to leave my farm and my share of the horse training business to you. Eben's three children inherited a sizeable sum of money from their mother's side of the family and from an insurance settlement when their mother passed away in an automobile accident when they were children. Eben set up individual trust funds for each of them and he continued to contribute graciously to those funds throughout his career. His children are also well established in their own careers now and have no interest in running a farm. Brian and I met in person with Eben's children after Eben passed away and allowed them to take any personal possessions they wanted. They agreed since I already had most of the assets on this farm when I met Eben, they would have no quarrel with my decision to choose someone who would help Brian keep the farm running.* signed *Vanessa*"

***

"Do you have any questions?" Mr. Bauer asked.

Aubrey had lots of questions but couldn't think of a single one a the time, so she quietly replied, "No," hesitated, then said, "thank you."

Aubrey remained silent, gathering her thoughts, while Mr. Bauer rearranged some papers on his desk.

Aubrey was curious about the book Vanity mentioned and assumed it was a go-to manual of sorts to help her run the farm.

Aubrey knew she could take the farm into the future, but she was only thirty-one and still had over nine years before she would be eligible for military retirement. She certainly would already have a solid base to start with at the farm.

The farm had long ago attracted a good, steady stream of clientele and had recently hired a former Olympian to teach most of the lessons, along with Brian's two assistant trainers doing most of the colt starting and finishing. Aubrey knew she was going to have to do some finagling and make some tough decisions, but her head was so full of information, ideas, and sadness right then, she knew it wasn't the time to do anything but get through this day.

Riding horses and training horses was something Aubrey still loved. Her days of flying helicopters for the military were over and she had been moved into more of an administrative role, so her dedication to her Army career was wavering. There was just too much coming at her to make any immediate decisions. This was something she and Steve would have to discuss over time.

Vanity didn't want to let Brian down by leaving her portion of the farm to someone who would split it off from Brian's portion, or who would sell it to a builder. Subdivisions were popping up all around, as horse farms, boarding, and training facilities, one by one, were disappearing. And Brian wasn't getting any younger. He needed and would appreciate Aubrey and Steve's help. Carol, approaching eighty, still loved being outdoors and refused to live anywhere except on the farm, so she would welcome Aubrey and Steve to the farm operation with open arms.

"Ms. VanBuren also left you this book," Mr. Bauer continued. "She requested I ask you to read it, and the only stipulation in her will is that you read this entire book to your father."

"My father? Why?"

Aubrey couldn't imagine what her father had to do with Vanity or Vanity's death. None of this made any sense to her. Surely, Vanity had someone in her life she had been closer to than Aubrey. They enjoyed each other's company, and their feelings of friendship as kindred spirits remained strong, but the physical miles between them and time apart had weakened their bonds, or so Aubrey thought.

"There is a handwritten note inside the front cover of the book, from Ms. VanBuren to you. The book will explain everything."

Aubrey couldn't wait to call Steve. She was curious about the book and the note, however, so she decided to read the note from Aubrey without delay, quietly to herself, while sitting in front of Mr. Bauer.

Chapter Forty-One

Part IV – A Note for Aubrey

Dearest Aubrey,

If you are reading this, I have passed on to a beautiful, peaceful place surrounded by love and you need not worry about me. Please read this book privately, in its entirety, so you understand why you are my only suitable heir. Then read this book aloud to your dad so he knows I completed it. It was, after all, his idea. If you wish to have this book published, I've included the contact information of the publisher willing to proceed. I would like you to donate all the net proceeds of this book to veterinarians who spay and neuter shelter pets and continue the work you and I started in 2016. The attorney can help you with that. The book should answer most of your questions. I hope you forgive me for not telling you sooner. Vanessa

***

After reading the note, Aubrey signed the papers that Mr. Bauer had placed in front of her. He informed her they would need two or three more meetings to settle the estate entirely. She barely heard the words Mr. Bauer was speaking, as her thoughts drifted back to the book and the note. Why had her father told Vanity to write a book, she wondered.

Aubrey couldn't wait for her meeting with Mr. Bauer to conclude so she could walk out to her car and make a private call to her husband.

"Steve, you aren't going to believe this."

Aubrey proceeded to tell him about her trip to Mr. Bauer's office and about the inheritance, the items listed, the bottom-line amount of estimated assets and cash and life insurance proceeds. Steve was speechless. Aubrey noted she had never seen Steve like this because words usually flowed from Steve's mind to his lips in an unerring ebb and flow.

Steve and Aubrey were both taken aback by the generosity of the gift they had been given but they were even more curious about the book Vanity had left for Aubrey. It was more than a book she had left for them. It was a book Vanity had written, not for Aubrey, but for Aubrey's dad. Steve, of course, was as confused by that as Aubrey was when Mr. Bauer first handed her the book.

Aubrey then explained to Steve that Vanity's book was supposed to hold all the answers and the book had been her father's idea.

"Why would my dad have anything to do with a book written by Vanity?" Aubrey asked Steve. "None of this makes any sense."

Steve was even more confused and quite anxious to know the answers, as was Aubrey.

"Start reading and call me as soon as you learn anything," Steve said. "I'll get there as soon as I can."

Steve couldn't drive to New River with Aubrey the day prior because of his job, but he went to his commander and asked for leave and his leave was also granted. He booked a commercial flight to join Aubrey the following day.

Aubrey made it back to Vanessa's house and started to read the book. She didn't want to put it down when Brian and Carol called and invited her to dinner at Carol's house. Instead, she suggested they cook at Vanity's house, where Aubrey was staying. The sole topic of conversation that evening was Vanessa's amazing life and the secret she held for decades, the inheritance, and the book. Aubrey, Brian, and Carol could have chatted until morning, but Aubrey was anxious to read the rest of the book, quietly and to herself. She also promised to let Carol and Brian read it as soon as she finished it. She knew Vanity wouldn't mind if she shared it with them.

Aubrey called Steve after she read Chapter 22 – The Tearful Goodbye, the chapter about when Vanity had dropped off her dad at the Cincinnati airport thirty years earlier.

"My dad and Vanity were lovers in 1989," Aubrey said as soon as Steve answered the phone.

"What!!?" Steve said as he digested the enormity of that sentence.

"And they remained in love for the rest of their lives, although the only contact they had since 1989 was the random chance encounter they had when I took my parents to the barn to meet Vanity."

"No way, what?"

Steve was still not wrapping his head completely around the scenario.

"And it was my dad's idea that she write a book about their adventures."

"I can't believe this," Steve said. "And we never had a clue."

"I'm not finished with the book yet, there may be more we don't know. I'll let you go. I'm going to keep reading. Love you, honey. See you tomorrow."

Aubrey changed into comfortable pajamas, returned to the oversized leather living room couch, pulled a throw blanket over her legs, and signaled one of Vanity's cats to hop onto her lap. She read until the early-morning hours when sleep overcame her just after Chapter 25 – Aubrey, the chapter Vanity had written about her.

Chapter Forty-Two

Part V – Craig's Perspective

April to June 2023

Aubrey explained to her dad about Vanity's will and how Vanity had written a book and requested she read it to him. She also told him Vanity had left a literary agent's contact information for her to call for a potential publishing deal.

"She thought of everything but that's how she was," Aubrey told him.

Craig smiled to himself and his heart warmed thinking of Vanessa. Craig already knew all about Vanessa's personality and he loved her for it. She could try to micromanage situations all she wanted but it never quite worked for her when whe was with him. He thought she probably liked that most about him.

Aubrey also updated Craig about her mom's cancer, still not knowing whether he could process anything she was telling him. Sometimes talking to her dad about absolutely everything was healing for her, but not necessarily for him. Aubrey had no way of knowing that either.

Craig's mind was fully alert inside his body, a body that had now become his tomb. As Aubrey read to him, he enjoyed listening to what a pedestal Vanessa had put him on during their summer together. He was physically fit and handsome at the time of their relationship. He knew that.

He wondered, as Aubrey was reading to him, what Vanessa would think of him if she could see him now. He knew his once muscular physique had atrophied. He had lost most of his teeth, before the dentist finally pulled them all, as he had relied on other people to care for him and his teeth. Even the best care by others was far inferior to what he would have been doing to care for himself.

He could see parts of his own body, at times, while they moved him from bed to chair as he had no ability to move even his own head. He could feel the deterioration of his limbs and he felt life starting to drain from his body. He knew he didn't have much time left, but those thoughts were just his own private thoughts and a knowledge of his own sense of self, as he had no way to share them with anyone.

He had wanted to die many times since the accident and often hoped he was getting worse. His life as he knew it, and what a glorious, full life it had been, had for all intents and useful purposes ended on the side of Mont Blanc.

If he could just die, he would be free, but he was powerless to do anything about his situation except wait for death to come.

Listening to Aubrey read Vanity's book aloud to him was the most alive he had felt since that unfortunate day on Mont Blanc. He had loved Vanessa from the moment he saw her and had never stopped loving her or questioning why she didn't follow him and why he hadn't gone back to convince her to come live with him.

Now, he realized how much she loved him and why she made the decision to let him go. He regurgitated in his own mind all the comments he had made to her about how much he wanted to have children. He realized the extreme pressure she must have been under due to those comments, and he also realized, for the first time, the extreme sacrifice she made for him as a result. He wished he had known about her medical condition and her inability to have children, but he also thought about Aubrey and how Aubrey wouldn't exist if he hadn't met Leah.

He was proud of Vanessa for finishing the book. She nailed their time together. It was every bit as magical as she described. If only he could explain to her about Leah. He had wanted to contact Vanessa many times over the thirty years they were apart. He had picked up the phone and held it in his hand at least a dozen times. He wanted to dial her number to talk to her. He wanted to know if she still loved him as much as he still loved her.

He did reflect on the irony of them both loving each other more than seemed humanly possible even though they hadn't communicated and lived in different countries. He had nothing to do but reflect, in that useless body of his.

He never broke the promise he made to her in 1989 to love her forever and to always know she loved him. Over the years, when he would feel down, he reminded himself she still loved him and that always lifted his spirits. He thought she did anyway, but the book confirmed it and made his heart soar out of his chest and romp around the room, even if his legs couldn't follow.

Running into Vanessa at his daughter's boarding facility shook him to his core. He wanted to take her aside and explain everything. Mostly, he wanted to take her into his arms, hold her, and never let her go.

After Leah made those biting comments in the car in front of Vanessa, Craig realized Vanessa knew he met Leah on their vacation, and Vanessa thought he had married her, but he hadn't. That was something Aubrey didn't know, something he didn't think she would ever know, and he would be happy if she never discovered. Craig had never officially married Leah. They just developed a relationship over time. Leah got pregnant, gave birth to Aubrey, and neither of them ever broached the subject of tying the knot.

Norwegians don't necessarily put the same weight and urgency on proposals and marriage as Americans do, but he knew Vanessa would never move overseas without a permanent commitment from him. He had no hesitation or doubts when he bought an engagement ring for her, right before they left for their vacation, but somehow, he never found the right words or the right time. Vanessa had made it pretty clear to him she did not want to live in Norway, and he wondered if he was just being selfish to ask her to make a move like that to a cold climate so far away from her family. It was a decision he would spend the rest of his life questioning, never knowing if he truly made the right decision by walking away.

He even turned around and walked back outside the airport in Cincinnati, after Vanessa dropped him off on that painful day when they said goodbye. He saw Vanessa still sitting in her car, unable to pull away from the terminal. He wanted to run to her, tap on her window, and ask her to marry him and yet his feet remained frozen in place just outside the terminal doors.

He didn't know Leah would start writing to him and they would get to know each other through letters for almost two years before

Leah made her way to Norway to visit him. It wasn't love, at least not at first, and he had never been in love with anyone like he had been with Vanessa. Craig held back from committing himself fully to Leah due to his past relationship with Vanessa, who he still felt deeply connected to despite her being on the other side of the world. But then came the news that changed everything: Leah was pregnant with Craig's child and after that, Craig knew there was only one right thing to do. He committed to being the best father possible to his little Aubrey. Leah moved in with Craig and they set up house.

Right up to the time Aubrey was conceived, Craig had repeatedly considered calling Vanessa and asking her to marry him and move to Norway to be with him. He even considered moving to the States to be with her. In his heart, he knew she would say yes and would follow him or welcome him to live with her, but he had a budding career in Norway.

Instead, Craig took Vanessa with him, in his mind and heart, on every adventure he had up until the day of his accident. He had never found a more adventurous, loving partner than he had with Vanessa. He longed for her to just suddenly appear during each one of his adventures. He fantasized as he was climbing, he would look down, and there she would be, scaling the wall after him.

He never thought Vanessa would somehow find out about Leah and in such a heartbreaking way while she was driving them to the airport. He never dreamed his daughter Aubrey would meet Vanessa and become so incredibly close to her. He never dreamed any of that would happen.

He also had no physical way to react to the tearful goodbye at the airport part of the story, which Aubrey had just finished reading to him, although it stirred up tremendous emotions in him.

He agonized over what he should do about contacting Vanessa after he returned home with Leah. Then the accident prevented him from ever setting the record straight with Vanessa or reaching out to her to at least answer all her questions.

Leah's cancer had started in her breast and had spread to her lungs and liver. Craig's injuries and subsequent daily care had taken their toll on Leah. Other than genetics, medical science doesn't know how any person gets breast cancer, but Leah's stress level over Craig's illness didn't help.

Leah's cancer progressed quickly. She hadn't been paying attention to her own health and was diagnosed at a later stage. She wasn't taking time to get mammograms, but she felt a lump at least a year before informing her doctor. Part of her knew it was something bad and she didn't want to deal with any more bad news because of what she was already experiencing. It would only be a matter of time before Leah succumbed to it. They had already tried chemo and Keytruda, but the end was near. They had exhausted all treatment options.

She was in hospice care about three miles from Craig's long-term-care location. Aubrey had extended her family emergency leave to stay by her mother's side and visit her dad and read the book to him. It took Aubrey months to absorb the information she was learning about her dad and Vanity.

"I will never share this information with Mom," Aubrey told her dad shortly after reading Craig the part in the book about the car ride to the airport where Leah had talked openly about how she met Craig and unknowingly insulted Vanity in one of the worst ways possible. Inside, Craig was relieved about that.

Aubrey told her mom about Vanessa's will and how Vanessa had left her the farm, house, and life insurance proceeds. Even in her mom's weakened state, Leah was pleasantly shocked but relieved to know she wouldn't have to worry about Aubrey financially, and yet a bit suspicious of Vanity's generous gift to her daughter. Aubrey reminded her mom Vanity didn't have any living heirs.

It started to make a little more sense to Leah. Still, there were things Leah seemed to question. Aubrey did her best to answer Leah's questions without mentioning the book or Vanity's love affair with her dad.

Aubrey wondered if Leah had somehow sensed something or noticed the strange interaction between Craig and Vanity either during the reunion in the barn or the car ride to the airport. Had her mom seen and recognized Vanessa waving to the plane from the highway that day, or had she noticed tears in Craig's eyes after he checked the luggage? He could have played that off as missing Aubrey.

Did her mom sense Craig's need for quiet alone time on the plane? Or did her mom leave her dad alone with Vanessa at the airport for a reason? Were the words she said in the car to Vanessa random or did she know? Her mom had an unkind streak that she rarely let anyone see. Did she recognize Vanessa after all those years? Aubrey doubted it. Aubrey never got the answers to these questions, yet they lingered in her mind.

Aubrey, once she absorbed the book and the enormity of the message in it, got to know her dad in a new and unique way. Before the book, she never realized her dad was really that handsome or so much fun. She pulled out old photo albums with pictures of her dad and saw him in an entirely new light.

She noticed, as she had never noticed before, he always had something like ski poles, a snow board, or climbing gear. She also found a picture of him standing alone on the Golden Gate Bridge. He looked so young and happy. She didn't remember any stories of her parents ever going to San Francisco, so she pictured, in her mind, Vanity snapping that photo and her father saving it.

She once again thought of her dad as an adventurous spirit, not defining him by his accident that had consumed her thoughts of him in recent years. One minute he was just her dad, who she was mostly just ignoring because of her own industrious career, and the next minute he's gone and done something a man his age shouldn't have been doing and gotten himself hurt. She had been mad at him for getting injured, but now, she was mad at herself for not seeing the real him until it was too late.

Aubrey was no longer mad at her dad for climbing Mont Blanc. She now knew she was more like her dad than she had ever realized. She had let their parent-child relationship cloud her view of him.

The book became harder for Aubrey to read aloud to her dad. It was not an ideal time to read such a book because of her mom's failing health. The enjoyment she got from Vanity's story came with a high dose of guilt and shame. She decided to pause and take a break from it so she could tend to her mom instead.

Aubrey stopped visiting her father as frequently as her mom's health declined even further. Her mom was now dying in hospice. The book would have to wait.

Craig already knew the ending, but parts of the story were a surprise to him and saddened him, like knowing how afraid Vanity had really been on some of their adventures and learning of Annie's death due to COVID-19.

He had an odd sense of jealousy when he learned about Vanessa marrying Eben, but he was also happy for her. His happiness for her overshadowed any sense of possessiveness he had. He didn't realize she had waited over thirty years to move on with her life. That troubled him a great deal. He was heartbroken for Vanessa when he learned of Eben's passing.

He questioned if he had done the right thing by calling Vanessa when they returned from the New River rafting trip. He wondered what Vanessa's life would have been if they had never met, or if he had not pursued her when they got home. Vanessa had wondered about that as well, but she knew her approach to life and life's unexpected twists and turns had always been easier for her to navigate because of Craig's influence.

***

Leah passed away on a Saturday in June of 2023. She was only fifty-six. Aubrey delivered the news to Craig, still not knowing if he could hear or comprehend anything she was telling him. She sat and cried in the chair next to his bed. She saw a tear run down her dad's cheek. She was positive she saw life in there and in that moment, she knew for sure.

He did, of course. He knew.

Chapter Forty-Three

Part VI – The Final Reading

August 2023

Three weeks after Leah was laid to rest, during one of Aubrey's daily visits to her father, she noticed something unusual. Under the covers, it looked like Craig's arms were crossed and that he was hugging a small pillow. Craig's arms were usually placed next to him flat on the bed except when they turned him slightly side to side every four hours. He had a mattress with air that automatically inflated and deflated to increase his circulation and keep him from getting bed sores. She had never seen his arms crossed on his chest, pillow or no pillow, as they would usually just fall back to his side.

After scrolling through her phone and answering some text messages and video chatting with Steve and having Steve say hello to her dad, Aubrey glanced over to the side table for Vanessa's book, but it was missing. She knew she had left it there with a bookmark to mark the place to resume reading. It made her nervous as she hoped a nurse hadn't tossed it, or removed it to read it, or taken it to the family waiting lobby, or even to another patient's room.

She hopped up and looked in the small closet in his room and under the small sink. Aubrey, wishing she had taken the book home with her, started to get terribly upset with herself for not doing just that. It had been three weeks, so the book could be anywhere. Aubrey chastised herself for not taking it home and keeping it in a safe place. She had just gotten distracted with her mom's death and temporarily forgotten about it.

She was beside herself with worry and frustration and on the verge of tears over losing the book. Aubrey noticed tears flowed freer and more often since her mom died and she tried to step out of the room to not worry her father with her unleashed emotions.

Before she did, she lifted her dad's sheet to locate the call button next to his bed. Although Craig was unable to push a panic button, it was connected to the bed just the same for the nurses to use when necessary. It often got stuck under the sheet or pillow while the nurses repositioned Craig.

Aubrey couldn't believe what she saw when she pulled back the sheet. Craig wasn't clutching a pillow; he was clutching Vanity's book. How was he clutching anything, she wondered again. He hadn't grasped anything since the accident. She located the panic button under the covers and summoned the nurse.

Two nurses rushed into the room. Aubrey pointed to Craig. One of the nurses Aubrey knew had worked there for fifteen years. Her name was Berta. The other nurse, Olin, had only started his training two weeks prior, so he wasn't aware of the significance of this event. Aubrey felt silly for pushing a panic button over a lost, now found, book, but the astonishment she was feeling at Craig's ability to grip got the best of her. She wanted the nursing staff to see it for themselves before it vanished. She needed witnesses to see the miracle and to confirm she wasn't exaggerating Craig's sudden improvement.

Berta called Craig's doctor, at home, to let him know what they were witnessing. There was nothing anyone could do but wait and wonder and talk about it. They had to pry the book out of Craig's hand. He had a grip. It didn't make any sense. There was no medical explanation his doctor could come up with to explain it. If any motor function was going to return, it would usually be in the first year, not in year four.

"It must be a reflex action," Olin volunteered.

"We just don't know. I spoke to the doctor. He doesn't have an explanation for it."

"I was reading it to him," Olin admitted. "When I got paged to help a patient in room 210, I stopped reading and Mr. Eriksen seemed like he wanted me to hand him the book, so I did. I'm really sorry. I didn't know I did something wrong."

"You didn't," Berta reassured him.

"It was nice you were reading to him," Aubrey said.

"He reached for the book. I'm certain he reached for it," Olin said, "or I never would have handed it to him."

Everyone in the room remained baffled. Aubrey welcomed any sign of improvement in Craig's condition and was joyful for even a shred of good news regarding her father.

Aubrey decided to finish reading the book to him. She had a renewed energy and the sight of her dad holding that book warmed her heart. Holding anything, in her mind, was a major accomplishment, a milestone that represented hope. She read for over an hour before reaching the final chapter.

She was surprised her dad had not drifted off to sleep before she finished as she expected he would, but as long as he remained awake, she decided to keep reading. Aubrey finally got to the very last chapter of Vanity's memoir and looked over again to make sure Craig was not sleeping. In a soothing voice she began to read it to him.

***

The Final Chapter of Vanity's Memoir

Always by My Side

In February of 2023, I was still nowhere near recovered from losing Eben, but I found writing and editing gave me a sense of peace. It gave my mind a place to wander freely, and I found it to be cathartic.

I envisioned Craig touching and holding the book and Aubrey reading it to him. It was special to me because I knew it was the last thread weaving my world and Craig's world together. I hoped it would be as special for him to hear as it was for me to write, and as special as it was for me to have experienced it.

If I had to live life over again, is this the life I would have chosen? Would I make changes? I would have asked Carol to introduce me to Eben ten years earlier. I would have begged Annie to get the Covid vaccines, which she was entirely against doing. I would have saved my friends John and Kyle and Gene and Luke from running out of gas a half mile from their runway. I would have tried to make a difference wherever I could, but as for my time with Craig, I wouldn't have changed a thing.

Our experiment is ending as we both approach the final season of our lives. It was a success. Craig and I tested our hypothesis that love can last forever, and indeed it can. Although I haven't spoken to Craig for years, I feel confident I speak for both of us when I tell you true love does last forever.

When I look back at all the options I had, decisions I made, forks in the road that took me one way or another, or I envision traveling on an entirely different journey with Craig by my side, I remind myself that he was always by my side.

From the moment we met, I was never alone. I was always loved. It's easy to go through the pain life throws at you when you love someone and when someone loves you. Love makes life BEAR-able, endurable, and happy. You don't have to be physically with a person to reap the benefits of love.

Love transcends time and space and wraps around you like a warm blanket; it supports you like a comfortable chair; and stays with you to keep you alive, long after the physical relationship has ended. I hope you find true and everlasting love.

Chapter Forty-Four

Part VII – The Reunion

Aubrey closed the book and placed her hand on its leather cover and said, "That was the end of Vanity's book, Dad,"

She looked up at Craig with a tear in her eye. She saw what she thought was eye contact, but her dad was looking right through her as if he were looking at someone else, someone only he could see.

"Vanessa," he said.

Craig had spoken.

A second passed as Aubrey processed the fact that her dad had just spoken Vanessa's name.

"Dad, it's me. Aubrey," she said.

"It's okay, Vanessa's here to help me," Craig replied.

Happy tears came quickly for Aubrey. Her dad was still looking past her, his eyes were fixated on something or someone to her right. She looked around as if she were expecting to see Vanessa standing right beside her, but she knew that was impossible.

Craig had a surprised yet strangely pleasant look on his face. This was a huge improvement in his condition. He had not been able to hold eye contact or even appear to really be looking at anything or anyone since the accident, yet he had just spoken a complete sentence with noticeable emotion and expression on his face.

"Dad," she said again.

Craig exhaled a long breath. It lasted longer than normal and made a strange sound. She noticed no inhalation followed it.

"Dad," she cried. Her happy tears turned into tears of heartbreak.

She stepped forward, standing over him, and held him in her arms and touched his face with her cheek.

"Dad," she called out again.

Craig was gone.

Aubrey's tears landed on his face.

A feeling of love more powerful than anything Aubrey had ever experienced enveloped the room and surrounded her with peace. It dried her tears, filled her heart with calmness, and dispelled her feeling of despair. It was surreal and spiritual. Although Aubrey wasn't an overtly religious person, it was a fork in the road for Aubrey. At that moment she realized there was an afterlife and although she was firmly planted in the physical world, she could feel the light and energy in the room. Aubrey couldn't have known Vanity had been there with her all along and yet, somehow, she knew.

***

Craig and Vanity had always communicated on a higher frequency than everyone else, so right before he passed, Craig could finally see her. Vanessa had not only been in the room the entire time but had held Craig in her arms and slept next to him every night since she died. She had held Craig's arms in place around the book because she knew that was what he wanted. She had nothing to do with him seeing her, saying her name, or speaking his first sentence. That was a power beyond her abilities. That was the power of passion.

Passion itself is supernatural. It transcends time and space and gives us extraordinary abilities we aren't capable of understanding or denying.

Epilogue

During Aubrey's extended visit to Norway, Aubrey decided to say farewell to Army life, become a civilian, and take care of the farm. Steve decided to remain in the military for another seven years until his retirement date, because he was able to get transferred back to Fort Liberty a year after Vanessa's death. He wanted to stay in the military until his retirement, mainly for insurance purposes, but also because he was teaching fellow soldiers to fly, and he loved flying.

Steve and Brian had always gotten along well and another person around to help Brian with the farm, even on weekends, was welcomed.

Aubrey contacted the agent on the card Vanity had left for her. She proceeded to get Vanity's book published, not only to raise money for their Dog Days of Summer charity, but also to honor Vanity. Vanity had gifted her with a beautiful farm, but more than that she gifted Aubrey with financial freedom. Financial freedom gave Aubrey the ability to live her life the way she wanted and have time to make a difference in the lives of people and animals around her. Vanity knew Aubrey wouldn't squander such an opportunity and gift.

Aubrey was completely content with her life, except for losing so many people she loved in a relatively brief period of time. She knew her parents would want her to move past her grief and live a joyful life, so Aubrey decided to do just that.

The *New River Times* posted an article Aubrey wrote called "What I Learned from My Father's True Love." Aubrey realized her father and horses weren't the only things she had in common with Vanity. Aubrey discovered her passion for the written word. What started as a tribute to Vanity turned into a journey of self-discovery for Aubrey and an exploration of her own creative writing abilities.

That was the start of Aubrey's career as a writer. The success of her tribute article led her to publish many more articles, with a focus on finding deeper meaning in life by exploring human emotions, relationships, and experiences. Her writing was authentic, introspective, deeply personal, and eventually became so successful Aubrey couldn't help but think Vanity had a hand in it.

A Note from The Author

Thank you for reading New River Vanity. I sincerely appreciate you. A few characters from New River Vanity will be making an appearance in my next novel. Please follow my page: facebook.com/TamiNoftz and please post a review.

Acknowledgments

A special thanks to:

Developmental editor, Laurie Chittenden

Copy editor, Brooks Becker

Author cover photo: Jamie Loomis Photography